FRANCIS LYNDE
THE TAMING OF RED BUTTE WESTERN

FRANCIS LYNDE
THE TAMING OF RED BUTTE WESTERN

THE TAMING OF RED BUTTE WESTERN

BY FRANCIS LYNDE

CONTENTS

I   1

II   9

III   15

IV   23

V   33

VI   43

VII   53

VIII   61

IX   69

X   79

XI   83

XII   89

XIII   99

XIV   111

XV   117

XVI   123

XVII   131

XVIII   137

XIX   145

XX   155

XXI   165

XXII   171

XXIII   179

The windows of the division head-quarters of the Pacific Southwestern at Copah look northward over bald, brown mesas, and across the Pannikin to the eroded cliffs of the Uintah Hills. The prospect, lacking vegetation, artistic atmosphere, and color, is crude and rather harshly aggressive; and to Lidgerwood, glooming thoughtfully out upon it through the weather-worn panes scratched and bedimmed by many desert sandstorms, it was peculiarly depressing.

"No, Ford; I hate to disappoint you, but I'm not the man you are looking for," he said, turning back to things present and in suspense, and speaking as one who would add a reason to unqualified refusal. "I've been looking over the ground while you were coming on from New York. It isn't in me to flog the Red Butte Western into a well-behaved division of the P. S-W."

The grave-eyed man who had borrowed Superintendent Leckhard's pivot-chair nodded intelligence.

"That is what you have been saying, with variations, for the last half-hour. Why?"

"Because the job asks for gifts that I don't possess. At the present moment the Red Butte Western is the most hopelessly demoralized three hundred miles of railroad west of the Rockies. There is no system, no discipline, no respect for authority. The men run the road as if it were a huge joke. Add to these conditions the fact that the Red Desert is a country where the large-calibred revolver is——"

"Yes, I know all that," interrupted the man in the chair. "The road and the region need civilizing—need it badly. That is one of the reasons why I am trying to persuade you to take hold. You are long on civilization, Howard."

"Not on the kind which has to be inculcated by main strength and a cheerful disregard for consequences. I'm no scrapper."

To the eye of appraisal, Lidgerwood's personal appearance bore out the peaceable assertion to the final well-groomed detail. Compactly built and neatly, brawn and bulk were conspicuously lacking; and the thin, intellectual face was made to appear still thinner by the pointed cut of the closely trimmed brown beard. The eyes were alert and not wanting in steadfastness; but they had a trick of seeming to look beyond, rather than directly at, the visual object. A physiognomist would have classified him as a man of studious habit with the leisure to indulge it, and unconsciously he dressed the part.

In his outspoken moments, which were rare, he was given to railing against the fate which had made him a round peg in a square hole; a technical engineer and a man of action, when his earlier tastes and inclinations had drawn him in other directions. But the temperamental qualities; the niceties, the exactness, the thoroughness, which, finding no outlet in an artistic calling, had made him a master in his unchosen profession, were well known to Mr. Stuart Ford, first vice-president of the Pacific Southwestern System. And, it was largely for the sake of these qualities that Ford locked his hands over one knee and spoke as a man and a comrade.

"Let me tell you, Howard—you've no idea what a savage fight we've had in New York, absorbing these same demoralized three hundred miles. You know why we were obliged to have them. If the

Transcontinental had beaten us, it meant that our competitor would build over here from Jack's Canyon, divide the Copah business with us, and have a line three hundred miles nearer to the Nevada gold-fields than ours."

"I understand," said Lidgerwood; and the vice-president went on.

"Since the failure of the Red Butte 'pocket' mines, the road and the country it traverses have been practically given over to the cowmen, the gulch miners, the rustlers, and the drift from the big camps elsewhere. In New York and on the Street, Red Butte Western was regarded as an exploded cartridge—a kite without a tail. It was only a few weeks ago that it dawned upon our executive committee that this particular kite without a tail offered us a ready-made jump of three hundred miles toward Tonopah and Goldfield. We began buying quietly for the control with the stock at nineteen. Naturally the Transcontinental people caught on, and in twenty-four hours we were at it, hammer and tongs."

Lidgerwood nodded. "I kept up with it in the newspapers," he cut in.

"The newspapers didn't print the whole story; not by many chapters," was the qualifying rejoinder. "When the stock had gone to par and beyond, our own crowd went back on us; and after it had passed the two-hundred mark, Adair and I were fighting it practically alone. Even President Brewster lost his nerve. He wanted to make a hedging compromise with the Transcontinental brokers just before we swung over the summit with the final five hundred shares we needed."

Again Lidgerwood made the sign of assent.

"Mr. Brewster is a level-headed Westerner. He doubtless knew, to the dotting of an 'i,' the particular brand of trouble you two expansionists were so eager to acquire."

"He did. He has a copper property somewhere in the vicinity of Angels, and he knows the road. He contended that we were buying two streaks of rust and a right-of-way in the Red Desert. More than that, he asserted that the executive officer didn't live who could bring order out of the chaos into which bad management and a peculiarly tough environment had plunged the Red Butte Western. That's where I had him bested, Howard. All through the hot fight I kept saying over and over to myself that I knew the man."

"But you don't know him, Stuart; that is the weak link in the chain."

Lidgerwood turned away to the scratched window-panes and the crude prospect, blurred now by the gathering shadows of the early evening. In the yards below, a long freight-train was pulling in from the west, with a switching-engine chasing it to begin the cutting out of the Copah locals. Over in the Red Butte yard a road-locomotive, turning on the table, swept a wide arc with the beam of its electric headlight in the graying dusk. Through the half-opened door in the despatcher's room came the diminished chattering of the telegraph instruments; this, with the outer clamor of trains and engines, made the silence in the private office more insistent.

When Lidgerwood faced about again after the interval of abstraction there were fine lines of harassment between his eyes, and his words came as if speech were costing him a conscious effort.

"If it were merely a matter of technical fitness, I suppose I might go over to Angels and do what you want done with the three hundred miles of demoralization. But the Red Butte proposition asks for more; for something that I can't give it. Stuart, there is a yellow streak in me that you seem never to have discovered. I am a coward."

The ghost of an incredulous smile wrinkled about the tired eyes of the big man in the pivot-chair.

"You put it with your usual exactitude," he assented slowly; "I hadn't discovered it." Then: "You forget that I have known you pretty much all your life, Howard."

"You haven't known me at all," was the sober reply.

"Oh, yes, I have! Let me recall one of the boyhood pictures that has never faded. It was just after school, one hot day, in the Illinois September. Our crowd had gone down to the pond back of the school-house, and two of us were paddling around on a raft made of sawmill slabs. One of the two— who always had more dare-deviltry than sense under his skull thatch—was silly enough to 'rock the boat,' and it went to pieces. You couldn't swim, Howard, but if you hadn't forgotten that trifling handicap and wallowed in to pull poor Billy Mimms ashore, I should have been a murderer."

Lidgerwood shook his head.

"You think you have made your case, but you haven't. What you say is true enough; I wasn't afraid of drowning—didn't think much about it, either way, I guess. But what I say is true, also. There are many kinds of courage, and quite as many kinds of cowardice. I am a coward of men."

"Oh, no, you're not: you only think you are," protested the one who thought he knew. But Lidgerwood would not let that stand.

"I know I am. Hear me through, and then judge for yourself. What I am going to tell you I have never told to any living man; but it is your right to hear it.... I have had the symptoms all my life, Stuart. You have spoken of the schoolboy days: you may remember how you used to fight my battles for me. You thought I took the bullying of the bigger boys because I wasn't strong enough physically to hold up my end. That wasn't it: it was fear, pure and simple. Are you listening?"

The man in the chair nodded and said, "Go on." He was of those to whom fear, the fear of what other men might do to him, was as yet a thing unlearned, and he was trying to attain the point of view of one to whom it seemed very real.

"It followed me up to manhood, and after a time I found myself constantly and consciously deferring to it. It was easy enough after the habit was formed. Twentieth-century civilization is decently peaceable, and it isn't especially difficult to dodge the personal collisions. I have succeeded in dodging them, for the greater part, paying the price in humiliation and self-abasement as I went along. God, Stuart, you don't know what that means!—the degradation; the hot and cold chills of self-loathing; the sickening misery of having your own soul turn upon you to rend and tear you like a rabid dog!"

"No, I don't know what it means," said the other man, moved more than he cared to admit by the abject confession.

3

"Of course you don't. Nobody else can know. I am alone in my pit of wretchedness, Ford ... as one born out of time; apprehending, as well as you or any one, what is required of a man and a gentleman, and yet unable to answer when my name is called. I said I had been paying the price; I am paying it here and now. This is the fourth time I have had to refuse a good offer that carried with it the fighting chance."

The vice-president's heavy eyebrows slanted in questioning surprise.

"You knew in advance that you were going to turn me down? Yet you came a thousand miles to meet me here; and you admit that you have gone the length of looking the ground over."

Lidgerwood's smile was mirthless.

"A regular recurring phase of the disease. It manifests itself in a determination to break away and do or die in the effort to win a little self-respect. I can't take the plunge. I know beforehand that I can't ... which brings us down to Copah, the present exigency, and the fact that you'll have to look farther along for your Red Butte Western man-queller. The blood isn't in my veins, Stuart. It was left out in the assembling."

The vice-president was still a young man and he was confronting a problem that annoyed him. He had been calling himself, and not without reason, a fair judge of men. Yet here was a man whom he had known intimately from boyhood, who was but just now revealing a totally unsuspected quality.

"You say you have been dodging the collisions. How do you know you wouldn't buck up when the real pinch comes?" he demanded.

"Because the pinch came once—and I didn't buck up. It was over a year ago, and to this good day I can't think calmly about it. You will understand when I say that it cost me the love of the one woman in the world."

The vice-president did understand. Being a married lover himself, he could measure the depth of the abyss into which Lidgerwood was looking. His voice was as sympathetic as a woman's when he said: "Go ahead and ease your mind; tell me about it, if you can, Howard. It's barely possible that you are not the best judge of your own act."

There was something approaching the abandonment of the shameless in Lidgerwood's manner when he went on.

"It was in the Montana mountains. I was going in to do a bit of expert engineering for her father. Incidentally, I was escorting her and her mother from the railroad terminus to the summer camp in the hills, where they were to join a coaching party of their friends for the Yellowstone tour. We had to drive forty miles in a stage, and there were six of us—the two women and four men. On the way the talk turned upon stage-robbings and hold-ups. With the chance of the real thing as remote as a visit from Mars, I could be an ass and a braggart. One of the men, a salesman for a powder company, gave me the rope wherewith to hang myself. He argued for non-resistance, and I remember that I grew sarcastic over the spectacle afforded by a grown man, armed and in possession of his five senses, permitting himself to be robbed without attempting to resist. You can guess what followed?"

"I'd rather hear you tell it," said the listener at Superintendent Leckhard's desk. "Go on."

Lidgerwood waited until the switching-engine, with its pop-valve open and screaming like a liberated devil of the noise pit, had passed.

"Three miles beyond the supper station we had our hold-up; the cut-and-dried, melodramatic sort of thing you read about, or used to read about, in the early days, with a couple of Winchesters poking through the scrub pines to represent the gang in hiding, and one lone, crippled desperado to come down to the footlights in the speaking part. You get the picture?"

"Yes; I've seen the original."

"Of course, it struck every soul of us with the shock of the incredible—the totally unexpected. It was a rank anachronism, twenty-five years out of date in that particular locality. Before anybody realized what was happening, the cripple had us lined up in a row beside the stage, and I was reaching for the stars quite as anxiously as the little Jew hat salesman, who was swearing by all the patriarchs that the twenty-dollar bill in his right-hand pocket was his entire fortune."

"Naturally," Ford commented. "You needn't rawhide yourself for that. You've been West often enough and long enough at a time to know the rules of the game—not to be frivolous when the other fellow has the drop on you."

"Wait," said Lidgerwood. "One minute later the cripple had sized us up for what we were. The other three men were not armed. I was, and Miss El—the young woman knew it. Also the cripple knew it. He tapped the gun bulging in my pocket and said, in good-natured contempt, 'Watch out that thing don't go off and hurt you some time when you ain't lookin', stranger.' Ford, I think I must have been hypnotized. I stood there like a frozen image, and let that crippled cow-rustler rob those two women—take the rings from their fingers!"

"Oh, hold on; there's another side to all that, and you know it," the vice-president began; but Lidgerwood would not listen.

"No," he protested; "don't try to find excuses for me; there were none. The fellow gave me every chance; turned his back on me as an absolutely negligible factor while he was going through the others. I'm quick enough when the crisis doesn't involve a fighting man's chance; and I can handle a gun, too, when the thing to be shot at isn't a human being. But to save my soul from everlasting torments I couldn't go through the simple motions of pulling the pistol from my pocket and dropping that fellow in his tracks; couldn't and didn't."

"Why, of course you couldn't, after it had got that far along," asserted Ford. "I doubt if any one could. That little remark about the gun in your pocket did you up. When a man gets you pacified to the condition in which he can safely josh you, he has got you going and he knows it—and knows you know it. You may be twice as hot and bloodthirsty as you were before, but you are just that much less able to strike back. It's not a theory; it is a psychological demonstration."

"But the fact remained," said Lidgerwood, sparing himself not at all. "I was weighed and found wanting; that is the only point worth considering."

"Well?" queried Ford, when the self-condemned culprit turned again to the dusk-darkened window, "what came of it?"

"That which was due to come. I was told many times and in many different ways what the one woman thought of me. For the few days during which she and her mother waited at her father's mine for the coming of the Yellowstone party, she used me for a door-mat, as I deserved. That was a year ago last spring. I haven't seen her since; haven't tried to."

The vice-president reached up and snapped the key of the electric bulb over the desk, and the lurking shadows in the corners of the room fled away.

"Sit down," he said shortly; and when Lidgerwood had found a chair: "You treat it as an incident closed, Howard. Do you mean to go on leaving it up in the air like that?"

"It was left in the air a year ago last spring. I can't pull it down now."

"Yes, you can. You haven't exaggerated the conditions on the Red Butte line an atom. As you say, the operating force is as godless a lot of outlaws as ever ran trains or ditched them. They all know that the road has been bought and sold, and that pretty sweeping changes are impending. They are looking for trouble, and are quite ready to help make it. If you could discharge them in a body, you couldn't replace them—the Red Desert having nothing to offer as a dwelling-place for civilized men; and this they know, too. Howard, I'm telling you right now that it will require a higher brand of courage to go over to Angels and manhandle the Red Butte Western as a division of the P. S-W. than it would to face a dozen highwaymen, if every individual one of the dozen had the drop on you!"

Lidgerwood left his chair and began to pace the narrow limits of the private office, five steps and a turn. The noisy switching-engine had gone clattering and shrieking down the yard again before he said, "You mean that you are still giving me the chance to make good over yonder in the Red Desert—after what I have told you?"

"I do; only I'll make it more binding. It was optional with you before; it's a sheer necessity now. You've *got* to go."

Again Lidgerwood took time to reflect, tramping the floor, with his head down and his hands in the pockets of the correct coat. In the end he yielded, as the vice-president's subjects commonly did.

"I'll go, if you still insist upon it," was the slowly spoken decision. "There will doubtless be plenty of trouble, and I shall probably show the yellow streak—for the last time, perhaps. It's the kind of an outfit to kill a coward for the pure pleasure of it, if I'm not mistaken."

"Well," said the man in the swing-chair, calmly, "maybe you need a little killing, Howard. Had you ever thought of that?"

A gray look came into Lidgerwood's face.

"Maybe I do."

A little silence supervened. Then Ford plunged into detail.

"Now that you are fairly committed, sit down and let me give you an idea of what you'll find at Angels in the way of a head-quarters outfit. Draw up here and we'll go over the lay-out together."

A busy hour had elapsed, and the gong of the station dining-room below was adding its raucous clamor to the drumming thunder of the incoming train from Green Butte, when the vice-president concluded his outline sketch of the Red Butte Western conditions.

"Of course, you know that you will have a free hand. We have already cleared the decks for you. As an independent road, the Red Butte line had the usual executive organization in miniature: Cumberley had the title of general superintendent, but his authority, when he cared to assert it, was really that of general manager. Under him, in the head-quarters staff at Angels, there was an auditor—who also acted as paymaster, a general freight and passenger agent, and a superintendent of motive power. Operating the line as a branch of the P. S-W System, we can simplify the organization. We have consolidated the auditing and traffic departments with our Colorado-lines head-quarters at Denver. This will leave you with only the operating, telegraph, train-service, and engineering departments to handle from Angels. With one exception, your authority will be absolute; you will hire and discharge as you see fit, and there will be no appeal from your decision."

"That applies to my own departments—the operating, telegraph, train-service, and engineering; but how about the motive power?" asked the new incumbent.

Ford threw down the desk-knife, with which he had been sharpening a pencil, with a little gesture indicative of displeasure.

"There lies the exception, and I wish it didn't. Gridley, the master-mechanic, will be nominally under your orders, of course; but if it should come to blows between you, you couldn't fire him. In the regular routine he will report to the Colorado-lines superintendent of motive power at Denver. But in a quarrel with you he could make a still longer arm and reach the P. S-W. board of directors in New York."

"How is that?" inquired Lidgerwood.

"It's a family affair. He is a widower, and his wife was a sister of the Van Kensingtons. He got his job through the family influence, and he'll hold it in the same way. But you are not likely to have any trouble with him. He is a brute in his own peculiar fashion; but when it comes to handling shopmen and keeping the engines in service, he can't be beat."

"That is all I shall ask of him," said the new superintendent. "Anything else?" looking at his watch.

"Yes, there is one other thing. I spoke of Hallock, the man you will find holding down the head-quarters office at Angels. He was Cumberley's chief clerk, and long before Cumberley resigned he was the real superintendent of the Red Butte Western in everything but the title, and the place on the pay-roll. Naturally he thought he ought to be considered when we climbed into the saddle, and he has already written to President Brewster, asking for the promotion in fact. He happens to be a New Yorker—like Gridley; and, again like Gridley, he has a friend at court. Magnus knows him, and he recommended him for the superintendency when Mr. Brewster referred the application to me. I couldn't agree, and I had to turn him down. I am telling you this so you'll be easy with him—as easy as you can. I don't know him personally, but if you can keep him on——"

"I shall be only too glad to keep him, if he knows his business and will stay," was Lidgerwood's reply. Then, with another glance at his watch, "Shall we go up-town and get dinner? Afterward you can give me your notion in the large about the future extension of the road across the second Timanyoni, and I'll order out the service-car and an engine and go to my place. A man can die but once; and maybe I shall contrive to live long enough to set a few stakes for some better fellow to drive. Let's go."

At ten o'clock that night Engine 266, Williams, engineer, and Blackmar, fireman, was chalked up on the Red Butte Western roundhouse bulletin-board to go west at midnight with the new superintendent's service-car, running as a special train.

Svenson, the caller, who brought the order from the Copah sub-despatcher's office, unloaded his news upon the circle of R.B.W. engineers, firemen, and roundhouse roustabouts lounging on the benches in the tool-room and speculating morosely upon the probable changes which the new management would bring to pass.

"Ve bane got dem new boss, Ay vant to tal you fallers," he drawled.

"Who is he?" demanded Williams, who had been looking on sourly while the engine-despatcher chalked his name on the board for the night run with the service-car.

"Ay couldn't tal you his name. Bote he is dem young faller bane goin' 'round hare dees two, t'ree days, lukin' lak preacher out of a yob. Vouldn'd dat yar you?"

Williams rose up to his full height of six-feet-two, and flung his hands upward in a gesture that was more expressive than many oaths.

"*Collars-and-Cuffs, by God!*" he said.

II

In the beginning the Red Desert, figuring unpronounceably under its Navajo name of Tse-nastci—Circle-of-Red-Stones—was shunned alike by man and beast, and the bravest of the gold-hunters, seeking to penetrate to the placer ground in the hill gulches between the twin Timanyoni ranges, made a hundred-mile détour to avoid it.

Later, the discoveries of rich "pocket" deposits in the Red Butte district lifted the intermontane hill country temporarily to the high plane of a bonanza field. In the rush that followed, a few prudent ones chose the longer détour; others, hardier and more temerarious, outfitted at Copah, and assaulting the hill barrier of the Little Piñons at Crosswater Gap, faced the jornada through the Land of Thirst.

Of these earliest of the desert caravans, the railroad builders, following the same trail and pointing toward the same destination in the gold gulches, found dismal reminders. In the longest of the thirsty stretches there were clean-picked skeletons, and they were not always the relics of the patient pack-animals. In which event Chandler, chief of the Red Butte Western construction, proclaimed himself Eastern-bred and a tenderfoot by compelling the grade contractors to stop and bury them.

Why the railroad builders, with Copah for a starting-point and Red Butte for a terminus, had elected to pitch their head-quarters camp in the western edge of the desert, no later comer could ever determine. Lost, also, is the identity of the camp's sponsor who, visioning the things that were to be, borrowed from the California pioneers and named the halting-place on the desert's edge "Angels." But for the more material details Chandler was responsible. It was he who laid out the division yards on the bald plain at the foot of the first mesa, planting the "Crow's Nest" head-quarters building on the mesa side of the gridironing tracks, and scattering the shops and repair plant along the opposite boundary of the wide right-of-way.

The town had followed the shops, as a sheer necessity. First and always the railroad nucleus, Angels became in turn, and in addition, the forwarding station for a copper-mining district in the Timanyoni foot-hills, and a little later, when a few adventurous cattlemen had discovered that the sun-cured herbage of the desert borders was nutritious and fattening, a stock-shipping point. But even in the day of promise, when the railroad building was at its height and a handful of promoters were plotting streets and town lots on the second mesa, and printing glowing tributes—for strictly Eastern distribution—to the dry atmosphere and the unfailing sunshine, the desert leaven was silently at work. A few of the railroad men transplanted their families; but apart from these, Angels was a man's town with elemental appetites, and with only the coarse fare of the frontier fighting line to satisfy them.

Farther along, the desert came more definitely to its own. The rich Red Butte "pockets" began to show signs of exhaustion, and the gulch and ore mining afforded but a precarious alternative to the thousands who had gone in on the crest of the bonanza wave. Almost as tumultuously as it had swept into the hill country, the tide of population swept out. For the gulch hamlets between the Timanyonis there was still an industrial reason for being; but the railroad languished, and Angels became the weir to catch and retain many of the leavings, the driftwood stranded in the slack water of the outgoing tide. With the railroad, the Copperette Mine, and the "X-bar-Z" pay-days to bring regularly recurring moments of flushness, and with every alternate door in Mesa Avenue the entrance to a bar, a dance-hall, a gambling den, or the three in combination, the elemental appetites grew avid, and the hot breath of the desert fanned slow fires of brutality that ate the deeper when they penetrated to the punk heart of the driftwood.

It was during this period of deflagration and dry rot that the Eastern owners of the railroad lost heart. Since the year of the Red Butte inrush there had been no dividends; and Chandler, summoned from another battle with the canyons in the far Northwest, was sent in to make an expert report on the property. "Sell it for what it will bring," was the substance of Chandler's advice; but there were no bidders, and from this time on a masterless railroad was added to the spoils of war—the inexpiable war of the Red Desert upon its invaders.

At the moment of the moribund railroad's purchase by the Pacific Southwestern, the desert was encroaching more and more upon the town planted in its western border. In the height of Angels's prosperity there had been electric lights and a one-car street tramway, a bank, and a Building and Loan Association attesting its presence in rows of ornate cottages on the second mesa—alluring bait thrown out to catch the potential savings of the railroad colonists.

But now only the railroad plant was electric-lighted; the single ramshackle street-car had been turned into a *chile-con-carne* stand; the bank, unable to compete with the faro games and the roulette wheels, had gone into liquidation; the Building and Loan directors had long since looted the treasury and sought fresh fields, and the cottages were chiefly empty shells.

Of the charter members of the Building and Loan Association, shrewdest of the many boom-time schemes for the separation of the pay-roll man from his money, only two remained as residents of Angels the decadent. One of these was Gridley, the master-mechanic, and the other was Hallock, chief clerk for a diminishing series of imported superintendents, and now for the third time the disappointed applicant for the headship of the Red Butte Western.

Associated for some brief time in the real-estate venture, and hailing from the same far-away Eastern State and city, these two had been at first yoke-fellows, and afterward, as if by tacit consent, inert enemies. As widely separated as the poles in characteristics, habits, and in their outlook upon life, they had little in common, and many antipathies.

Gridley was a large man, virile of face and figure, and he marched in the ranks of the full-fed and the self-indulgent. Hallock was big-boned and cadaverous of face, but otherwise a fair physical match for the master-mechanic; a dark man with gloomy eyes and a permanent frown. Jovial good-nature went with the master-mechanic's gray eyes twinkling easily to a genial smile, but it stopped rather abruptly at the straight-lined, sensual mouth, and found a second negation in the brutal jaw which was only thinly masked by the neatly trimmed beard. Hallock's smile was bitter, and if he had a social side no one in Angels had ever discovered it. In a region where fellowship in some sort, if it were only that of the bottle and the card-table, was any man's for the taking, he was a hermit, an ascetic; and his attitude toward others, all others, so far as Angels knew, was that of silent and morose ferocity.

It was in an upper room of the "Crow's Nest" head-quarters building that these two, the master-mechanic and the acting superintendent, met late in the evening of the day when Vice-President Ford had kept his appointment in Copah with Lidgerwood.

Gridley, clad like a gentleman, and tilting comfortably in his chair as he smoked a cigar that neither love nor money could have bought in Angels, was jocosely sarcastic. Hallock, shirt-sleeved, unkempt, and with the permanent frown deepening the furrow between his eyes, neither tilted nor smoked.

"They tell me you have missed the step up again, Hallock," said the smoker lazily, when the purely technical matter that had brought him to Hallock's office had been settled.

"Who tells you?" demanded the other; and a listener, knowing neither, would have remarked the curious similarity of the grating note in both voices as infallibly as a student of human nature would have contrasted the two men in every other personal characteristic.

"I don't remember," said Gridley, good-naturedly refusing to commit his informant, "but it's on the wires. Vice-President Ford is in Copah, and the new superintendent is with him."

Hallock leaned forward in his chair.

"Who is the new man?" he asked.

"Nobody seems to know him by name. But he is a friend of Ford's all right. That is how he gets the job."

Hallock took a plug of black tobacco from his pocket, and cut a small sliver from it for a chew. It was his one concession to appetite, and he made it grudgingly.

"A college man, I suppose," he commented. "Otherwise Ford wouldn't be backing him."

"Oh, yes, I guess it's safe to count on that."

"And a man who will carry out the Ford policy?"

Gridley's eyes smiled, but lower down on his face the smile became a cynical baring of the strong teeth.

"A man who may try to carry out the Ford idea," he qualified; adding, "The desert will get hold of him and eat him alive, as it has the others."

"Maybe," said Hallock thoughtfully. Then, with sudden heat, "It's hell, Gridley! I've hung on and waited and done the work for their figure-heads, one after another. The job belongs to me!"

This time Gridley's smile was a thinly veiled sneer.

"What makes you so keen for it, Hallock?" he asked. "You have no use for the money, and still less for the title."

"How do you know I don't want the salary?" snapped the other. "Because I don't have my clothes made in New York, or blow myself across the tables in Mesa Avenue, does it go without saying that I have no use for money?"

"But you haven't, you know you haven't," was the taunting rejoinder. "And the title, when you have, and have always had, the real authority, means still less to you."

"Authority!" scoffed the chief clerk, his gloomy eyes lighting up with slow fire, "this maverick railroad don't know the meaning of the word. By God! Gridley, if I had the club in my hands for a few months I'd show 'em!"

"Oh, I guess not," said the cigar-smoker easily. "You're not built right for it, Hallock; the desert would give you the horse-laugh."

"Would it? Not before I had squared off a few old debts, Gridley; don't you forget that."

There was a menace in the harsh retort, and the chief clerk made no attempt to conceal it.

"Threatening, are you?" jeered the full-fed one, still good-naturedly sarcastic. "What would you do, if you had the chance, Rankin?"

"I'd kill out some of the waste and recklessness, if it took the last man off the pay-rolls; and I'd break even with at least one man over in the Timanyoni, if I had to use the whole Red Butte Western to pry him loose!"

"Flemister again?" queried the master-mechanic. And then, in mild deprecation, "You are a bad loser, Hallock, a damned bad loser. But I suppose that is one of your limitations."

A silence settled down upon the upper room, but Gridley made no move to go. Out in the yards the night men were making up a westbound freight, and the crashing of box-cars carelessly "kicked" into place added its note to the discord of inefficiency and destructive breakage.

Over in the town a dance-hall piano was jangling, and the raucous voice of the dance-master calling the figures came across to the Crow's Nest curiously like the barking of a distant dog. Suddenly the barking voice stopped, and the piano clamor ended futilely in an aimless tinkling. For climax a pistol-shot rang out, followed by a scattering volley. It was a precise commentary on the time and the place that neither of the two men in the head-quarters upper room gave heed to the pistol-shots, or to the yelling uproar that accompanied them.

It was after the shouting had died away in a confused clatter of hoofs, and the pistol cracklings were coming only at intervals and from an increasing distance, that the corridor door opened and the night despatcher's off-trick man came in with a message for Hallock.

It was a mere routine notification from the line-end operator at Copah, and the chief clerk read it sullenly to the master-mechanic.

"Engine 266, Williams, engineer, and Blackmar, fireman, with service-car Naught-One, Bradford, conductor, will leave Copah at 12:01 A.M., and run special to Angels. By order of Howard Lidgerwood, General Superintendent."

Gridley's pivot-chair righted itself with a snap. But he waited until the off-trick man was gone before he said, "Lidgerwood! Well, by all the gods!" then, with a laugh that was more than half a snarl, "There is a chance for you yet, Rankin."

"Why, do you know him?"

"No, but I know something about him. I've got a line on New York, the same as you have, and I get a hint now and then. I knew that Lidgerwood had been considered for the place, but I was given to understand that he would refuse the job if it were offered to him."

"Why should he refuse?" demanded Hallock.

"That is where my wire-tapper fell down; he couldn't tell."

"Then why do you say there is still a chance for me?"

"Oh, on general principles, I guess. If it was an even break that he would refuse, it is still more likely that he won't stay after he has seen what he is up against, don't you think?"

Hallock did not say what he thought. He rarely did.

"Of course, you made inquiries about him when you found out he was a possible; I'd trust you to do that, Gridley. What do you know?"

"Not much that you can use. He is out of the Middle West; a young man and a graduate of Purdue. He took the Civil degree, but stayed two years longer and romped through the Mechanical. He ought to be pretty well up on theory, you'd say."

"Theory be damned!" snapped the chief clerk. "What he'll need in the Red Desert will be nerve and a good gun. If he has the nerve, he can buy the gun."

"But having the gun he couldn't always be sure of buying the nerve, eh? I guess you are right, Rankin; you usually are when you can forget to be vindictive. And that brings us around to the jumping-off place again. Of course, you will stay on with the new man—if he wants you to?"

"I don't know. That is my business, and none of yours."

It was a bid for a renewal of the quarrel which was never more than half veiled between these two. But Gridley did not lift the challenge.

"Let it go at that," he said placably. "But if you should decide to stay, I want you to let up on Flemister."

The morose antagonism died out of Hallock's eyes, and in its place came craft.

"I'd kill Flemister on sight, if I had the sand; you know that, Gridley. Some day it may come to that. But in the meantime——"

"In the meantime you have been snapping at his heels like a fice-dog, Hallock; holding out ore-cars on him, delaying his coal supplies, stirring up trouble with his miners. That was all right, up to yesterday. But now it has got to stop."

"Not for any orders that you can give," retorted the chief clerk, once more opening the door for the quarrel.

The master-mechanic got up and flicked the cigar ash from his coat-sleeve with a handkerchief that was fine enough to be a woman's.

"I am not going to come to blows with you. Rankin—not if I can help it," he said, with his hand on the door-knob. "But what I have said will have to go as it lies. Shoot Flemister out of hand, if you feel like it, but quit hampering his business."

Hallock stood up, and when he was on his feet his big frame made him look still more a fair match physically for the handsome master-mechanic.

"Why?" The single word shot out of the loose-lipped mouth like an explosive bullet.

Gridley opened the door and turned upon the threshold.

"I might borrow the word from you and say that Flemister's business and mine are none of yours. But I won't do that. I'll merely say that Flemister may need a little Red Butte Western nursing in the Ute Valley irrigation scheme he is promoting, and I want you to see that he gets it. You may take that as a word to the wise, or as a kicked-in hint to a blind mule; whichever you please. You can't afford to fight me, Hallock, and you know it. Sleep on it a few hours, and you'll see it in that way, I'm sure. Good-night."

III

Crosswater Gap, so named because the high pass over which the railroad finds its way is anything but a gap, and, save when the winter snows are melting, there is no water within a day's march, was in sight from the loopings of the eastern approach. Lidgerwood, scanning the grades as the service-car swung from tangent to curve and curve to tangent up the steep inclines, was beginning to think of breakfast. The morning air was crisp and bracing, and he had been getting the full benefit of it for an hour or more, sitting under the umbrella roof at the observation end of the car.

With the breakfast thought came the thing itself, or the invitation to it. As a parting kindness the night before, Ford had transferred one of the cooks from his own private car to Lidgerwood's service, and the little man, Tadasu Matsuwari by name, and a subject of the Mikado by race and birth, came to the car door to call his new employer to the table.

It was an attractive table, well appointed and well served; but Lidgerwood, temperamentally single-eyed in all things, was diverted from his reorganization problem for the moment only. Since early dawn he had been up and out on the observation platform, noting, this time with the eye of mastership, the physical condition of the road; the bridges, the embankments, the cross-ties, the miles of steel unreeling under the drumming trucks, and the object-lesson was still fresh in his mind.

To a disheartening extent, the Red Butte demoralization had involved the permanent way. Originally a good track, with heavy steel, easy grades compensated for the curves, and a mathematical alignment, the roadbed and equipment had been allowed to fall into disrepair under indifferent supervision and the short-handing of the section gangs—always an impractical directory's first retrenchment when the dividends begin to fail. Lidgerwood had seen how the ballast had been suffered to sink at the rail-joints, and he had read the record of careless supervision at each fresh swing of the train, since it is the section foreman's weakness to spoil the geometrical curve by working it back, little by little, into the adjoining tangent.

Reflecting upon these things, Lidgerwood's comment fell into speech over his cup of coffee and crisp breakfast bacon.

"About the first man we need is an engineer who won't be too exalted to get down and squint curves with the section bosses," he mused, and from that on he was searching patiently through the memory card-index for the right man.

At the summit station, where the line leaves the Pannikin basin to plunge into the western desert, there was a delay. Lidgerwood was still at the breakfast-table when Bradford, the conductor, black-shirted and looking, in his slouch hat and riding-leggings, more like a horse-wrangler than a captain of railroad trains, lounged in to explain that there was a hot box under the 266's tender. Bradford was not of any faction of discontent, but the spirit of morose insubordination, born of the late change in management, was in the air, and he spoke gruffly. Hence, with the flint and steel thus provided, the spark was promptly evoked.

"Were the boxes properly overhauled before you left Copah?" demanded the new boss.

Bradford did not know, and the manner of his answer implied that he did not care. And for good measure he threw in an intimation that roundhouse dope kettles were not in his line.

Lidgerwood passed over the large impudence and held to the matter in hand.

"How much time have we on 201?" he asked, Train 201 being the westbound passenger overtaken and left behind in the small hours of the morning by the lighter and faster special.

"Thirty minutes, here," growled the little brother of the cows; after which he took himself off as if he considered the incident sufficiently closed.

Fifteen minutes later Lidgerwood finished his breakfast and went back to his camp-chair on the observation platform of the service-car. A glance over the side rail showed him his train crew still working on the heated axle-bearing. Another to the rear picked up the passenger-train storming around the climbing curves of the eastern approach to the summit. There was a small problem impending for the division despatcher at Angels, and the new superintendent held aloof to see how it would be handled.

It was handled rather indifferently. The passenger-train was pulling in over the summit switches when Bradford, sauntering into the telegraph office as if haste were the last thing in the world to be considered, asked for his clearance card, got it, and gave Williams the signal to go.

Lidgerwood got up and went into the car to consult the time-table hanging in the office compartment. Train 201 had no dead time at Crosswater; hence, if the ten-minute interval between trains of the same class moving in the same direction was to be preserved, the passenger would have to be held.

The assumption that the passenger-train would be held aroused all the railroad martinet's fury in the new superintendent. In Lidgerwood's calendar, time-killing on regular trains stood next to an infringement of the rules providing for the safety of life and property. His hand was on the signal-cord when, chancing to look back, he saw that the passenger-train had made only the momentary time-card stop at the summit station, and was coming on.

This turned the high crime into a mere breach of discipline, common enough even on well-managed railroads when the leading train can be trusted to increase the distance interval. But again the martinet in Lidgerwood protested. It was his theory that rules were made to be observed, and his experience had proved that little infractions paved the way for great ones. In the present instance, however, it was too late to interfere; so he drew a chair out in line with one of the rear observation windows and sat down to mark the event.

Pitching over the hilltop summit, within a minute of each other, the two trains raced down the first few curving inclines almost as one. Mile after mile was covered, and still the perilous situation remained unchanged. Down the short tangents and around the constantly recurring curves the special seemed to be towing the passenger at the end of an invisible but dangerously short drag-rope.

Lidgerwood began to grow uneasy. On the straight-line stretches the following train appeared to be rushing onward to an inevitable rear-end collision with the one-car special; and where the track swerved to right or left around the hills, the pursuing smoke trail rose above the intervening hill-shoulders near and threatening. With the parts of a great machine whirling in unison and nicely timed to escape destruction, a small accident to a single cog may spell disaster.

Lidgerwood left his chair and went again to consult the time-table. A brief comparison of miles with minutes explained the effect without excusing the cause. Train 201's schedule from the summit station to the desert level was very fast; and Williams, nursing his hot box, either could not, or would not, increase his lead.

At first, Lidgerwood, anticipating rebellion, was inclined to charge the hazardous situation to intention on the part of his own train crew. Having a good chance to lie out of it if they were accused, Williams and Bradford might be deliberately trying the nerve of the new boss. The presumption did not breed fear; it bred wrath, hot and vindictive. Two sharp tugs at the signal-cord brought Bradford from the engine. The memory of the conductor's gruff replies and easy impudence was fresh enough to make Lidgerwood's reprimand harsh.

"Do you call this railroading?" he rasped, pointing backward to the menace. "Don't you know that we are on 201's time?"

Bradford scowled in surly antagonism.

"That blamed hot box—" he began, but Lidgerwood cut him off short.

"The hot box has nothing to do with the case. You are not hired to take chances, or to hold out regular trains. Go forward and tell your engineer to speed up and get out of the way."

"I got my clearance at the summit, and I ain't despatchin' trains on this jerk-water railroad," observed the conductor coolly. Then he added, with a shade less of the belligerent disinterest: "Williams can't speed up. That housin' under the tender is about ready to blaze up and set the woods afire again, right now."

Once more Lidgerwood turned to the time-card. It was twenty miles farther along to the next telegraph station, and he heaped up wrath against the day of wrath in store for a despatcher who would recklessly turn two trains loose and out of his reach under such critical conditions, for thirty hazardous mountain miles.

Bradford, looking on sullenly, mistook the new boss's frown for more to follow, with himself for the target, and was moving away. Lidgerwood pointed to a chair with a curt, "Sit down!" and the conductor obeyed reluctantly.

"You say you have your clearance card, and that you are not despatching trains," he went on evenly, "but neither fact relieves you of your responsibility. It was your duty to make sure that the despatcher fully understood the situation at Crosswater, and to refuse to pull out ahead of the passenger without something more definite than a formal permit. Weren't you taught that? Where did you learn to run trains?"

It was an opening for hard words, but the conductor let it pass. Something in the steady, business-like tone, or in the shrewdly appraisive eyes, turned Bradford the potential mutineer into Bradford the possible partisan.

"I reckon we are needing a *rodeo* over here on this jerk-water mighty bad, Mr. Lidgerwood," he said, half humorously. "Take us coming and going, about half of us never had the sure-enough railroad brand put onto us, nohow. But, Lord love you! this little *pasear* we're making down this hill ain't anything! That's the old 210 chasin' us with the passenger, and she couldn't catch Bat Williams and the '66 in a month o' Sundays if we didn't have that doggoned spavined leg under the tender. She sure couldn't."

Lidgerwood smiled in spite of his annoyance, and wondered at what page in the railroad primer he would have to begin in teaching these men of the camps and the round-ups.

"But it isn't railroading," he insisted, meeting his first pupil half-way, and as man to man. "You might do this thing ninety-nine times without paying for it, and the hundredth time something would turn up to slow or to stop the leading train, and there you are."

"Sure!" said the ex-cowboy, quite heartily.

"Now, if there should happen to be——"

The sentence was never finished. The special, lagging a little now in deference to the smoking hot box, was rounding one of the long hill curves to the left. Suddenly the air-brakes ground sharply upon the wheels, shrill whistlings from the 266 sounded the stop signal, and past the end of the slowing service-car a trackman ran frantically up the line toward the following passenger, yelling and swinging his stripped coat like a madman.

Lidgerwood caught a fleeting glimpse of a section gang's green "slow" flag lying toppled over between the rails a hundred feet to the rear. Measuring the distance of the onrushing passenger-train against the life-saving seconds remaining, he called to Bradford to jump, and then ran forward to drag the Japanese cook out of his galley.

It was all over in a moment. There was time enough for Lidgerwood to rush the little Tadasu to the forward vestibule, to fling him into space, and to make his own flying leap for safety before the crisis came. Happily there was no wreck, though the margin of escape was the narrowest. Williams stuck to his post in the cab of the 266, applying and releasing the brakes, and running as far ahead as he dared upon the loosened timbers of the culvert, for which the section gang's slowflag was out. Carter, the engineer on the passenger-train, jumped; but his fireman was of better mettle and stayed with the machine, sliding the wheels with the driver-jams, and pumping sand on the rails up to the moment when the shuddering mass of iron and steel thrust its pilot under the trucks of Lidgerwood's car, lifted them, dropped them, and drew back sullenly in obedience to the pull of the reverse and the recoil of the brake mechanism.

It was an excellent opportunity for eloquence of the explosive sort, and when the dust had settled the track and trainmen were evidently expecting the well-deserved tongue-lashing. But in crises like this the new superintendent was at his self-contained best. Instead of swearing at the men, he gave his orders quietly and with the brisk certainty of one who knows his trade. The passenger-train was to keep ten minutes behind its own time until the next siding was passed, making up beyond that point if its running orders permitted. The special was to proceed on 201's time to the siding in question, at which point it would side-track and let the passenger precede it.

Bradford was in the cab of 266 when Williams eased his engine and the service-car over the unsafe culvert, and inched the throttle open for the speeding race down the hill curves toward the wide valley plain of the Red Desert.

"Turn it loose, Andy," said the big engineman, when the requisite number of miles of silence had been ticked off by the space-devouring wheels. "What-all do you think of Mister Collars-and-Cuffs by this time?"

Bradford took a leisurely minute to whittle a chewing cube from his pocket plug of hard-times tobacco.

"Well, first dash out o' the box, I allowed he was some locoed; he jumped me like a jack-rabbit for takin' a clearance right under Jim Carter's nose that-a-way. Then we got down to business, and I was just beginning to get onto his gait a little when the green flag butted in."

"Gait fits the laundry part of him?" suggested Williams.

"It does and it don't. I ain't much on systems and sure things, Bat, but I can make out to guess a guess, once in a while, when I have to. If that little tailor-made man don't get his finger mashed, or something, and have to go home and get somebody to poultice it, things are goin' to have a spell of happenings on this little old cow-trail of a railroad. That's my ante."

"What sort of things?" demanded Williams.

"When it comes to that, your guess is as good as mine, but they'll spell trouble for the amatoors and the trouble-makers, I reckon. I ain't placin' any bets yet, but that's about the way it stacks up to me."

Williams let the 266 out another notch, hung out of his window to look back at the smoking hot box, and, in the complete fulness of time, said, "Think he's got the sand, Andy?"

"This time you've got me goin'," was the slow reply. "Sizing him up one side and down the other when he called me back to pull my ear, I said, 'No, my young bronco-buster; you're a bluffer—the kind that'll put up both hands right quick when the bluff is called.' Afterward, I wasn't so blamed sure. One kind o' sand he's got, to a dead moral certainty. When he saw what was due to happen back yonder at the culvert, he told me '23,' all right, but he took time to hike up ahead and yank that Jap cook out o' the car-kitchen before he turned his own little handspring into the ditch."

The big engineer nodded, but he was still unconvinced when he made the stop for the siding at Last Chance. After the fireman had dropped off to set the switch for the following train, Williams put the unconvincement into words.

"That kind of sand is all right in God's country, Andy, but out here in the nearer edges of hell you got to know how to fight with pitchforks and such other tools as come handy. The new boss may be that kind of a scrapper, but he sure don't look it. You know as well as I do that men like Rufford and 'Cat' Biggs and Red-Light Sammy'll eat him alive, just for the fun of it, if he can't make out to throw lead quicker'n they can. And that ain't saying anything about the hobo outfit he'll have to go up against on this make-b'lieve railroad."

"No," agreed Bradford, ruminating thoughtfully. And then, by way of rounding out the subject: "Here's hopin' his nerve is as good as his clothes. I don't love a Mongolian any better'n you do, Bat, but the way he hustled to save that little brown man's skin sort o' got next to me; it sure did. Says I, 'A man that'll do that won't go round hunting a chance to kick a fice-dog just because the fice don't happen to be a blooded bull-terrier.'"

Williams, brawny and broad-chested, leaned against his box, his bare arms folded and his short pipe at the disputatious angle.

"He'd better have nerve, or get some," he commented. "T'otherways it's him for an early wooden overcoat and a trip back home in the express-car. After which, let me tell you, Andy, that man Ford'll sift this cussed country through a flour-shaker but what he'll cinch the outfit that does it. You write that out in your car-report."

Back in the service-car Lidgerwood was sitting quietly in the doorway, smoking his delayed after-breakfast cigar, and timing the up-coming passenger-train, watch in hand. Carter was ten minutes, to the exact second, behind his schedule time when the train thundered past on the main track, and Lidgerwood pocketed his watch with a smile of satisfaction. It was the first small victory in the campaign for reform.

Later, however, when the special was once more in motion westward, the desert laid hold upon him with the grip which first benumbs, then breeds dull rage, and finally makes men mad. Mile after mile the glistening rails sped backward into a shimmering haze of red dust. The glow of the breathless forenoon was like the blinding brightness of a forge-fire. To right and left the great treeless plain rose to bare buttes, backed by still barer mountains. Let the train speed as it would, there was always the same wearying prospect, devoid of interest, empty of human landmarks. Only the blazing sun swung from side to side with the slow veerings of the track: what answered for a horizon seemed never to change, never to move.

At long intervals a siding, sometimes with its waiting train, but oftener empty and deserted, slid into view and out again. Still less frequently a telegraph station, with its red, iron-roofed office, its water-tank cars and pumping machinery, and its high-fenced corral and loading chute, moved up out of the distorting heat haze ahead, and was lost in the dusty mirages to the rear. But apart from the crews of the waiting trains, and now and then the desert-sobered face of some telegraph operator staring from his window at the passing special, there were no signs of life: no cattle upon the distant hills, no loungers on the station platforms.

Lidgerwood had crossed this arid, lifeless plain twice within the week on his preliminary tour of inspection, but both times he had been in the Pullman, with fellow-passengers to fill the nearer field of vision and to temper the awful loneliness of the waste. Now, however, the desert with its heat, its stillness, its vacancy, its pitiless barrenness, claimed him as its own. He wondered that he had been impatient with the men it bred. The wonder now was that human virtue of any temper could long withstand the blasting touch of so great and awful a desolation.

It was past noon when the bowl-like basin, in which the train seemed to circle helplessly without gaining upon the terrifying horizons, began to lose its harshest features. Little by little, the tumbled hills drew nearer, and the red-sand dust of the road-bed gave place to broken lava. Patches of gray, sun-dried mountain grass appeared on the passing hill slopes, and in the arroyos trickling threads of water glistened, or, if the water were hidden, there were at least paths of damp sand to hint at the blessed moisture underneath.

Lidgerwood began to breathe again; and when the shrill whistle of the locomotive signalled the approach to the division head-quarters, he was thankful that the builders of Angels had pitched their tents and driven their stakes in the desert's edge, rather than in its heart.

Truly, Angels was not much to be thankful for, as the exile from the East regretfully admitted when he looked out upon it from the windows of his office in the second story of the Crow's Nest. A many-tracked railroad yard, flanked on one side by the repair shops, roundhouse, and coal-chutes; and on the other by a straggling town of bare and commonplace exteriors, unpainted, unfenced, treeless, and wind-swept: Angels stood baldly for what it was—a mere stopping-place in transit for the Red Butte Western.

The new superintendent turned his back upon the depressing outlook and laid his hand upon the latch of the door opening into the adjoining room. There was a thing to be said about the reckless bunching of trains out of reach of the wires, and it might as well be said now as later, he determined. But at the moment of door-opening he was made to realize that a tall, box-like contrivance in one corner of the office was a desk, and that it was inhabited.

The man who rose up to greet him was bearded, heavy-shouldered, and hollow-eyed, and he was past middle age. Green cardboard cones protecting his shirt-sleeves, and a shade of the same material visoring the sunken eyes, were the only clerkly suggestions about him. Since he merely stood up and ran his fingers through his thick black hair, with no more than an abstracted "Good-afternoon" for speech, Lidgerwood was left to guess at his identity.

"You are Mr. Hallock?" Lidgerwood made the guess without offering to shake hands, the high, box-like desk forbidding the attempt.

"Yes." The answer was neither antagonistic nor placatory; it was merely colorless.

"My name is Lidgerwood. You have heard of my appointment?"

Again the colorless "Yes."

Lidgerwood saw no good end to be subserved by postponing the inevitable.

"Mr. Ford spoke to me about you last night. He told me that you had been Mr. Cumberley's chief clerk, and that since Cumberley's resignation you have been acting superintendent of the Red Butte Western. Do you want to stay on as my lieutenant?"

For the long minute that Hallock took before replying, the loose-lipped mouth under the shaggy mustache seemed to have lost the power of speech. But when the words finally came, they were shorn of all euphemism.

"I suppose I ought to tell you to go straight to hell, Mr. Lidgerwood, put on my coat and walk out," said this most singular of all railway subordinates. "By all the rules of the game, this job belongs to me. What I've gone through to earn it, you nor any other man will ever know. If I stay, I'll wish I hadn't; and so will you. You'd better give me a time-check and let me go."

Lidgerwood walked to the window and once more stared out upon the dreary prospect, bounded by the bluffs of the second mesa. A horseman was ambling down the single street of the town, weaving in his saddle, and giving vent to a series of Indian war-whoops. Lidgerwood saw the drunken cowboy only with the outward eye. And when he turned back to the man in the rifle-pit desk, he could not have told why the words of regret and dismissal which he had made up his mind to say, refused to come. But they did refuse, and what he said was not at all what he had intended to say.

"If I can't quite match your frankness, Mr. Hallock, it is because my early education was neglected. But I'll say this: I appreciate your disappointment; I know what it means to a man situated as you are. Notwithstanding, I want you to stay with me. I'll say more; I shall take it as a personal favor if you will stay."

"You'll be sorry for it if I do," was the ungracious rejoinder.

"Not because you will do anything to make me sorry, I am sure," said the new superintendent, in his evenest tone. And then, as if the matter were definitely settled: "I'd like to have a word with the trainmaster, Mr. McCloskey. May I trouble you to tell me which is his office?"

Hallock waved a hand toward the door which Lidgerwood had been about to open a few minutes earlier.

"You'll find him in there," he said briefly, adding, with his altogether remarkable disregard for the official proprieties: "If he gives you the same chance that I did, don't take him up. He is the one man in this outfit worth more than the powder it would take to blow him to the devil."

IV

The matter to be taken up with McCloskey, master of trains and chief of the telegraph department, was not altogether disciplinary. In the summarizing conference at Copah, Vice-President Ford had spoken favorably of the trainmaster, recommending him to mercy in the event of a general beheading in the Angels head-quarters. "A lame duck, like most of the desert exiles, and the homeliest man west of the Missouri River," was Ford's characterization. "He is as stubborn as a mule, but he is honest and outspoken. If you can win him over to your side, you will have at least one lieutenant whom you can trust—and who will, I think, be duly grateful for small favors. Mac couldn't get a job east of the Crosswater Hills, I'm afraid."

Lidgerwood had not inquired the reason for the eastern disability. He had lived in the West long enough to know that it is an ill thing to pry too curiously into any man's past. So there should be present efficiency, no man in the service should be called upon to recite in ancient history, much less one for whom Ford had spoken a good word.

Like all the other offices in the Crow's Nest, that of the trainmaster was bare and uninviting. Lidgerwood, passing beyond the door of communication, found himself in a dingy room, with cobwebs festooning the ceiling and a pair of unwashed windows looking out upon the open square called, in the past and gone day of the Angelic promoters, the "railroad plaza." Two chairs, a cheap desk, and a pine table backed by the "string-board" working model of the current time-table, did duty as the furnishings, serving rather to emphasize than to relieve the dreariness of the place.

McCloskey was at his desk at the moment of door-opening, and Lidgerwood instantly paid tribute to Vice-President Ford's powers of characterization. The trainmaster was undeniably homely—and more; his hard-featured face was a study in grotesques. There was fearless honesty in the shrewd gray eyes, and a good promise of capability in the strong Scotch jaw and long upper lip, but the grotesque note was the one which persisted, and the trainmaster seemed wilfully to accentuate it. His coat, in a region where shirt-sleeves predominated, was a close-buttoned gambler's frock, and his hat, in the country of the sombrero and the soft Stetson, was a derby.

Lidgerwood was striving to estimate the man beneath these outward eccentricities when McCloskey rose and thrust out a hand, great-jointed and knobbed like a laborer's.

"You're Mr. Lidgerwood, I take it?" said he, tilting the derby to the back of his head. "Come to tell me to pack my kit and get out?"

"Not yet, Mr. McCloskey," laughed Lidgerwood, getting his first real measure of the man in the hearty hand-grip. "On the contrary, I've come to thank you for not dropping things and running away before the new management could get on the ground."

The trainmaster's rejoinder was outspokenly blunt. "I've nowhere to run to, Mr. Lidgerwood, and that's no joke. Some of the backcappers will be telling you presently that I was a train despatcher over in God's country, and that I put two trains together. It's your right to know that it's true."

"Thank you, Mr. McCloskey," said Lidgerwood simply; "that sounds good to me. And take this for yourself: the man who has done that once won't do it again. That is one thing, and another is this: we start with a clean slate on the Red Butte Western. No man in the service who will turn in and help us make a real railroad out of the R.B.W. need worry about his past record: it won't be dug up against him."

"That's fair—more than fair," said the trainmaster, mouthing the words as if the mere effort of speech were painful, "and I wish I could promise you that the rank and file will meet you halfway. But I can't. You'll find a plucked pigeon, Mr. Lidgerwood—with plenty of hawks left to pick the bones. The road has been running itself for the past two years and more."

"I understand," said Lidgerwood; and then he spoke of the careless despatching.

"That will be Callahan, the day man," McCloskey broke in wrathfully. "But that's the way of it. When we get through the twenty-four hours without killing somebody or smashing something, I thank God, and put a red mark on that calendar over my desk."

"Well, we won't go back of the returns," declared Lidgerwood, meaning to be as just as he could to his predecessors in office. "But from now on——"

The door leading into the room beyond the trainmaster's office opened squeakily on dry hinges, and a chattering of telegraph instruments heralded the incoming of a disreputable-looking office-man, with a green patch over one eye and a blackened cob-pipe between his teeth. Seeing Lidgerwood, he ducked and turned to McCloskey. Bradley, reporting in, had given his own paraphrase of the new superintendent's strictures on Red Butte Western despatching and the criticism had lost nothing in the recasting.

"Seventy-one's in the ditch at Gloria Siding," he said, speaking pointedly to the trainmaster. "Goodloe reports it from Little Butte; says both enginemen are in the mix-up, but he doesn't know whether they are killed or not."

"There you are!" snarled McCloskey, wheeling upon Lidgerwood. "They couldn't let you get your chair warmed the first day!"

With the long run from Copah to Angels to his credit, and with all the head-quarters loose ends still to be gathered up, Lidgerwood might blamelessly have turned over the trouble call to his trainmaster. But a wreck was as good a starting-point as any, and he took command at once.

"Go and clear for the wrecking-train, and have some one in your office notify the shops and the yard," he said briskly, compelling the attention of the one-eyed despatcher; and when Callahan was gone: "Now, Mac, get out your map and post me. I'm a little lame on geography yet. Where is Gloria Siding?"

McCloskey found a blue-print map of the line and traced the course of the western division among the foot-hills to the base of the Great Timanyonis, and through the Timanyoni Canyon to a park-like valley, shut in by the great range on the east and north, and by the Little Timanyonis and the Hophras on the west and south. At a point midway of the valley his stubby forefinger rested.

"That's Gloria," he said, "and here's Little Butte, twelve miles beyond."

"Good ground?" queried Lidgerwood.

24

"As pretty a stretch as there is anywhere west of the desert; reminds you of a Missouri bottom, with the river on one side and the hills a mile away on the other. I don't know what excuse those hoboes could find for piling a train in the ditch there."

"We'll hear the excuse later," said Lidgerwood. "Now, tell me what sort of a wrecking-plant we have?"

"The best in the bunch," asserted the trainmaster. "Gridley's is the one department that has been kept up to date and in good fighting trim. We have one wrecking-crane that will pick up any of the big freight-pullers, and a lighter one that isn't half bad."

"Who is your wrecking-boss?"

"Gridley—when he feels like going out. He can clear a main line quicker than any man we've ever had."

"He will go with us to-day?"

"I suppose so. He is in town and he's—sober."

The new superintendent caught at the hesitant word.

"Drinks, does he?"

"Not much while he is on the job. But he disappears periodically and comes back looking something the worse for wear. They tell tough stories about him over in Copah."

Lidgerwood dropped the master-mechanic as he had dropped the offending trainmen who had put Train 71 in the ditch at Gloria where, according to McCloskey, there should be no ditch.

"I'll go and run through my desk mail and fill Hallock up while you are making ready," he said. "Call me when the train is made up."

Passing through the corridor on the way to his private office back of Hallock's room, Lidgerwood saw that the wreck call had already reached the shops. A big, bearded man with a soft hat pulled over his eyes was directing the make-up of a train on the repair track, and the yard engine was pulling an enormous crane down from its spur beyond the coal-chutes. Around the man in the soft hat the wrecking-crew was gathering: shopmen for the greater part, as a crew of a master mechanic's choosing would be.

As the event proved, there was little time for the doing of the preliminary work which Lidgerwood had meant to do. In the midst of the letter-sorting, McCloskey put his head in at the door of the private office.

"We're ready when you are, Mr. Lidgerwood," he interrupted; and with a few hurried directions to Hallock, Lidgerwood joined the trainmaster on the Crow's Nest platform. The train was backing up to get its clear-track orders, and on the tool-car platform stood the big man whom Lidgerwood had already identified presumptively as Gridley.

McCloskey would have introduced the new superintendent when the train paused for the signal from the despatcher's window, but Gridley did not wait for the formalities.

"Come aboard, Mr. Lidgerwood," he called, genially. "It's too bad we have to give you a sweat-box welcome. If there are any of Seventy-one's crew left alive, you ought to give them thirty days for calling you out before you could shake hands with yourself."

Being by nature deliberate in forming friendships, and proportionally tenacious of them when they were formed, Lidgerwood's impulse was to hold all men at arm's length until he was reasonably assured of sincerity and a common ground. But the genial master-mechanic refused to be put on probation. Lidgerwood made the effort while the rescue train was whipping around the hill shoulders and plunging deeper into the afternoon shadows of the great mountain range. The tool-car was comfortably filled with men and working tackle, and for seats there were only the blocking timbers, the tool-boxes, and the coils of rope and chain cables. Sharing a tool-box with Gridley and smoking a cigar out of Gridley's pocket-case, Lidgerwood found it difficult to be less than friendly.

It was to little purpose that he recalled Ford's qualified recommendation of the man who had New York backing and who, in Ford's phrase, was a "brute after his own peculiar fashion." Brute or human, the big master-mechanic had the manners of a gentleman, and his easy good-nature broke down all the barriers of reserve that his somewhat reticent companion could interpose.

"You smoke good cigars, Mr. Gridley," said Lidgerwood, trying, as he had tried before, to wrench the talk aside from the personal channel into which it seemed naturally to drift.

"Good tobacco is one of the few luxuries the desert leaves a man capable of enjoying. You haven't come to that yet, but you will. It is a savage life, Mr. Lidgerwood, and if a man hasn't a good bit of the blood of his stone-age ancestors in him, the desert will either kill him or make a beast of him. There doesn't seem to be any medium."

The talk was back again in the personal channel, and this time Lidgerwood met the issue fairly.

"You have been saying that, in one form or another, ever since we left Angels: are you trying to scare me off, Mr. Gridley, or are you only giving me a friendly warning?" he asked.

The master-mechanic laughed easily.

"I hope I wouldn't be impudent enough to do either, on such short acquaintance," he protested. "But now that you have opened the door, perhaps a little man-to-man frankness won't be amiss. You have tackled a pretty hard proposition, Mr. Lidgerwood."

"Technically, you mean?"

"No, I didn't mean that, because, if your friends tell the truth about you, you can come as near to making bricks without straw as the next man. But the Red Butte Western reorganization asks for something more than a good railroad officer."

"I'm listening," said Lidgerwood.

Gridley laughed again.

"What will you do when a conductor or an engineer whom you have called on the carpet curses you out and invites you to go to hell?"

"I shall fire him," was the prompt rejoinder.

"Naturally and properly, but afterward? Four out of five men in this human scrap-heap you've inherited will lay for you with a gun to play even for the discharge. What then?"

It was just here that Lidgerwood, staring absently at the passing panorama of shifting hill shoulders framing itself in the open side-door of the tool-car, missed a point. If he had been less absorbed in the personal problem he could scarcely have failed to mark the searching scrutiny in the shrewd eyes shaded by Gridley's soft hat.

"I don't know," he said, half hesitantly. "Civilization means something—or it should mean something—even in the Red Desert, Mr. Gridley. I suppose there is some semblance of legal protection in Angels, as elsewhere, isn't there?"

The master-mechanic's smile was tolerant.

"Surely. We have a town marshal, and a justice of the peace; one is a blacksmith and the other the keeper of the general store."

The good-natured irony in Gridley's reply was not thrown away upon his listener, but Lidgerwood held tenaciously to his own contention.

"The inadequacy of the law, or of its machinery, hardly excuses a lapse into barbarism," he protested. "The discharged employee, in the case you are supposing, might hold himself justified in shooting at me; but if I should shoot back and happen to kill him, it would be murder. We've got to stand for something, Mr. Gridley, you and I who know the difference between civilization and savagery."

Gridley's strong teeth came together with a little snap.

"Certainly," he agreed, without a shade of hesitation; adding, "I've never carried a gun and have never had to." Then he changed the subject abruptly, and when the train had swung around the last of the hills and was threading its tortuous way through the great canyon, he proposed a change of base to the rear platform from which Chandler's marvel of engineering skill could be better seen and appreciated.

The wreck at Gloria Siding proved to be a very mild one, as railway wrecks go. A broken flange under a box-car had derailed the engine and a dozen cars, and there were no casualties—the report about the involvement of the two enginemen being due to the imagination of the excited flagman who had propelled himself on a hand-car back to Little Butte to send in the call for help.

Since Gridley was on the ground, Lidgerwood and McCloskey stood aside and let the master-mechanic organize the attack. Though the problem of track-clearing, on level ground and with a convenient siding at hand for the sorting and shifting, was a simple one, there was still a chance for an exhibition of time-saving and speed, and Gridley gave it. There was never a false move made or a tentative one, and when the huge lifting-crane went into action, Lidgerwood grew warmly enthusiastic.

"Gridley certainly knows his business," he said to McCloskey. "The Red Butte Western doesn't need any better wrecking-boss than it has right now."

"He can do the job, when he feels like it," admitted the trainmaster sourly.

"But he doesn't often feel like it? You can't blame him for that. Picking up wrecks isn't fairly a part of a master-mechanic's duty."

"That is what he says, and he doesn't trouble himself to go when it isn't convenient. I have a notion he wouldn't be here to-day if you weren't."

It was plainly evident that McCloskey meant more than he said, but once again Lidgerwood refused to go behind the returns. He felt that he had been prejudiced against Gridley at the outset, unduly so, he was beginning to think, and even-handed fairness to all must be the watchword in the campaign of reorganization.

"Since we seem to be more ornamental than useful on this job, you might give me another lesson in Red Butte geography, Mac," he said, purposely changing the subject. "Where are the gulch mines?"

The trainmaster explained painstakingly, squatting to trace a rude map in the sand at the track-side. Hereaway, twelve miles to the westward, lay Little Butte, where the line swept a great curve to the north and so continued on to Red Butte. Along the northward stretch, and in the foot-hills of the Little Timanyonis, were the placers, most of them productive, but none of them rich enough to stimulate a rush.

Here, where the river made a quick turn, was the butte from which the station of Little Butte took its name—the superintendent might see its wooded summit rising above the lower hills intervening. It was a long, narrow ridge, more like a hogback than a true mountain, and it held a silver mine, Flemister's, which was a moderately heavy shipper. The vein had been followed completely through the ridge, and the spur track in the eastern gulch, which had originally served it, had been abandoned and a new spur built up along the western foot of the butte, with a main line connection at Little Butte. Up here, ten miles above Little Butte, was a bauxite mine, with a spur; and here....

McCloskey went on, industriously drawing lines in the sand, and Lidgerwood sat on a cross-tie end and conned his lesson. Below the siding the big crane was heaving the derailed cars into line with methodical precision, but now it was Gridley's shop foreman who was giving the orders. The master-mechanic had gone aside to hold converse with a man who had driven up in a buckboard, coming from the direction in which Little Butte lay.

"Goodloe told me the wreck-wagons were here, and I thought you would probably be along," the buckboard driver was saying. "How are things shaping up? I haven't cared to risk the wires since Bigsby leaked on us."

Gridley put a foot on the hub of the buckboard wheel and began to whittle a match with a penknife that was as keen as a razor.

"The new chum is in the saddle; look over your shoulder to the left and you'll see him sitting on a cross-tie beside McCloskey," he said.

"I've seen him before. He was over the road last week, and I happened to be in Goodloe's office at Little Butte when he got off to look around," was the curt rejoinder. "But that doesn't help any. What do you know?"

"He is a gentleman," said Gridley slowly.

"Oh, the devil! what do I care about——"

"And a scholar," the master-mechanic went on imperturbably.

The buckboard driver's black eyes snapped. "Can you add the rest of it—'and he isn't very bright'?"

"No," was the sober reply.

"Well, what are we up against?"

Gridley snapped the penknife shut and began to chew the sharpened end of the match.

"Your pop-valve is set too light; you blow off too easily, Flemister," he commented. "So far we—or rather you—are up against nothing worse than the old proposition. Lidgerwood is going to try to make a silk purse out of a sow's ear, beginning with the pay-roll contingent. If I have sized him up right, he'll be kept busy; too busy to remember your name—or mine."

"What do you mean? in just so many words."

"Nothing more than I have said. Mr. Lidgerwood is a gentleman and a scholar."

"Ha!" said the man in the buckboard seat. "I believe I'm catching on, after so long a time. You mean he hasn't the sand."

Gridley neither denied nor affirmed. He had taken out his penknife again and was resharpening the match.

"Hallock is the man to look to," he said. "If we could get him interested ..."

"That's up to you, damn it; I've told you a hundred times that I can't touch him!"

"I know; he doesn't seem to love you very much. The last time I talked to him he mentioned something about shooting you off-hand, but I guess he didn't mean, it. You've got to interest him in some way, Flemister."

"Perhaps you can tell me how," was the sarcastic retort.

"I think perhaps I can, now. Do you remember anything about the sky-rocketing finish of the Mesa Building and Loan Association, or is that too much of a back number for a busy man like you?"

"I remember it," said Flemister.

"Hallock was the treasurer," put in Gridley smoothly.

"Yes, but——"

"Wait a minute. A treasurer is supposed to treasure something, isn't he? There are possibly twenty-five or thirty men still left in the Red Butte Western service who have never wholly quit trying to find out why Hallock, the treasurer, failed so signally to treasure anything."

"Yah! that's an old sore."

"I know, but old sores may become suddenly troublesome—or useful—as the case may be. For some reason best known to himself, Hallock has decided to stay and continue playing second fiddle."

"How do you know?"

The genial smile was wrinkling at the corners of Gridley's eyes.

"There isn't very much going on under the sheet-iron roof of the Crow's Nest that I don't know, Flemister, and usually pretty soon after it happens. Hallock will stay on as chief clerk, and, naturally, he is anxious to stand well with his new boss. Are you beginning to see daylight?"

"Not yet."

"Well, we'll open the shutters a little wider. One of the first things Lidgerwood will have to wrestle with will be this Loan Association business. The kickers will put it up to him, as they have put it up to every new man who has come out here. Ferguson refused to dig into anybody's old graveyard, and so did Cumberley. But Lidgerwood won't refuse. He is going to be the just judge, if not the very terrible."

"Still, I don't see," persisted Flemister.

"Don't you? Hallock will be obliged to justify himself to Lidgerwood, and he can't. In fact, there is only one man living to-day who could fully justify him."

"And that man is——"

"—Pennington Flemister, ex-president of the defunct Building and Loan. You know where the money went, Flemister."

"Maybe I do. What of that?"

"I can only offer a suggestion, of course. You are a pretty smooth liar, Pennington; it wouldn't be much trouble for you to fix up a story that would satisfy Lidgerwood. You might even show up a few documents, if it came to the worst."

"Well?"

"That's all. If you get a good, firm grip on that club, you'll have Hallock, coming and going. It's a dead open and shut. If he falls in line, you'll agree to pacify Lidgerwood; otherwise the law will have to take its course."

The man in the buckboard was silent for a long minute before he said: "It won't work, Gridley. Hallock's grudge against me is too bitter. You know part of it, and part of it you don't know. He'd hang himself in a minute if he could get my neck in the same noose."

The master-mechanic threw the whittled match away, as if the argument were closed.

"That is where you are lame, Flemister: you don't know your man. Put it up to Hallock barehanded: if he comes in, all right; if not, you'll put him where he'll wear stripes. That will fetch him."

The men of the derrick gang were righting the last of the derailed box-cars, and the crew of the wrecking-train was shifting the cripples into line for the return run to Angels.

"We'll be going in a few minutes," said the master-mechanic, taking his foot from the wheel-hub. "Do you want to meet Lidgerwood?"

"Not here—or with you," said the owner of the Wire-Silver; and he had turned his team and was driving away when Gridley's shop foreman came up to say that the wrecking-train was ready to leave.

Lidgerwood found a seat for himself in the tool-car on the way back to Angels, and put in the time smoking a short pipe and reviewing the events of his first day in the new field.

The outlook was not wholly discouraging, and but for the talk with Gridley he might have smoked and dozed quite peacefully on his coiled hawser, in the corner of the car. But, try as he would, the importunate demon of distrust, distrust of himself, awakened by the master-mechanic's warning, refused to be quieted; and when, after the three hours of the slow return journey were out-worn, McCloskey came to tell him that the train was pulling into the Angels yard, the explosion of a track torpedo under the wheels made him start like a nervous woman.

V

For the first few weeks after the change in ownership and the arrival of the new superintendent, the Red Butte Western and its nerve-centre, Angels, seemed disposed to take Mr. Howard Lidgerwood as a rather ill-timed joke, perpetrated upon a primitive West and its people by some one of the Pacific Southwestern magnates who owned a broad sense of humor.

During this period the sardonic laugh was heard in the land, and the chuckling appreciation of the joke by the Red Butte rank and file, and by the Angelic soldiers of fortune who, though not upon the company's pay-rolls, still throve indirectly upon the company's bounty, lacked nothing of completeness. The Red Desert grinned like the famed Cheshire cat when an incoming train from the East brought sundry boxes and trunks, said to contain the new boss's wardrobe. Its guffaws were long and uproarious when it began to be noised about that the company carpenters and fitters were installing a bath and other civilizing and softening appliances in the alcove opening out of the superintendent's sleeping-room in the head-quarters building.

Lidgerwood slept in the Crow's Nest, not so much from choice as for the reason that there seemed to be no alternative save a room in the town tavern, appropriately named "The Hotel Celestial." Between his sleeping-apartment and his private office there was only a thin board partition; but even this gave him more privacy than the Celestial could offer, where many of the partitions were of building-paper, muslin covered.

It is a railroad proverb that the properly inoculated railroad man eats and sleeps with his business; Lidgerwood exemplified the saying by having a wire cut into the despatcher's office, with the terminals on a little table at his bed's head, and with a tiny telegraph relay instrument mounted on the stand. Through the relay, tapping softly in the darkness, came the news of the line, and often, after the strenuous day was ended, Lidgerwood would lie awake listening.

Sometimes the wire gossiped, and echoes of Homeric laughter trickled through the relay in the small hours; as when Ruby Creek asked the night despatcher if it were true that the new boss slept in what translated itself in the laborious Morse of the Ruby Creek operator as "pijjimmies"; or when Navajo, tapping the same source of information, wished to be informed if the "Chink"—doubtless referring to Tadasu Matsuwari—ran a laundry on the side and thus kept His Royal Highness in collars and cuffs.

At the tar-paper-covered, iron-roofed Celestial, where he took his meals, Lidgerwood had a table to himself, which he shared at times with McCloskey, and at other times with breezy Jack Benson, the young engineer whom Vice-President Ford had sent, upon Lidgerwood's request and recommendation, to put new life into the track force, and to make the preliminary surveys for a possible western extension of the road.

When the superintendent had guests, the long table on the opposite side of the dining-room restrained itself. When he ate alone, Maggie Donovan, the fiery-eyed, heavy-handed table-girl who ringed his plate with the semicircle of ironstone portion dishes, stood between him and the men who were still regarding him as a joke. And since Maggie's displeasure manifested itself in cold coffee and tough cuts of the beef, the long table made its most excruciating jests elaborately impersonal.

On the line, and in the roundhouse and repair-shops, the joke was far too good to be muzzled. The nickname, "Collars-and-Cuffs," became classical; and once, when Brannagan and the 117 were ordered out on the service-car, the Irishman wore the highest celluloid collar he could find in Angels, rounding out the clownery with a pair of huge wickerware cuffs, which had once seen service as the coverings of a pair of Maraschino bottles.

No official notice having been taken of Brannagan's fooling, Buck Tryon, ordered out on the same duty, went the little Irishman one better, decorating his engine headlight and handrails with festoonings of colored calico, the decoration figuring as a caricature of Lidgerwood's college colors, and calico being the nearest approach to bunting obtainable at Jake Schleisinger's emporium, two doors north of Red-Light Sammy's house of call.

All of which was harmless enough, one would say, however subversive of dignified discipline it might be. Lidgerwood knew. The jests were too broad to be missed. But he ignored them good-naturedly, rather thankful for the playful interlude which gave him a breathing-space and time to study the field before the real battle should begin.

That a battle would have to be fought was evident enough. As yet, the demoralization had been scarcely checked, and sooner or later the necessary radical reforms would have to begin. Gridley, whose attitude toward the new superintendent continued to be that of a disinterested adviser, assured Lidgerwood that he was losing ground by not opening the campaign of severity at once.

"You'll have to take a club to these hoboes before you can ever hope to make railroad men out of them," was Gridley's oft-repeated assertion; and the fact that the master-mechanic was continually urging the warfare made Lidgerwood delay it.

Just why Gridley's counsel should have produced such a contrary effect, Lidgerwood could not have explained. The advice was sound, and the man who gave it was friendly and apparently ingenuous. But prejudices, like prepossessions, are sometimes as strong as they are inexplicable, and while Lidgerwood freely accused himself of injustice toward the master-mechanic, a certain feeling of distrust and repulsion, dating back to his first impressions of the man, died hard.

Oddly enough, on the other hand, there was a prepossession, quite as unreasoning, for Hallock. There was absolutely nothing in the chief clerk to inspire liking, or even common business confidence; on the contrary, while Hallock attended to his duties and carried out his superior's instructions with the exactness of an automaton, his attitude was distinctly antagonistic. As the chief subaltern on Lidgerwood's small staff he was efficient and well-nigh invaluable. But as a man, Lidgerwood felt that he might easily be regarded as an enemy whose designs could never be fathomed or prefigured.

In spite of Hallock's singular manner, which was an abrupt challenge to all comers, Lidgerwood acknowledged a growing liking for the chief clerk. Under the crabbed and gloomy crust of the man the superintendent fancied he could discover a certain savage loyalty. But under the loyalty there was a deeper depth—of misery, or tragedy, or both; and to this abysmal part of him there was no key that Lidgerwood could find.

McCloskey, who had served under Hallock for a number of months before the change in management, confessed that he knew the gloomy chief clerk only as a man in authority, and exceedingly hard to please. Questioned more particularly by Lidgerwood, McCloskey added that Hallock was married; that after the first few months in Angels his wife, a strikingly beautiful young woman, had disappeared, and that since her departure Hallock had lived alone in two rooms over the freight station, rooms which no one, save himself, ever entered.

These, and similar bits of local history, were mere gatherings by the way for the superintendent, picked up while the Red Desert was having its laugh at the new bath-room, the pajamas, and the clean linen. They weighed lightly, because the principal problem was, as yet, untouched. For while the laugh endured, Lidgerwood had not found it possible to breach many of the strongholds of lawlessness.

Orders, regarded by disciplined railroad men as having the immutability of the laws of the Medes and Persians, were still interpreted as loosely as if they were but the casual suggestions of a bystander. Rules were formulated and given black-letter emphasis in their postings on the bulletin boards, only to be coolly ignored when they chanced to conflict with some train crew's desire to make up time or to kill it. Directed to account for fuel and oil consumed, the enginemen good-naturedly forged reports and the storekeepers blandly O.K.'d them. Instructed to keep an accurate record of all material used, the trackmen jocosely scattered more spikes than they drove, made fire-wood of the stock cross-ties, and were not above underpinning the section-houses with new dimension timbers.

In countless other ways the waste was prodigious and often mysteriously unexplainable. The company supplies had a curious fashion of disappearing in transit. Two car-loads of building lumber sent to repair the station at Red Butte vanished somewhere between the Angels shipping-yards and their billing destination. Lime, cement, and paint were exceedingly volatile. House hardware, purchased in quantities for company repairs, figured in the monthly requisition sheet as regularly as coal and oil; and the lost-tool account roughly balanced the pay-roll of the company carpenters and bridge-builders.

In such a chaotic state of affairs, track and train troubles were the rule rather than the exception, and it was a Red Butte Western boast that the fire was never drawn under the wrecking-train engine. For the first few weeks Lidgerwood let McCloskey answer the "hurry calls" to the various scenes of disaster, but when three sections of an eastbound cattle special, ignoring the ten-minute-interval rule, were piled up in the Piñon Hills, he went out and took personal command of the track-clearers.

This happened when the joke was at flood-tide, and the men of the wrecking-crew took a ten-gallon keg of whiskey along wherewith to celebrate the first appearance of the new superintendent in character as a practical wrecking-boss. The outcome was rather astonishing. For one thing, Lidgerwood's first executive act was to knock in the head of the ten-gallon celebration with a striking-hammer, before it was even spiggoted; and for another he quickly proved that he was Gridley's equal, if not his master, in the gentle art of track-clearing; lastly, and this was the most astonishing thing of all, he demonstrated that clean linen and correct garmentings do not necessarily make for softness and effeminacy in the wearer. Through the long day and the still longer night of toil and stress the new boss was able to endure hardship with the best man on the ground.

This was excellent, as far as it went. But later, with the offending cattle-train crews before him for trial and punishment, Lidgerwood lost all he had gained by being too easy.

"We've got him chasin' his feet," said Tryon, one of the rule-breaking engineers, making his report to the roundhouse contingent at the close of the "sweat-box" interview. "It's just as I've been tellin' you mugs all along, he hain't got sand enough to fire anybody."

Likewise Jack Benson, though from a friendlier point of view. The "sweat-box" was Lidgerwood's private office in the Crow's Nest, and Benson happened to be present when the reckless trainmen were told to go and sin no more.

"I'm not running your job, Lidgerwood, and you may fire the inkstand at me if the spirit moves you to, but I've got to butt in. You can't handle the Red Desert with kid gloves on. Those fellows needed an artistic cussing-out and a thirty-day hang-up at the very lightest. You can't hold 'em down with Sunday-school talk."

Lidgerwood was frowning at his blotting-pad and pencilling idle little squares on it—a habit which was insensibly growing upon him.

"Where would I get the two extra train-crews to fill in the thirty-day lay-off, Jack? Had you thought of that?"

"I had only the one think, and I gave you that one," rejoined Benson carelessly. "I suppose it is different in your department. When I go up against a thing like that on the sections, I fire the whole bunch and import a few more Italians. Which reminds me, as old Dunkenfeld used to say when there wasn't either a link or a coupling-pin anywhere within the four horizons: what do you know about Fred Dawson, Gridley's shop draftsman?"

"Next to nothing, personally," replied Lidgerwood, taking Benson's abrupt change of topic as a matter of course. "He seems a fine fellow; much too fine a fellow to be wasting himself out here in the desert. Why?"

"Oh, I just wanted to know. Ever met his mother and sister?"

"No."

"Well, you ought to. The mother is one of the only two angels in Angels, and the sister is the other. Dawson, himself, is a ghastly monomaniac."

Lidgerwood's brows lifted, though his query was unspoken.

"Haven't you heard his story?" asked Benson; "but of course you haven't. He is a lame duck, you know—like every other man this side of Crosswater Summit, present company excepted."

"A lame duck?" repeated Lidgerwood.

"Yes, a man with a past. Don't tell me you haven't caught onto the hall-mark of the Red Desert. It's notorious. The blacklegs and tin-horns and sure-shots go without saying, of course, but they haven't a monopoly on the broken records. Over in the ranch country beyond the Timanyonis they lump us all together and call us the outlaws."

"Not without reason," said Lidgerwood.

"Not any," asserted Benson with cheerful pessimism. "The entire Red Butte Western outfit is tarred with the same stick. You haven't a dozen operators, all told, who haven't been discharged for incompetence, or worse, somewhere else; or a dozen conductors or engineers who weren't good and comfortably blacklisted before they climbed Crosswater. Take McCloskey: you swear by him, don't you? He was a chief despatcher back East, and he put two passenger-trains together in a head-on collision the day he resigned and came West to grow up with the Red Desert."

"I know," said Lidgerwood, "and I did not have to learn it at second-hand. Mac was man enough to tell me himself, before I had known him five minutes." Then he suggested mildly, "But you were speaking of Dawson, weren't you?"

"Yes, and that's what makes me say what I'm saying; he is one of them, though he needn't be if he weren't such a hopelessly sensitive ass. He's a B.S. in M.E., or he would have been if he had stayed out his senior year in Carnegie, but also he happened to be a foot-ball fiend, and in the last intercollegiate game of his last season he had the horrible luck to kill a man—and the man was the brother of the girl Dawson was going to marry."

"Heavens and earth!" exclaimed Lidgerwood. "Is he *that* Dawson?"

"The same," said the young engineer laconically. "It was the sheerest accident, and everybody knew it was, and nobody blamed Dawson. I happen to know, because I was a junior in Carnegie at the time. But Fred took it hard; let it spoil his life. He threw up everything, left college between two days, and came to bury himself out here. For two years he never let his mother and sister know where he was; made remittances to them through a bank in Omaha, so they shouldn't be able to trace him. Care to hear any more?"

"Yes, go on," said the superintendent.

"*I* found him," chuckled Benson, "and I took the liberty of piping his little game off to the harrowed women. Next thing he knew they dropped in on him; and he is just crazy enough to stay here, and to keep them here. That wouldn't be so bad if it wasn't for Gridley, Fred's boss and your peach of a master-mechanic."

"Why 'peach'? Gridley is a pretty decent sort of a man-driver, isn't he?" said Lidgerwood, doing premeditated and intentional violence to what he had come to call his unjust prejudice against the handsome master-mechanic.

"You won't believe it," said Benson hotly, "but he has actually got the nerve to make love to Dawson's sister! and he a widow-man, old enough to be her father!"

Lidgerwood smiled. It is the privilege of youth to be intolerant of age in its rival. Gridley was, possibly, forty-two or three, but Benson was still on the sunny slope of twenty-five. "You are prejudiced, Jack," he criticized. "Gridley is still young enough to marry again, if he wants to—and to live long enough to spoil his grandchildren."

"But he doesn't begin to be good enough for Faith Dawson," countered the young engineer, stubbornly.

"Isn't he? or is that another bit of your personal grudge? What do you know against him?"

Pressed thus sharply against the unyielding fact, Benson was obliged to confess that he knew nothing at all against the master-mechanic, nothing that could be pinned down to day and date. If Gridley had the weaknesses common to Red-Desert mankind, he did not parade them in Angels. As the head of his department he was well known to be a hard hitter; and now and then, when the blows fell rather mercilessly, the railroad colony called him a tyrant, and hinted that he, too, had a past that would not bear inspection. But even Benson admitted that this was mere gossip.

Lidgerwood laughed at the engineer's failure to make his case, and asked quizzically, "Where do I come in on all this, Jack? You have an axe to grind, I take it."

"I have. Mrs. Dawson wants me to take my meals at the house. I'm inclined to believe that she is a bit shy of Gridley, and maybe she thinks I could do the buffer act. But as a get-between I'd be chiefly conspicuous by my absence."

"Sorry I can't give you an office job," said the superintendent in mock sympathy.

"So am I, but you can do the next best thing. Get Fred to take you home with him some of these fine evenings, and you'll never go back to Maggie Donovan and the Celestial's individual hash-holders; not if you can persuade Mrs. Dawson to feed you. The alternative is to fire Gridley out of his job."

"This time you are trying to make the tail wag the dog," said Lidgerwood. "Gridley has twice my backing in the P. S-W. board of directors. Besides, he is a good fellow; and if I go up on the mesa and try to stand him off for you, it will be only because I hope you are a better fellow."

"Prop it up on any leg you like, only go," said Benson simply. "I'll take it as a personal favor, and do as much for you, some time. I suppose I don't have to warn you not to fall in love with Faith Dawson yourself—or, on second thought, perhaps I *had* better."

This time Lidgerwood's laugh was mirthless.

"No, you don't have to, Jack. Like Gridley, I am older than I look, and I have had my little turn at that wheel; or rather, perhaps I should say that the wheel has had its little turn at me. You can safely deputize me, I guess."

"All right, and many thanks. Here's 202 coming in, and I'm going over to Navajo on it. Don't wait too long before you make up to Dawson. You'll find him well worth while, after you've broken through his shell."

The merry jest on the Red Butte Western ran its course for another week after the three-train wreck in the Piñons—for a week and a day. Then Lidgerwood began the drawing of the net. A new time-card was strung with McCloskey's cooperation, and when it went into effect a notice on all bulletin boards announced the adoption of the standard "Book of Rules," and promised penalties in a rising scale for unauthorized departure therefrom.

Promptly the horse-laugh died away and the trouble storm was evoked. Grievance committees haunted the Crow's Nest, and the insurrectionary faction, starting with the trainmen and spreading to the track force, threatened to involve the telegraph operators—threatened to become a protest unanimous and in the mass. Worse than this, the service, haphazard enough before, now became a maddening chaos. Orders were misunderstood, whether wilfully or not no court of inquiry could determine; wrecks were of almost daily occurrence, and the shop track was speedily filled to the switches with crippled engines and cars.

In such a storm of disaster and disorder the captain in command soon finds and learns to distinguish his loyal supporters, if any such there be. In the pandemonium of untoward events, McCloskey was Lidgerwood's right hand, toiling, smiting, striving, and otherwise approving himself a good soldier. But close behind him came Gridley; always suave and good-natured, making no complaints, not even when the repair work made necessary by the innumerable wrecks grew mountain-high, and always counselling firmness and more discipline.

"This is just what we have been needing for years, Mr. Lidgerwood," he took frequent occasion to say. "Of course, we have now to pay the penalty for the sins of our predecessors; but if you will persevere, we'll pull through and be a railroad in fact when the clouds roll by. Don't give in an inch. Show these muckers that you mean business, and mean it all the time, and you'll win out all right."

Thus the master-mechanic; and McCloskey, with more at stake and a less insulated point of view, took it out in good, hard blows, backing his superior like a man. Indeed, in the small head-quarters staff, Hallock was the only non-combatant. From the beginning of hostilities he seemed to have made a pact with himself not to let it be known by any act or word of his that he was aware of the suddenly precipitated conflict. The routine duties of a chief clerk's desk are never light; Hallock's became so exacting that he rarely left his office, or the pen-like contrivance in which he entrenched himself and did his work.

When the fight began, Lidgerwood observed Hallock closely, trying to discover if there were any secret signs of the satisfaction which the revolt of the rank and file might be supposed to awaken in an unsuccessful candidate for the official headship of the Red Butte Western. There were none. Hallock's gaunt face, with the loose lips and the straggling, unkempt beard, was a blank; and the worst wreck of the three which promptly followed the introduction of the new rules, was noted in his reports with the calm indifference with which he might have jotted down the breakage of a section foreman's spike-maul.

McCloskey, being of Scottish blood and desert-seasoned, was a cool in-fighter who could take punishment without wincing overmuch. But at the end of the first fortnight of the new time-card, he cornered his chief in the private office and freed his mind.

"It's no use, Mr. Lidgerwood; we can't make these reforms stick with the outfit we've got," he asserted, in sharp discouragement. "The next thing on the docket will be a strike, and you know what that will mean, in a country where the whiskey is bad and nine men out of every ten go fixed for trouble."

"I know; nevertheless the reforms have got to stick," returned Lidgerwood definitively. "We are going to run this railroad as it should be run, or hang it up in the air. Did you discharge that operator at Crow Canyon? the fellow who let Train 76 get by him without orders night before last?"

"Dick Rufford? Oh yes, I fired him, and he came in on 202 to-day lugging a piece of artillery and shooting off his mouth about what he was going to do to me ... and to you. I suppose you know that his brother Bart, they call him 'the killer', is the lookout at Red-Light Sammy Faro's game, and the meanest devil this side of the Timanyonis?"

"I didn't know it, but that cuts no figure." Lidgerwood forced himself to say it, though his lips were curiously dry. "We are going to have discipline on this railroad while we stay here, Mac; there are no two ways about that."

McCloskey tilted his hat to the bridge of his nose, his characteristic gesture of displeasure.

"I promised myself that I wouldn't join the gun-toters when I came out here," he said, half musingly, "but I've weakened on that. Yesterday, when I was calling Jeff Cummings down for dropping that new shifting-engine out of an open switch in broad daylight, he pulled on me out of his cab window. What I had to take while he had me 'hands up' is more than I'll take from any living man again."

As in other moments of stress and perplexity, Lidgerwood was absently marking little pencil squares on his desk blotter.

"I wouldn't get down to the desert level, if I were you, Mac," he said thoughtfully.

"I'm down there right now, in self-defence," was the sober rejoinder. "And if you'll take a hint from me you'll heel yourself, too, Mr. Lidgerwood. I know this country better than you do, and the men in it. I don't say they'll come after you deliberately, but as things are now you can't open your face to one of them without taking the chance of a quarrel, and a quarrel in a gun-country——"

"I know," said Lidgerwood patiently, and the trainmaster gave it up.

It was an hour or two later in the same day when McCloskey came into the private office again, hat tilted to nose, and the gargoyle face portraying fresh soul agonies.

"They've taken to pillaging now!" he burst out. "The 316, that new saddle-tank shifting-engine, has disappeared. I saw Broderick using the '95, and when I asked him why, he said he couldn't find the '16."

"Couldn't find it?" echoed Lidgerwood.

"No; nor I can't, either. It's nowhere in the yards, the roundhouse, or back shop, and none of Gridley's foremen know anything about it. I've had Callahan wire east and west, and if they're all telling the truth, nobody has seen it or heard of it."

"Where was it, at last accounts?"

"Standing on the coal track under chute number three, where the night crew left it at midnight, or thereabouts."

"But certainly somebody must know where it has gone," said Lidgerwood.

"Yes; and by grapples! I think I know who the somebody is."

"Who is it?"

"If I should tell you, you wouldn't believe it, and besides I haven't got the proof. But I'm going to get the proof," shaking a menacing forefinger, "and when I do——"

The interruption was the entrance of Hallock, coming in with the pay-rolls for the superintendent's approval. McCloskey broke off short and turned to the door, but Lidgerwood gave him a parting command.

"Come in again, Mac, in about half an hour. There is another matter that I want to take up with you, and to-day is as good a time as any."

The trainmaster nodded and went out, muttering curses to the tilted hat brim.

VI

"This switching-engine mystery opens up a field that I've been trying to get into for some little time, Mac," the superintendent began, after the half-hour had elapsed and the trainmaster had returned to the private office. "Sit down and we'll thresh it out. Here are some figures showing loss and expense in the general maintenance account. Look them over and tell me what you think."

"Wastage, you mean?" queried the trainmaster, glancing at the totals in the auditor's statement.

"That is what I have been calling it; a reckless disregard for the value of anything and everything that can be included in a requisition. There is a good deal of that, I know; the right-of-way is littered from end to end with good material thrown aside. But I'm afraid that isn't the worst of it."

The trainmaster was nursing a knee and screwing his face into the reflective scheme of distortion.

"Those things are always hard to prove. Short of a military guard, for instance, you couldn't prevent Angels from raiding the company's coal-yard for its cook-stoves. That's one leak, and the others are pretty much like it. If a company employee wants to steal, and there isn't enough common honesty among his fellow-employees to hold him down, he can steal fast enough and get away with it."

"By littles, yes, but not in quantity," pursued Lidgerwood.

"'Mony a little makes a mickle,' as my old grandfather used to say," McCloskey went on. "If everybody gets his fingers into the sugar-bowl——"

Lidgerwood swung his chair to face McCloskey.

"We'll pass up the petty thieveries, for the present, and look a little higher," he said gravely. "Have you found any trace of those two car-loads of company lumber lost in transit between here and Red Butte two weeks ago?"

"No, nor of the cars themselves. They were reported as two Transcontinental flats, initials and numbers plainly given in the car-record. They seem to have disappeared with the lumber."

"Which means?" queried the superintendent.

"That the numbers, or the initials, or both, were wrongly reported. It means that it was a put-up job to steal the lumber."

"Exactly. And there was a mixed car-load of lime and cement lost at about the same time, wasn't there?"

"Yes."

Lidgerwood's swing-chair "righted itself to the perpendicular with a snap."

"Mac, the Red Butte mines are looking up a little, and there is a good bit of house-building going on in the camp just now: tell me, what man or men in the company's service would be likely to be taking a flyer in Red Butte real estate?"

"I don't know of anybody. Gridley used to be interested in the camp. He went in pretty heavily on the boom, and lost out—so they all say. So did your man out there in the pig-pen desk," with a jerk of his thumb to indicate the outer office.

"They are both out of it," said Lidgerwood shortly. Then: "How about Sullivan, the west-end supervisor of track? He has property in Red Butte, I am told."

"Sullivan is a thief, all right, but he does it openly and brags about it; carries off a set of bridge-timbers, now and then, for house-sills, and makes a joke of it with anybody who will listen."

Lidgerwood dismissed Sullivan abruptly.

"It is an organized gang, and it must have its members pretty well scattered through the departments—and have a good many members, too," he said conclusively. "That brings us to the disappearance of the switching-engine again. No one man made off with that, single-handed, Mac."

"Hardly."

"It was this gang we are presupposing—the gang that has been stealing lumber and lime and other material by the car-load."

"Well?"

"I believe we'll get to the bottom of all the looting on this switching-engine business. They have overdone it this time. You can't put a locomotive in your pocket and walk off with it. You say you've wired Copah?"

"Yes."

"Who was at the Copah key—Mr. Leckhard?"

"No. I didn't want to advertise our troubles to a main-line official. I got the day-despatcher, Crandall, and told him to keep his mouth shut until he heard of it some other way."

"Good. And what did Crandall say?"

"He said that the '16 had never gone out through the Copah yards; that it couldn't get anywhere if it had without everybody knowing about it."

Lidgerwood's abstracted gaze out of the office window became a frown of concentration.

"But the object, McCloskey—what possible profit could there be in the theft of a locomotive that can neither be carried away nor converted into salable junk?"

The trainmaster shook his head. "I've stewed over that till I'm threatened with softening of the brain," he confessed.

"Never mind, you have a comparatively easy job," Lidgerwood went on. "That engine is somewhere this side of the Crosswater Hills. It is too big to be hidden under a bushel basket. Find it, and you'll be hot on the trail of the car-load robbers."

McCloskey got upon his feet as if he were going at once to begin the search, but Lidgerwood detained him.

"Hold on; I'm not quite through yet. Sit down again and have a smoke."

The trainmaster squinted sourly at the extended cigar-case. "I guess not," he demurred. "I cut it out, along with the toddies, the day I put on my coat and hat and walked out of the old F. & P.M. offices without my time-check."

"If it had to be both or neither, you were wise; whiskey and railroading don't go together very well. But about this other matter. Some years ago there was a building and loan association started here in Angels, the ostensible object being to help the railroad men to own their homes. Ever hear of it?"

"Yes, but it was dead and buried before my time."

"Dead, but not buried," corrected Lidgerwood. "As I understand it, the railroad company fathered it, or at all events, some of the officials took stock in it. When it died there was a considerable deficit, together with a failure on the part of the executive committee to account for a pretty liberal cash balance."

"I've heard that much," said the trainmaster.

"Then we'll bring it down to date," Lidgerwood resumed. "It appears that there are twenty-five or thirty of the losers still in the employ of this company, and they have sent a committee to me to ask for an investigation, basing the demand on the assertion that they were coerced into giving up their money to the building and loan people."

"I've heard that, too," McCloskey admitted. "The story goes that the house-building scheme was promoted by the old Red Butte Western bosses, and if a man didn't take stock he got himself disliked. If he did take it, the premiums were held out on the pay-rolls. It smells like a good, old-fashioned graft, with the lid nailed on."

"There wouldn't seem to be any reasonable doubt about the graft," said the superintendent. "But my duty is clear. Of course, the Pacific Southwestern Company isn't responsible for the side-issue schemes of the old Red Butte Western officials. But I want to do strict justice. These men charge the officials of the building and loan company with open dishonesty. There was a balance of several thousand dollars in the treasury when the explosion came, and it disappeared."

"Well?" said the trainmaster.

"The losers contend that somebody ought to make good to them. They also call attention to the fact that the building and loan treasurer, who was never able satisfactorily to explain the disappearance of the cash balance, is still on the railroad company's pay-rolls."

McCloskey sat up and tilted the derby to the back of his head. "Gridley?" he asked.

"No; for some reasons I wish it were Gridley. He is able to fight his own battles. It comes nearer home, Mac. The treasurer was Hallock."

McCloskey rose noiselessly, tiptoed to the door of communication with the outer office, and opened it with a quick jerk. There was no one there.

"I thought I heard something," he said. "Didn't you think you did?"

Lidgerwood shook his head.

"Hallock has gone over to the storekeeper's office to check up the time-rolls. He won't be back to-day."

McCloskey closed the door and returned to his chair.

"If I say what I think, you'll be asking me for proofs, Mr. Lidgerwood, and I have none. Besides, I'm a prejudiced witness. I don't like Hallock."

Quite unconsciously Lidgerwood picked up a pencil and began adding more squares to the miniature checker-board on his desk blotter. It was altogether subversive of his own idea of fitness to be discussing his chief clerk with his trainmaster, but McCloskey had proved himself an honest partisan and a fearless one, and Lidgerwood was at a pass where the good counsel of even a subordinate was not to be despised.

"I don't want to do Hallock an injustice," he went on, after a hesitant pause, "neither do I wish to dig up the past, for him or for anybody. I was hoping that you might know some of the inside details, and so make it easier for me to get at the truth. I can't believe that Hallock was culpably responsible for the disappearance of the money."

By this time McCloskey had his hat tilted to the belligerent angle.

"I'm not a fair witness," he reiterated. "There's been gossip, and I've listened to it."

"About this building and loan mess?"

"No; about the wife."

"To Hallock's discredit, you mean?"

"You'd think so: there was a scandal of some sort; I don't know what it was—never wanted to know. But there are men here in Angels who hint that Hallock killed the woman and sunk her body in the Timanyoni."

"Heavens!" exclaimed Lidgerwood, under his breath. "I can't believe that, Mac."

"I don't know as I do, but I can tell you a thing that I do know, Mr. Lidgerwood: Hallock is a devil out of hell when it comes to paying a grudge. There was a freight-conductor named Jackson that he had a shindy with in Mr. Ferguson's time, and it came to blows. Hallock got the worst of the fist-fight, but Ferguson made a joke of it and wouldn't fire Jackson. Hallock bided his time like an Indian, and worked it around so that Jackson got promoted to a passenger run. After that it was easy."

"How so?"

"It was the devil's own game. Jackson was a handsome young fellow, and Hallock set a woman on him—a woman out of Cat Biggs's dance-hall. From that to holding out fares to get more money to squander was only a step for the young fool, and he took it. Having baited the trap and set it, Hallock sprung it. One fine day Jackson was caught red-handed and turned over to the company lawyers. There had been a good bit of talk and they made an example of him. He's got a couple of years to serve yet, I believe."

Lidgerwood was listening thoughtfully. The story which had ended so disastrously for the young conductor threw a rather lurid sidelight upon Jackson's accuser. Fairness was the superintendent's fetish, and the revenge which would sleep on its wrongs and go about deliberately and painstakingly to strike a deadly blow in the dark was revolting to him. Yet he was just enough to distinguish between gross vindictiveness and an evil which bore no relation to the vengeful one.

"A financially honest man might still have a weakness for playing even in a personal quarrel," he commented. "Your story proves nothing more than that."

"I know it."

"But I am going to run the other thing down, too," Lidgerwood insisted. "Hallock shall have a chance to clear himself, but if he can't do it, he can't stay with me."

At this the trainmaster changed front so suddenly that Lidgerwood began to wonder if his estimate of the man's courage was at fault.

"Don't do that, Mr. Lidgerwood, for God's sake don't stir up the devil in that long-haired knife-fighter at such a time as this!" he begged. "The Lord knows you've got trouble enough on hand as it is, without digging up something that belongs to the has-beens."

"I know, but justice is justice," was the decisive rejoinder. "The question is still a live one, as the complaint of the grievance committee proves. If I dodge, my refusal to investigate will be used against us in the labor trouble which you say is brewing. I'm not going to dodge, McCloskey."

The contortions of the trainmaster's homely features indicated an inward struggle of the last-resort nature. When he had reached a conclusion he spat it out.

"You haven't asked my advice, Mr. Lidgerwood, but here it is anyway. Flemister, the owner of the Wire-Silver mine over in Timanyoni Park, was the president of that building and loan outfit. He and Hallock are at daggers drawn, for some reason that I've never understood. If you could get them together, perhaps they could make some sort of a statement that would quiet the kickers for the time being, at any rate."

Lidgerwood looked up quickly. "That's odd," he said. "No longer ago than yesterday, Gridley suggested precisely the same thing."

McCloskey was on his feet again and fumbling behind him for the door-knob.

"I'm all in," he grimaced. "When it comes to figuring with Gridley and Flemister and Hallock all in the same breath, I'm done."

Lidgerwood made a memorandum on his desk calendar to take the building and loan matter up with Hallock the following day. But another wreck intervened, and after the wreck a conference with the Red Butte mine-owners postponed all office business for an additional twenty-four hours. It was late in the evening of the third day when the superintendent's special steamed home from the west, and Lidgerwood, who had dined in his car, went directly to his office in the Crow's Nest.

He had scarcely settled himself at his desk for an attack upon the accumulation of mail when Benson came in. It was a trouble call, and the young engineer's face advertised it.

"It's no use talking, Lidgerwood," he began, "I can't do business on this railroad until you have killed off some of the thugs and highbinders."

Lidgerwood flung the paper-knife aside and whirled his chair to face the new complaint.

"What is the matter now, Jack?" he snapped.

"Oh, nothing much—when you're used to it; only about a thousand dollars' worth of dimension timber gone glimmering. That's all."

"Tell it out," rasped the superintendent. The mine-owners' conference, from which he had just returned, had been called to protest against the poor service given by the railroad, and knowing his present inability to give better service, he had temporized until it needed but this one more touch of the lash to make him lose his temper hopelessly.

"It's the Gloria bridge," said Benson. "We had the timbers all ready to pull out the old and put in the new, and the shift was to be made to-day between trains. Last night every stick of the new stock disappeared."

Lidgerwood was not a profane man, but what he said to Benson in the coruscating minute or two which followed resolved itself into a very fair imitation of profanity, inclusive and world-embracing.

"And you didn't have wit enough to leave a watchman on the job!" he chafed—this by way of putting an apex to the pyramid of objurgation. "By heavens! this thing has got to stop, Benson. And it's going to stop, if we have to call out the State militia and picket every cursed mile of this rotten railroad!"

"Do it," said Benson gruffly, "and when it's done you notify me and I'll come back to work." And with that he tramped out, and was too angry to remember to close the door.

Lidgerwood turned back to his desk, savagely out of humor with Benson and with himself, and raging inwardly at the mysterious thieves who were looting the company as boldly as an invading army might. At this, the most inauspicious moment possible, his eye fell upon the calendar memorandum, "See Hallock about B/L.," and his finger was on the chief clerk's bell-push before he remembered that it was late, and that there had been no light in Hallock's room when he had come down the corridor to his own door.

The touch of the push-button was only a touch, and there was no answering skirl of the bell in the adjoining room. But, as if the intention had evoked it, a shadow crossed behind the superintendent's chair and came to rest at the end of the roll-top desk. Lidgerwood looked up with his eyes aflame. It was Hallock who was standing at the desk's end, and he was pointing to the memorandum on the calendar pad.

"You made that note three days ago," he said abruptly. "I saw your train come in and your light go on. What bill of lading was it you wanted to see me about?"

For an instant Lidgerwood failed to understand. Then he saw that in abbreviating he had unconsciously used the familiar sign, "B/L," the common abbreviation of "bill of lading." At another time he would have turned Hallock's very natural mistake into an easy introduction to a rather delicate subject. But now he was angry.

"Sit down," he rapped out. "That isn't 'bill of lading'; it's 'building and loan.'"

Hallock dragged the one vacant chair into the circle illuminated by the shaded desk-electric, and sat on the edge of it, with his hands on his knees. "Well?" he said, in the grating voice that was so curiously like the master-mechanic's.

"We can cut out the details," this from the man who, under other conditions, would have gone diplomatically into the smallest details. "Some years ago you were the treasurer of the Mesa Building and Loan Association. When the association went out of business, its books showed a cash balance in the treasury. What became of the money?"

Hallock sat as rigid as a carved figure flanking an Egyptian propylon, which his attitude suggested. He was silent for a time, so long a time that Lidgerwood burst out impatiently, "Why don't you answer me?"

"I was just wondering if it is worth while for you to throw me overboard," said the chief clerk, speaking slowly and quite without heat. "You are needing friends pretty badly just now, if you only knew it, Mr. Lidgerwood."

The cool retort, as from an equal in rank, added fresh fuel to the fire.

"I'm not buying friends with concessions to injustice and crooked dealing," Lidgerwood exploded. "You were in the railroad service when the money was paid over to you, and you are in the railroad service now. I want to know where the money went."

"It is none of your business, Mr. Lidgerwood," said the carved figure with the gloomy eyes that never blinked.

"By heavens! I'm making it my business, Hallock! These men who were robbed say that you are an embezzler, a thief. If you are not, you've got to clear yourself. If you are, you can't stay in the Red Butte service another day: that's all."

Again there was a silence surcharged with electric possibilities. Lidgerwood bit the end from a cigar and lost three matches before he succeeded in lighting it. Hallock sat perfectly still, but the sallow tinge in his gaunt face had given place to a stony pallor. When he spoke, it was still without anger.

"I don't care a damn for your chief clerkship," he said calmly, "but for reasons of my own I am not ready to quit on such short notice. When I am ready, you won't have to discharge me. Upon what terms can I stay?"

"I've stated them," said the one who was angry. "Discharge your trust; make good in dollars and cents, or show cause why you were caught with an empty cash-box."

For the first time in the interview the chief clerk switched the stare of the gloomy eyes from the memorandum desk calendar, and fixed it upon his accuser.

"You seem to take it for granted that I was the only grafter in the building and loan business," he objected. "I wasn't; on the contrary, I was only a necessary cog in the wheel. Somebody had to make the deductions from the pay-rolls, and——"

"I'm not asking you to make excuses," stormed Lidgerwood. "I'm telling you that you've got to make good! If the money was used legitimately, you, or some of your fellow-officers in the company, should be able to show it. If the others left you to hold the bag, it is due to yourself, to the men who were held up, and to me, that you set yourself straight. Go to Flemister—he was your president, wasn't he?—and get him to make a statement that I can show to the grievance committee. That will let you out, and me, too."

Hallock stood up and leaned over the desk end. His saturnine face was a mask of cold rage, but his eyes were burning.

"If I thought you knew what you're saying," he began in the grating voice, "but you don't— you *can't* know!" Then, with a sudden break in the fierce tone: "Don't send me to Flemister for my clearance—don't do it, Mr. Lidgerwood. It's playing with fire. I didn't steal the money; I'll swear it on a stack of Bibles a mile high. Flemister will tell you so if he is paid his price. But you don't want me to pay the price. If I do——"

"Go on," said Lidgerwood, frowning, "if you do, what then?"

Hallock leaned still farther over the desk end.

"If I do, you'll get what you are after—and a good deal more. Again I am going to ask you if it is worth while to throw me overboard."

Lidgerwood was still angry enough to resent this advance into the field of the personalities.

"You've had my last word, Hallock, and all this talk about consequences that you don't explain is beside the mark. Get me that statement from Flemister, and do it soon. I am not going to have it said that we are fighting graft in one place and covering it up in another."

Hallock straightened up and buttoned his coat.

"I'll get you the statement," he said, quietly; "and the consequences won't need any explaining." His hand was on the door-knob when he finished saying it, and Lidgerwood had risen from his chair. There was a pause, while one might count five.

"Well?" said the superintendent.

"I was thinking again," said the man at the door. "By all the rules of the game—the game as it is played here in the desert—I ought to be giving you twenty-four hours to get out of gunshot, Mr. Lidgerwood. Instead of that I am going to do you a service. You remember that operator, Rufford, that you discharged a few days ago?"

"Yes."

"Bart Rufford, his brother, the 'lookout' at Red Light's place, has invited a few of his friends to take notice that he intends to kill you. You can take it straight. He means it. And that was what brought me up here to-night—not that memorandum on your desk calendar."

For a long time after the door had jarred to its shutting behind Hallock, Lidgerwood sat at his desk, idle and abstractedly thoughtful. Twice within the interval he pulled out a small drawer under the roll-top and made as if he would take up the weapon it contained, and each time he closed the drawer to break with the temptation to put the pistol into his pocket.

Later, after he had forced himself to go to work, a door slammed somewhere in the despatcher's end of the building, and automatically his hand shot out to the closed drawer. Then he made his decision and carried it out. Taking the nickel-plated thing from its hiding-place, and breaking it to eject the cartridges, he went to the end door of the corridor, which opened into the unused space under the rafters, and flung the weapon to the farthest corner of the dark loft.

VII

Lidgerwood had found little difficulty in getting on the companionable side of Dawson, so far as the heavy-muscled, silent young draftsman had a companionable side; and an invitation to the family dinner-table at the Dawson cottage on the low mesa above the town had followed, as a matter of course.

Once within the home circle, with Benson to plead his cause with the meek little woman whose brown eyes held the shadow of a deep trouble, Lidgerwood had still less difficulty in arranging to share Benson's permanent table welcome. Though Martha Dawson never admitted it, even to her daughter, she stood in constant terror of the Red Desert and its representative town of Angels, and the presence of the superintendent as the member of the household promised to be an added guaranty of protection.

Lidgerwood's acceptance as a table boarder in the cottage on the mesa being hospitably prompt, he was coming and going as regularly as his oversight of the three hundred miles of demoralization permitted before the buffoonery of the Red Butte Western suddenly laughed itself out, and war was declared. In the interval he had come to concur very heartily in Benson's estimate of the family, and to share—without Benson's excuse, and without any reason that could be set in words—the young engineer's opposition to Gridley as Miss Faith's possible choice.

There was little to be done in this field, however. Gridley came and went, not too often, figuring always as a friend of the family, and usurping no more of Miss Dawson's time and attention than she seemed willing to bestow upon him. Lidgerwood saw no chance to obstruct and no good reason for obstructing. At all events, Gridley did not furnish the reason. And the first time Lidgerwood found himself sitting out the sunset hour after dinner on the tiny porch of the mesa cottage, with Faith Dawson as his companion—this while the joke was still running its course—his talk was not of Gridley, nor yet of Benson; it was of himself.

"How long is it going to be before you are able to forget that I am constructively your brother's boss, Miss Faith?" he asked, when she had brought him a cushion for the back of the hard veranda chair in which he was trying to be luxuriously lazy.

"Oh, do I remember it?—disagreeably?" she laughed. And then, with charming naïveté: "I am sure I try not to."

"I am beginning to wish you would try a little harder," he ventured, endeavoring to put her securely upon the plane of companionship. "It is pretty lonesome sometimes, up here on the top round of the Red-Butte-Western ladder of authority."

"You mean that you would like to leave your official dignity behind you when you come to us here on the mesa?" she asked.

"That's the idea precisely. You have no conception how strenuous it is, wearing the halo all the time, or perhaps I should say, the cap and bells."

She smiled. Frederic Dawson, the reticent, had never spoken of the attitude of the Red Butte Western toward its new boss, but Gridley had referred to it quite frequently and had made a joke of it. Without knowing just why, she had resented Gridley's attitude; this notwithstanding the master-mechanic's genial affability whenever Lidgerwood and his difficulties were the object of discussion.

"They are still refusing to take you seriously?" she said. "I hope you don't mind it too much."

"Personally, I don't mind it at all," he assured her—which was sufficiently true at the moment. "The men are acting like a lot of foolish schoolboys bent on discouraging the new teacher. I am hoping they will settle down to a sensible basis after a bit, and take me and the new order of things for granted."

Miss Dawson had something on her mind; a thing not gathered from Gridley or from any one else in particular, but which seemed to take shape of itself. The effect of setting it in speech asked for a complete effacement of Lidgerwood the superintendent, and that was rather difficult. But she compassed it.

"I don't think you ought to take them so much for granted—the men, I mean," she cautioned. "I can't help feeling afraid that some of the joking is not quite good-natured."

"I fancy very little of it is what you would call good-natured," he rejoined evenly. "Very much of it is thinly disguised contempt."

"For your authority?"

"For me, personally, first; and for my authority as a close second."

"Then you are anticipating trouble when the laugh is over?"

He shook his head. "I'm hoping No, as I said a moment ago, but I'm expecting Yes."

"And you are not afraid?"

It would have been worth a great deal to him if he could have looked fearlessly into the clear gray eyes of questioning, giving her a brave man's denial. But instead, his gaze went beyond her and he said: "You surely wouldn't expect me to confess it if I were afraid, would you? Don't you despise a coward, Miss Dawson?"

The sun was sinking behind the Timanyonis, and the soft glow of the western sky suffused her face, illuminating it with rare radiance. It was not, in the last analysis, a beautiful face, he told himself, comparing it with another whose outlines were bitten deeply and beyond all hope of erasure into the memory page. Yet the face warming softly in the sunset glow was sweet and winsome, attractive in the best sense of the overworked word. At the moment Lidgerwood rather envied Benson—or Gridley, whichever one of the two it was for whom Miss Dawson cared the most.

"There are so many different kinds of cowards," she said, after the reflective interval.

"But they are all equally despicable?" he suggested.

"The real ones are, perhaps. But our definitions are often careless. My grandfather, who was a captain of volunteers in the Civil War, used to say that real cowardice is either a psychological condition or a soul disease, and that what we call the physical symptoms of it are often misleading."

"For example?" said Lidgerwood.

"Grandfather used to be fond of contrasting the camp-fire bully and braggart, as one extreme, with the soldier who was frankly afraid of getting killed, as the other. It was his theory that the man who dodged the first few bullets in a battle was quite likely to turn out to be the real hero."

Lidgerwood could not resist the temptation to probe the old wound.

"Suppose, under some sudden stress, some totally unexpected trial, a man who was very much afraid of being afraid found himself morally and physically unable to do the courageous thing. Wouldn't he be, to all intents and purposes, a real coward?"

She took time to think.

"No," she said finally, "I wouldn't say that. I should wait until I had seen the same man tried under conditions that would give him time, to think first and to act afterward."

"Would you really do that?" he asked doubtfully.

"Yes, I should. A trial of the kind you describe isn't quite fair. Acute presence of mind in an emergency is not a supreme test of anything except of itself; least of all, perhaps, is it a test of courage—I mean courage of that quality which endures to-day and faces without flinching the threatening to-morrow."

"And you think the man who might be surprised into doing something very disgraceful on the spur of the moment might still have that other kind of courage, Miss Faith?"

"Certainly." She was far enough from making any personal application of the test case suggested by the superintendent. But in a world which took its keynote from the harsh discords of the Red Desert, these little thoughtful talks with a man who was most emphatically not of the Red Desert were refreshing. And she could scarcely have been Martha Dawson's daughter or Frederic Dawson's sister without having a thoughtful cast of mind.

Lidgerwood rose and felt in his pockets for his after-dinner cigar.

"You are much more charitable than most women, Miss Dawson," he said gravely; after which he left abruptly, and went back to his desk in the Crow's Nest.

As we have seen, this bit of confidential talk between the superintendent and Faith Dawson fell in the period of the jesting horse-laugh; fell, as it chanced, on a day when the horse-laugh was at its height. Later, after the storm broke, there were no more quiet evenings on the cottage porch for a harassed superintendent. Lidgerwood came and went as before, when the rapidly recurring wrecks did not keep him out on the line, but he scrupulously left his troubles behind him when he climbed to the cottage on the mesa.

Quite naturally, his silence on the one topic which was stirring the Red Desert from the Crosswater Hills to Timanyoni Canyon was a poor mask. The increasing gravity of the situation wrote itself plainly enough in his face, and Faith Dawson was sorry for him, giving him silent sympathy, unasked, if not wholly unexpected. The town talk of Angels, what little of it reached the cottage, was harshly condemnatory of the new superintendent; and public opinion, standing for what it was worth, feared no denial when it asserted that Lidgerwood was doing what he could to earn his newer reputation.

After the mysterious disappearance of the switching-engine, mystery still unsolved and apparently unsolvable, he struck fast and hard, searching painstakingly for the leaders in the rebellion, reprimanding, suspending, and discharging until McCloskey warned him that, in addition to the evil of short-handing the road, he was filling Angels with a growing army of ex-employees, desperate and ripe for anything.

"I can't help it, Mac," was his invariable reply. "Unless they put me out of the fight I shall go on as I have begun, staying with it until we have a railroad in fact, or a forfeited charter. Do the best you can, but let it be plainly and distinctly understood that the man who isn't with us is against us, and the man who is against us is going to get a chance to hunt for a new job every time."

Whereupon the trainmaster's homely face would take on added furrowings of distress.

"That's all right, Mr. Lidgerwood; that is stout, two-fisted talk all right; and I'm not doubting that you mean every word of it. But, they'll murder you."

"That is neither here nor there, what they will do to me. I handled them with gloves at first, but they wanted the bare fist. They've got it now, and as I have said before, we are going to fight this thing through to a complete and artistic finish. Who goes east on 202 to-day?"

"It is Judson's run, but he is laying off."

"What is the matter with him, sick?"

"No; just plain drunk."

"Fire him. I won't have a single solitary man in the train service who gets drunk. Tell him so."

"All right; one more stick of dynamite, with a cap and fuse in it, turned loose under foot," prophesied McCloskey gloomily. "Judson goes."

"Never mind the dynamite. Now, what has been done with Johnston, that conductor who turned in three dollars as the total cash collections for a hundred-and-fifty-mile run?"

"I've had him up. He grinned and said that that was all the money there was, everybody had tickets."

"You don't believe it?"

"No; Grantby, the superintendent of the Ruby Mine, came in on Johnston's train that morning and he registered a kick because the Ruby Gulch station agent wasn't out of bed in time to sell him a ticket. He paid Johnston on the train, and that one fare alone was five dollars and sixty cents."

Lidgerwood was adding another minute square to the pencilled checker-board on his desk blotter.

"Discharge Johnston and hold back his time-check. Then have him arrested for stealing, and wire the legal department at Denver that I want him prosecuted."

Again McCloskey's rough-cast face became the outward presentment of a soul in anxious trouble.

"Call it done—and another stick of dynamite turned loose," he acquiesced. "Is there anything else?"

"Yes. What have you found out about that missing switch-engine?" This had come to be the stereotyped query, vocalizing itself every time the trainmaster showed his face in the superintendent's room.

"Nothing, yet. I'm hunting for proof."

"Against the men you suspect? Who are they, and what did they do with the engine?"

McCloskey became dumb.

"I don't dare to say part of it till I can say it all, Mr. Lidgerwood. You hit too quick and too hard. But tell me one thing: have you had to report the loss of that engine to anybody higher up?"

"I shall have to report it to General Manager Frisbie, of course, if we don't find it."

"But haven't you already reported it?"

"No; that is, I guess not. Wait a minute."

A touch of the bell-push brought Hallock to the door of the inner office. The green shade was pulled low over his eyes, and he held the pen he had been using as if it were a dagger.

"Hallock, have you reported the disappearance of that switching-engine to Mr. Frisbie?" asked the superintendent.

The answer seemed reluctant, and it was given in the single word of assent.

"When?" asked Lidgerwood.

"In the weekly summary for last week; you signed it," said the chief clerk.

"Did I tell you to include that particular item in the report?" Lidgerwood did not mean to give the inquiry the tang of an implied reproof, but the fight with the outlaws was beginning to make his manner incisive.

"You didn't need to tell me; I know my business," said Hallock, and his tone matched his superior's.

Lidgerwood looked at McCloskey, and, at the trainmaster's almost imperceptible nod, said, "That's all," and Hallock disappeared and closed the door.

"Well?" queried Lidgerwood sharply, when they had privacy again.

McCloskey was shifting uneasily from one foot to the other.

"My name's Scotch, and they tell me I've got Scotch blood in me," he began. "I don't like to shoot my mouth off till I know what I'm doing. I suppose I quarrelled with Hallock once a day, regular, before you came on the job, Mr. Lidgerwood, and I'll say again that I don't like him—never did. That's what makes me careful about throwing it into him now."

"Go on," said Lidgerwood.

"Well, you know he wanted to be superintendent of this road. He kept the wires to New York hot for a week after he found out that the P. S-W. was in control. He missed it, and you naturally took it over his head—at least, maybe that's the way he looks at it."

"Take it for granted and get to the point," urged Lidgerwood, always impatient of preliminary bush-beating.

"There isn't any point, if you don't see any," said McCloskey stubbornly. "But I can tell you how it would strike me, if I had to be wearing your shoes just now. You've got a man for your chief clerk who has kept this whole town guessing for two years. Some say he isn't all to the bad; some say he is a woman-killer; but they all agree that he's as spiteful as an Indian. He wanted your job: supposing he still wants it."

"Stick to the facts, Mac," said the superintendent. "You're theorizing now, you know."

"Well, by gravels, I will!" rasped McCloskey, pushed over the cautionary edge by Lidgerwood's indifference to the main question at issue. "What I know don't amount to much yet, but it all leans one way. Hallock puts in his daytime scratching away at his desk out there, and you'd think he didn't know it was this year. But when that desk is shut up, you'll find him at the roundhouse, over in the freight yard, round the switch shanties, or up at Biggs's—anywhere he can get half a dozen of the men together. I haven't found a man yet that I could trust to keep tab on him, and I don't know what he's doing; but I can guess."

"Is that all?" said Lidgerwood quietly.

"No, it isn't! That switch-engine dropped out two weeks ago last Tuesday night. I've been prying into this locked-up puzzle-box every way I could think of ever since. *Hallock knows where that engine went!*"

"What makes you think so?"

"I'll tell you. Robinson, the night-crew engineer, was a little late leaving her that night. His fireman had gone home, and so had the yardmen. After he had crossed the yard coming out, he saw a man sneaking toward the shifter, keeping in the shadow of the coal-chutes. He was just curious enough to want to know who it was, and he made a little sneak of his own. When he found it was Hallock, he went home and thought no more about it till I got him to talk."

Lidgerwood had gone back to the pencil and the blotting-pad and the making of squares.

"But the motive, Mac?" he questioned, without looking up. "How could the theft or the destruction of a locomotive serve any purpose that Hallock might have in view?"

McCloskey did not mean any disrespect to his superior officer when he retorted: "I'm no 'cyclopædia. There are lots of things I don't know. But unless you call it off, I'm going to know a few more of them before I quit."

"I don't call it off, Mac; find out what you can. But I can't believe that Hallock is heading this organized robbery and rebellion."

"Somebody is heading it, to a dead moral certainty, Mr. Lidgerwood; the licks are coming too straight and too well-timed."

"Find the man if you can, and we'll eliminate him. And, by the way, if it comes to the worst, how will Hepburn, the town marshal, stand?"

The trainmaster shook his head.

"I don't know. Jack's got plenty of sand, but he was elected out of the shops, and by the railroad vote. If it comes to a show-down against the men who elected him——"

"That is what I mean," nodded Lidgerwood. "It will come to a show-down sooner or later, if we can't nip the ringleaders. Young Rufford and a dozen more of the dropped employees are threatening to get even. That means train-wrecking, misplaced switches, arson—anything you like. At the first break there are going to be some very striking examples made of all the wreckers and looters we can land on."

McCloskey's chair faced the window, and he was scowling and mouthing at the tall chimney of the shop power-plant across the tracks. Where had he fallen upon the idea that this carefully laundered gentleman, who never missed his daily plunge and scrub, and still wore immaculate linen, lacked the confidence of his opinions and convictions? The trainmaster knew, and he thought Lidgerwood must also know, that the first blow of the vengeful ones would be directed at the man rather than at the company's property.

"I guess maybe Hepburn will do his duty when it comes to the pinch," he said finally. And the subject having apparently exhausted itself, he went about his business, which was to call up the telegraph operator at Timanyoni to ask why he had broken the rule requiring the conductor and engineer, both of them, to sign train orders in his presence.

Thereupon, quite in keeping with the militant state of affairs on a harassed Red Butte Western, ensued a sharp and abusive wire quarrel at long range; and when it was over, Timanyoni was temporarily stricken from the list of night telegraph stations pending the hastening forward of a relief operator, to take the place of the one who, with many profane objurgations curiously clipped in rattling Morse, had wired his opinion of McCloskey and the new superintendent, closely interwoven with his resignation.

It was after dark that evening when Lidgerwood closed his desk on the pencilled blotting-pad and groped his way down the unlighted stair to the Crow's Nest platform.

The day passenger from the east was in, and the hostler had just coupled Engine 266 to the train for the night run to Red Butte. Lidgerwood marked the engine's number, and saw Dawson talking to Williams, the engineer, as he turned the corner at the passenger-station end of the building. Later, when he was crossing the open plaza separating the railroad yard from the town, he thought he heard the draftsman's step behind him, and waited for Dawson to come up.

The rearward darkness, made blacker by contrast with the white beam of the 266's headlight, yielding no one and no further sounds, he went on, past the tar-paper-covered hotel, past the flanking of saloons and the false-fronted shops, past the "Arcade" with its crimson sidewalk eye setting the danger signal for all who should enter Red-Light Sammy's, and so up to the mesa and to the cottage of seven-o'clock dinners.

His hand was on the latch of the dooryard gate when a man rose out of the gloom—out of the ground at his feet, as it appeared to Lidgerwood—and in the twinkling of an eye the night and the starry dome of it were effaced for the superintendent in a flash of red lightning and a thunder-clap louder than the crash of worlds.

When he began to realize again, Dawson was helping him to his feet, and the draftsman's mother was calling anxiously from the door.

"What was it?" Lidgerwood asked, still dazed and half blinded.

"A man tried to kill you," said Dawson in his most matter-of-fact tone. "I happened along just in time to joggle his arm. That, and your quick drop, did the business. Not hurt, are you?"

Lidgerwood was gripping the gate and trying to steady himself. A chill, like a violent attack of ague, was shaking him to the bone.

"No," he returned, mastering the chattering teeth by the supremest effort of will. "Thanks to you, I guess—I'm—not hurt. Who w-was the man?"

"It was Rufford. He followed you from the Crow's Nest. Williams saw him and put me on, so I followed him."

"Williams? Then he isn't——"

"No," said Dawson, anticipating the query. "He is with us, and he is swinging the best of the engineers into line. But come into the house and let me give you a drop of whiskey. This thing has got on your nerves a bit—and no wonder."

But Lidgerwood clung to the gate-palings for yet another steadying moment.

"Rufford, you said: you mean the discharged telegraph operator?"

"Worse luck," said Dawson. "It was his brother Bart, the 'lookout' at Red-Light Sammy's; the fellow they call 'The Killer'."

VIII

It was on the morning following the startling episode at the Dawsons' gate that Benson, lately arrived from the west on train 204, came into the superintendent's office with the light of discovery in his eye. But the discovery, if any there were, was made to wait upon a word of friendly solicitude.

"What's this they were telling me down at the lunch-counter just now—about somebody taking a pot-shot at you last night?" he asked. "Dougherty said it was Bart Rufford; was it?"

Lidgerwood confirmed the gossip with a nod. "Yes, it was Rufford, so Dawson says. I didn't recognize him, though; it was too dark."

"Well, I'm mighty glad to see that he didn't get you. What was the row?"

"I don't know, definitely; I suppose it was because I told McCloskey to discharge his brother a while back. The brother has been hanging about town and making threats ever since he was dropped from the pay-rolls, but no one has paid any attention to him."

"A pretty close call, wasn't it?—or was Dougherty only putting on a few frills to go with my cup of coffee?"

"It was close enough," admitted Lidgerwood half absently. He was thinking not so much of the narrow escape as of the fresh and humiliating evidence it had afforded of his own wretched unreadiness.

"All right; you'll come around to my way of thinking after a while. I tell you, Lidgerwood, you've got to heel yourself when you live in a gun country. I said I wouldn't do it, but I have done it, and I'll tell you right now, when anybody in this blasted desert makes monkey-motions at me, I'm going to blow the top of his head off, quick."

Lidgerwood's gaze was resting on the little drawer in his desk which now contained nothing but a handful of loose cartridges.

"Hasn't it ever occurred to you, Jack, that I am the one man in the desert who cannot afford to go armed? I am supposed to stand for law and order. What would my example be worth if it should be noised around that I, too, had become a 'gun-toter'?"

"Oh, I'm not going to argue with you," laughed Benson. "You'll go your own way and do as you please, and probably get yourself comfortably shot up before you get through. But I didn't come up here to wrangle with you about your theoretical notions of law and order. I came to tell you that I have been hunting for those bridge-timbers of mine."

"Well?" queried Lidgerwood; "have you found them?"

"No, and I don't believe anybody will ever find them. It's going to be another case of Rachel weeping for her children and refusing to be comforted because they are not."

"But you have discovered something?"

"Partly yes, and partly no. I think I told you at the time that they vanished between two days like a puff of smoke, leaving no trace behind them. How it was done I couldn't imagine. There is a wagon-road paralleling the river over there at the Siding, as you know, and the first thing I did the next morning was to look for wagon-tracks. No set of wheels carrying anything as heavy as those twelve-by-twelve twenty-fours had gone over the road."

"How were they taken, then? They couldn't have been floated off down the river, could they?"

"It was possible, but not at all probable," said the engineer. "My theory was that they were taken away on somebody's railroad car. There were only two sources of information, at first—the night operator at Little Butte twelve miles west, and the track-walker at Point-of-Rocks, whose boat goes down to within two or three miles of the Gloria bridge. Goodloe, at Little Butte, reports that there was nothing moving on the main line after the passing of the midnight freight east; and Shaughnessy, the track-walker, is just a plain, unvarnished liar: he knows a lot more than he will tell."

"Still, you are looking a good bit more cheerful than you were last week," was Lidgerwood's suggestion.

"Yes; after I got the work started again with a new set of timbers, I spent three or four days on the ground digging for information like a dog after a woodchuck. There are some prospectors panning on the bar three miles up the Gloria, but they knew nothing—or if they knew they wouldn't tell. That was the case with every man I talked to on our side of the river. But over across the Timanyoni, nearly opposite the mouth of the Gloria, there is a little creek coming in from the north, and on this creek I found a lone prospector—a queer old chap who hails from my neck of woods up in Michigan."

"Go on," said Lidgerwood, when the engineer stopped to light his pipe.

"The old man told me a fairy tale, all right," Benson went on. "He was as full of fancies as a fig is of seeds. I have been trying to believe that what he told me isn't altogether a pipe-dream, but it sounds mightily like one. He says that about two o'clock in the morning of Saturday, two weeks ago, an engine and a single car backed down from the west to the Gloria bridge, and a crowd of men swarmed off the train, loaded those bridge-timbers, and ran away with them, going back up the line to the west. He tells it all very circumstantially, though he neglected to explain how he happened to be awake and on guard at any such unearthly hour."

"Where was he when he saw all this?"

"On his own side of the river, of course. It was a dark night, and the engine had no headlight. But the loading gang had plenty of lanterns, and he says they made plenty of noise."

"You didn't let it rest at that?" said the superintendent.

"Oh, no, indeed! I put in the entire afternoon that day on a hand-car with four of my men to pump it for me, and if there is a foot of the main line, side-tracks, or spurs, west of the Gloria bridge, that I haven't gone over, I don't know where it is. The next night I crossed the Timanyoni and tackled the old prospector again. I wanted to check him up—see if he had forgotten any of the little frills and details. He hadn't. On the contrary, he was able to add what seems to me a very important detail.

About an hour after the disappearance of the one-car train with my bridge-timbers, he heard something that he had heard many times before. He says it was the high-pitched song of a circular saw. I asked him if he was sure. He grinned and said he hadn't been brought up in the Michigan woods without being able to recognize that song wherever he might hear it."

"Whereupon you went hunting for saw-mills?" asked Lidgerwood.

"That is just what I did, and if there is one within hearing distance of that old man's cabin on Quartz Creek, I couldn't find it. But I am confident that there is one, and that the thieves, whoever they were, lost no time in sawing my bridge-timbers up into board-lumber, and I'll bet a hen worth fifty dollars against a no-account yellow dog that I have seen those boards a dozen times within the last twenty-four hours, without knowing it."

"Didn't see anything of our switch-engine while you were looking for your bridge-timbers and saw-mills and other things, did you?" queried Lidgerwood.

"No," was the quick reply, "no, but I have a think coming on that, too. My old prospector says he couldn't make out very well in the dark, but it seemed to him as if the engine which hauled away our bridge-timbers didn't have any tender. How does that strike you?"

Lidgerwood grew thoughtful. The missing engine was of the "saddle-tank" type, and it had no tender. It was hard to believe that it could be hidden anywhere on so small a part of the Red Butte Western system as that covered by the comparatively short mileage in Timanyoni Park. Yet if it had not been dumped into some deep pot-hole in the river, it was unquestionably hidden somewhere.

"Benson, are you sure you went over all the line lying west of the Gloria bridge?" he asked pointedly.

"Every foot of it, up one side and down the other ... No, hold on, there is that old spur running up on the eastern side of Little Butte; it's the one that used to serve Flemister's mine when the workings were on the eastern slope of the butte. I didn't go over that spur. It hasn't been used for years; as I remember it, the switch connections with the main line have been taken out."

"You're wrong about that," said Lidgerwood definitely. "McCloskey thought so too, and told me that the frogs and point-rails had been taken out at Silver Switch—at both of the main-line ends of the 'Y',—but the last time I was over the line I noticed that the old switch stands were there, and that the split rails were still in place."

Benson had been tilting comfortably in his chair, smoking his pipe, but at this he got up quickly and looked at his watch.

"Say, Lidgerwood, I'm going back to the Park on Extra 71, which ought to leave in about five minutes," he said hurriedly. "Tell me half a dozen things in just about as many seconds. Has Flemister used that spur since you took charge of the road?"

"No."

"Have you ever suspected him of being mixed up in the looting?"

"I haven't known enough about him to form an opinion."

Benson stepped to the door communicating with the outer office, and closed it quietly.

"Your man Hallock out there; how is he mixed up with Flemister?"

"I don't know. Why?"

"Because, the day before yesterday, when I was on the Little Butte station platform, talking with Goodloe, I saw Flemister and Hallock walking down the new spur together. When they saw me, they turned around and began to walk back toward the mine."

"Hallock had business with Flemister, I know that much, and he took half a day off Thursday to go and see him," said the superintendent.

"Do you happen to know what the business was?"

"Yes, I do. He went at my request."

"H'm," said Benson, "another string broken. Never mind; I've got to catch that train."

"Still after those bridge-timbers?"

"Still after the boards they have probably been sawed into. And before I get back I am going to know what's at the upper end of that old Silver Switch 'Y' spur."

The young engineer had been gone less than half an hour, and Lidgerwood had scarcely finished reading his mail, when McCloskey opened the door. Like Benson, the trainmaster also had the light of discovery in his eye.

"More thievery," he announced gloomily. "This time they have been looting my department. I had ten or twelve thousand feet of high-priced, insulated copper wire, and a dozen or more telephone sets, in the store-room. Mr. Cumberley had a notion of connecting up all the Angels departments by telephone, and it got as far as the purchasing of the material. The wire and all those telephone sets are gone."

"Well?" said Lidgerwood, evenly. The temptation to take it out upon the nearest man was still as strong as ever, but he was growing better able to resist it.

"I've done what I could," snapped McCloskey, seeming to know what was expected of him, "but nobody knows anything, of course. So far as I could find out, no one of my men has had occasion to go to the store-room for a week."

"Who has the keys?"

"I have one, and Spurlock, the line-chief, has one. Hallock has the third."

"Always Hallock!" was the half-impatient comment. "I hope you don't suspect him of stealing your wire."

McCloskey tilted his hat over his eyes, and looked truculent enough to fight an entire cavalry troop.

"That's just what I do," he gritted. "I've got him dead to rights this time. He was in that store-room day before yesterday, or rather night before last. Callahan saw him coming out of there."

Lidgerwood sat back in his chair and smiled. "I don't blame you much, Mac; this thing is getting to be pretty binding upon all of us. But I think you are mistaken in your conclusion, I mean. Hallock has been making an inventory of material on hand for the past week or more, and now that I think of it, I remember having seen your wire and the telephone sets included in his last sheet of telegraph supplies."

"There it goes again," said the trainmaster sourly. "Every time I get a half-hitch on that fellow, something turns up to make it slip. But if I had my way about twenty minutes I'd go and choke him till he'd tell me what he has done with that wire."

Lidgerwood was smiling again.

"Try to be as fair to him as you can," he advised good-naturedly. "I know you dislike him, and probably you have good reasons. But have you stopped to ask yourself what possible use he could make of the stolen material?"

Again McCloskey's hat went to the pugnacious angle. "I don't know anything any more; you couldn't prove it by me what day of the week it is. But I can tell you one thing, Mr. Lidgerwood"—shaking an emphatic finger—"Flemister has just put a complete system of wiring and telephones in his mine, and if he had the stuff for the system shipped in over our railroad, the agent at Little Butte doesn't know anything about it. I asked Goodloe, by grapples!"

But even this was unconvincing to the superintendent.

"That proves nothing against Hallock, Mac, as you will see when you cool down a little," he said.

"I know it doesn't," wrathfully; "nothing proves anything any more. I suppose I've got to say it again: I'm all in, down and out." And he went away, growling to his hat-brim.

Late in the evening of the same day, Benson returned from the west, coming in on a light engine that was deadheading from Red Butte to the Angels shops. He sought out Lidgerwood at once, and flinging himself wearily into a chair at the superintendent's elbow, made his report of the day's doings.

"I have, and I haven't," he said, beginning in the midst of things, as his habit was. "You were right about the track connection at Silver Switch. It is in; Flemister put it in himself a month ago when he had a car-load of coal taken up to the back door of his mine."

"Did you go up over the spur?"

"Yes; and I had my trouble for my pains. Before I go any further, Lidgerwood, I'd like to ask you one question: can we afford to quarrel with Mr. Pennington Flemister?"

"Benson, we sha'n't hesitate a single moment to quarrel with the biggest mine-owner or freight-shipper this side of the Crosswater Hills if we have the right on our side. Spread it out. What did you find?"

Benson sank a little lower in his chair. "The first thing I found was a couple of armed guards—a pair of tough-looking citizens with guns sagging at their hips, lounging around the Wire-Silver back door. There is quite a little nest of buildings at the old entrance to the Wire-Silver, and a stockade has been built to enclose them. The old spur runs through a gate in the stockade, and the gate was open; but the two toughs wouldn't let me go inside. I wrangled with them first, and tried to bribe them afterward, but it was no go. Then I started to walk around the outside of the stockade, which is only a high board fence, and they objected to that. Thereupon I told them to go straight to blazes, and walked away down the spur, but when I got out of sight around the first curve I took to the timber on the butte slope and climbed to a point from which I could look over into Flemister's carefully built enclosure."

"Well, what did you see?"

"Much or little, just as you happen to look at it. There are half a dozen buildings in the yard, and two of them are new and unpainted. Sizing them up from a distance, I said to myself that the lumber in them hadn't been very long out of the mill. One of them is evidently the power-house; it has an iron chimney set in the roof, and the power-plant was running."

For a little time after Benson had finished his report there was silence, and Lidgerwood had added many squares to the pencillings on his desk blotter before he spoke again.

"You say two of the buildings are new; did you make any inquiries about recent lumber shipments to the Wire-Silver?"

"I did," said the young engineer soberly. "So far as our station records show, Flemister has had no material, save coal, shipped in over either the eastern or the western spur for several months."

"Then you believe that he took your bridge-timbers and sawed them up into lumber?"

"I do—as firmly as I believe that the sun will rise to-morrow. And that isn't all of it, Lidgerwood. He is the man who has your switch-engine. As I have said, the power-plant was running while I was up there to-day. The power is a steam engine, and if you'd stand off and listen to it you'd swear it was a locomotive pulling a light train up an easy grade. Of course, I'm only guessing at that, but I think you will agree with me that the burden of proof lies upon Flemister."

Lidgerwood was nodding slowly. "Yes, on Flemister and some others. Who are the others, Benson?"

"I have no more guesses coming, and I am too tired to invent any. Suppose we drop it until to-morrow. I'm afraid it means a fight or a funeral, and I am not quite equal to either to-night."

For a long time after Benson had gone, Lidgerwood sat staring out of his office window at the masthead electrics in the railroad yard. Benson's news had merely confirmed his own and McCloskey's conclusion that some one in authority was in collusion with the thieves who were raiding the company. Sooner or later it must come to a grapple, and he dreaded it.

It was deep in the night when he closed his desk and went to the little room partitioned off in the rear of the private office as a sleeping-apartment. When he was preparing to go to bed, he noticed that the tiny relay on the stand at his bed's head was silent. Afterward, when he tried to adjust the instrument, he found it ruined beyond repair. Some one had connected its wiring with the electric lighting circuit, and the tiny coils were fused and burned into solid little cylinders of copper.

IX

Barton Rufford, ex-distiller of illicit whiskey in the Tennessee mountains, ex-welsher turned informer and betraying his neighbor law-breakers to the United States revenue officers, ex-everything which made his continued stay in the Cumberlands impossible, was a man of distinction in the Red Desert.

In the wider field of the West he had been successively a claim-jumper, a rustler of unbranded cattle, a telegraph operator in collusion with a gang of train-robbers, and finally a faro "lookout": the armed guard who sits at the head of the gaming-table in the untamed regions to kill and kill quickly if a dispute arises.

Angels acknowledged his citizenship without joy. A cold-blooded murderer, with an appalling record; and a man with a temper like smoking tow, an itching trigger-finger, the eye of a duck-hawk, and cat-like swiftness of movement, he tyrannized the town when the humor was on him; and as yet no counter-bully had come to chase him into oblivion.

For Lidgerwood to have earned the enmity of this man was considered equivalent to one of three things: the superintendent would throw up his job and leave the Red Desert, preferably by the first train; or Rufford would kill him; or he must kill Rufford. Red Butte Western opinion was somewhat divided as to which horn of the trilemma the victim of Rufford's displeasure would choose, all admitting that, for the moment, the choice lay with the superintendent. Would Lidgerwood fight, or run, or sit still and be slain? In the Angels roundhouse, on the second morning following the attempt upon Lidgerwood's life at the gate of the Dawson cottage, the discussion was spirited, not to say acrimonious.

"I'm telling you hyenas that Collars-and-Cuffs ain't going to run away," insisted Williams, who was just in from the all-night trip to Red Butte and return. "He ain't built that way."

Lester, the roundhouse foreman, himself a man-queller of no mean repute, thought differently. Lidgerwood would, most likely, take to the high grass and the tall timber. The alternative was to "pack a gun" for Rufford—an alternative quite inconceivable to Lester when it was predicated of the superintendent.

"I don't know about that," said Judson, the discharged—and consequently momentarily sobered—engineer of the 271. "He's fooled everybody more than once since he lit down in the Red Desert. First crack everybody said he didn't know his business, 'cause he wore b'iled shirts: he *does* know it. Next, you could put your ear to the ground and hear that he didn't have the sand to round up the maverick R.B.W. He's doing it. I don't know but he might even run a bluff on Bart Rufford, if he felt like it."

"Come off, John!" growled the big foreman. "You needn't be afraid to talk straight over here. He hit you when you was down, and we all know you're only waitin' for a chance to hit back."

Judson was a red-headed man, effusively good-natured when he was in liquor, and a quick-tempered fighter of battles when he was not.

"Don't you make any such mistake!" he snapped. "That's what McCloskey said when he handed me the 'good-by.' 'You'll be one more to go round feelin' for Mr. Lidgerwood's throat, I suppose,' says he. By cripes! what I said to Mac I'm sayin' to you, Bob Lester. I know good and well a-plenty when I've earned my blue envelope. If I'd been in the super's place, the 271 would have had a new runner a long time ago!"

"Oh, hell! *I* say he'll chase his feet," puffed Broadbent, the fat machinist who was truing off the valve-seats of the 195. "If Rufford doesn't make him, there's some others that will."

Judson flared up again.

"Who you quotin' now, Fatty? One o' the shop 'prentices? Or maybe it's Rank Hallock? Say, what's he doin' monkeyin' round the back shop so much lately? I'm goin' to stay round here till I get a chance to lick that scrub."

Broadbent snorted his derision of all mere enginemen.

"You rail-pounders'd better get next to Rankin Hallock," he warned. "He's the next sup'rintendent of the R.B.W. You'll see the 'pointment circular the next day after that jim-dandy over in the Crow's Nest gets moved off'n the map."

"Well, I'm some afeared Bart Rufford's likely to move him," drawled Clay, the six-foot Kentuckian who was filing the 195's brasses at the bench. "Which the same I ain't rejoicin' about, neither. That little cuss is shore a mighty good railroad man. And when you ain't rubbin' his fur the wrong way, he treats you white."

"For instance?" snapped Hodges, a freight engineer who had been thrice "on the carpet" in Lidgerwood's office for over-running his orders.

"Oh, they ain't so blame' hard to find," Clay retorted. "Last week, when we was out on the Navajo wreck, me and the boy didn't have no dinner-buckets. Bradford was runnin' the super's car, and when Andy just sort o' happened to mention the famine up along, the little man made that Jap cook o' his'n get us up a dinner that'd made your hair frizzle. He shore did."

"Why don't you go and take up for him with Bart Rufford?" sneered Broadbent, stopping his facing machine to set in a new cut on the valve-seat.

"Not me. I've got cold feet," laughed the Kentuckian. "I'm like the little kid's daddy in the Sunday-school song: I ain't got time to die yet—got too much to do."

It was Williams's innings, and what he said was cautionary.

"Dry up, you fellows; here comes Gridley."

The master-mechanic was walking down the planked track from the back shop, carrying his years, which showed only in the graying mustache and chin beard, and his hundred and eighty pounds of well-set-up bone and muscle, jauntily. Now, as always, he was the beau ideal of the industrial field-officer; handsome in a clean-cut masculine way, a type of vigor—but also, if the signs of the full face and the eager eyes were to be regarded, of the elemental passions.

Angelic rumor hinted that he was a periodic drunkard: he was both more and less than that. Like many another man, Henry Gridley lived a double life; or, perhaps it would be nearer the truth to say that there were two Henry Gridleys. Lidgerwood, the Dawsons, the little world of Angels at large, knew the virile, accomplished mechanical engineer and master of men, which was his normal personality. What time the other personality, the elemental barbarian, yawned, stretched itself, and came awake, the unspeakable dens of the Copah lower quarter engulfed him until the nether-man had gorged himself on degradation.

To his men, Gridley was a tyrant, exacting, but just; ruling them, as the men of the desert could only be ruled, with the mailed fist. Yet there was a human hand inside of the steel gauntlet, as all men knew. Having once beaten a bullying gang-boss into the hospital at Denver, he had promptly charged himself with the support of the man's family. Other generous roughnesses were recorded of him, and if the attitude of the men was somewhat tempered by wholesome fear, it was none the less loyal.

Hence, when he entered the roundhouse, industrious silence supplanted the discussion of the superintendent's case. Glancing at the group of enginemen, and snapping out a curt criticism of Broadbent's slowness on the valve-seats, he beckoned to Judson. When the discharged engineer had followed him across the turn-table, he faced about and said, not too crisply, "So your sins have found you out one more time, have they, John?"

Judson nodded.

"What is it this time, thirty days?"

Judson shook his head gloomily. "No, I'm down and out."

"Lidgerwood made it final, did he? Well, you can't blame him."

"You hain't heard me sayin' anything, have you?" was the surly rejoinder.

"No, but it isn't in human nature to forget these little things." Then, suddenly: "Where were you day before yesterday between noon and one o'clock, about the time you should have been taking your train out?"

Judson had a needle-like mind when the alcohol was out of it, and the sudden query made him dissemble.

"About ten o'clock I was playin' pool in Rafferty's place with the butt end of the cue. After that, things got kind o'hazy."

"Well, I want you to buckle down and think hard. Don't you remember going over to Cat Biggs's about noon, and sitting down at one of the empty card-tables to drink yourself stiff?"

Judson could not have told, under the thumbscrews, why he was prompted to tell Gridley a plain lie. But he did it.

"I can't remember," he denied. Then then needle-pointed brain got in its word, and he added, "Why?"

"I saw you there when I was going up to dinner. You called me in to tell me what you were going to do to Lidgerwood if he slated you for getting drunk. Don't you remember it?"

Judson was looking the master-mechanic fairly in the eyes when he said, "No, I don't remember a thing about that."

"Try again," said Gridley, and now the shrewd gray eyes under the brim of the soft-rolled felt hat held the engineer helpless.

"I guess—I do—remember it—now," said Judson, slowly, trying, still ineffectually, to break Gridley's masterful eyehold upon him.

"I thought you would," said the master-mechanic, without releasing him. "And you probably remember, also, that I took you out into the street and started you home."

"Yes," said Judson, this time without hesitation.

"Well, keep on remembering it; you went home to Maggie, and she put you to bed. That is what you are to keep in mind."

Judson had broken the curious eye-grip at last, and again he said, "Why?"

Gridley hooked his finger absently in the engineer's buttonhole.

"Because, if you don't, a man named Rufford says he'll start a lead mine in you. I heard him say it last night—overheard him, I should say. That's all."

The master-mechanic passed on, going out by the great door which opened for the locomotive entering-track. Judson hung upon his heel for a moment, and then went slowly out through the tool-room and across the yard tracks to the Crow's Nest.

He found McCloskey in his office above stairs, mouthing and grimacing over the string-board of the new time-table.

"Well?" growled the trainmaster, when he saw who had opened and closed the door. "Come back to tell me you've sworn off? That won't go down with Mr. Lidgerwood. When he fires, he means it."

"You wait till I ask you for my job back again, won't you, Jim McCloskey?" said the disgraced one hotly. "I hain't asked it yet; and what's more, I'm sober."

"Sure you are," muttered McCloskey. "You'd be better-natured with a drink or two in you. What's doing?"

"That's what I came over here to find out," said Judson steadily. "What is the boss going to do about this flare-up with Bart Rufford?"

The trainmaster shrugged.

"You've got just as many guesses as anybody, John. What you can bet on is that he will do something different."

Judson had slouched to the window. When he spoke, it was without turning his head.

"You said something yesterday morning about me feeling for the boss's throat along with that gang up-town that's trying to drink itself up to the point of hitting him back. It don't strike me that way, Mac."

"How does it strike you?"

Judson turned slowly, crossed the room, and sat down in the only vacant chair.

"You know what's due to happen, Mac. Rufford won't try it on again the way he tried it night before last. I heard up-town that he has posted his de-fi: Mr. Lidgerwood shoots him on sight or he shoots Mr. Lidgerwood on sight. You can figure that out, can't you?"

"Not knowing Mr. Lidgerwood much better than you do, John, I'm not sure that I can."

"Well, it's easy. Bart'll walk up to the boss in broad daylight, drop him, and then fill him full o'lead after he's down. I've seen him—saw him do it to Bixby, Mr. Brewster's foreman at the Copperette."

"Say the rest of it," commanded McCloskey.

"I've been thinking. While I'm laying round with nothing much to do, I believe I'll keep tab on Bart for a little spell. I don't love him much, nohow."

McCloskey's face contortion was intended to figure as a derisive smile. "Pshaw, John!" he commented, "he'd skin you alive. Why, even Jack Hepburn is afraid of him!"

"Jack is? How do you know that?"

McCloskey shrugged again.

"Are you with us, John?" he asked cautiously.

"I ain't with Bart Rufford and the tin-horns," said Judson negatively.

"Then I'll tell you a fairy tale," said the trainmaster, lowering his voice. "I gave you notice that Mr. Lidgerwood would do something different: he did it, bright and early this morning; went to Jake Schleisinger, who had to try twice before he could remember that he was a justice of the peace, and swore out a warrant for Rufford's arrest, on a charge of assault with intent to kill."

"Sure," said Judson, "that's what any man would do in a civilized country, ain't it?"

"Yes, but not here, John—not in the red-colored desert, with Bart Rufford's name in the body of the warrant."

"I don't know why not," insisted the engineer stubbornly. "But go on with the story; it ain't any fairy tale, so far."

"When he'd got the warrant, Schleisinger protesting all the while that Bart'd kill him for issuing it, Mr. Lidgerwood took it to Hepburn and told him to serve it. Jack backed down so fast that he fell over his feet. Said to ask him anything else under God's heavens and he'd do it—anything but that."

"Huh!" said Judson. "If I'd took an oath to serve warrants I'd serve 'em, if it did make me sick at my stomach." Then he got up and shuffled away to the window again, and when next he spoke his voice was the voice of a broken man.

"I lied to you a minute ago, Mac. I did want my job back. I came over here hopin' that you and Mr. Lidgerwood might be seein' things a little different by this time. I've quit the whiskey."

McCloskey wagged his shaggy head.

"So you've said before, John, and not once or twice either."

"I know, but every man gets to the bottom, some time. I've hit bed-rock, and I've just barely got sense enough to know it. Let me tell you, Mac, I've pulled trains on mighty near every railroad in this country—and then some. The Red Butte is my last ditch. With my record I couldn't get an engine anywhere else in the United States. Can't you see what I'm up against?"

The trainmaster nodded. He was human.

"Well, it's Maggie and the babies now," Judson went on. "They don't starve, Mac, not while I'm on top of earth. Don't you reckon you could make some sort of a play for me with the boss, Jim? He's got bowels."

McCloskey did not resent the familiarity of the Christian name, neither did he hold out any hope of reinstatement.

"No, John. One or two things I've learned about Mr. Lidgerwood: he doesn't often hit when he's mad, and he doesn't take back anything he says in cold blood. I'm afraid you've cooked your last goose."

"Let me go in and see him. He ain't half as hard-hearted as you are, Jim."

The trainmaster shook his head. "No, it won't do any good. I heard him tell Hallock not to let anybody in on him this morning."

"Hallock be—Say, Mac, what makes him keep that—" Judson broke off abruptly, pulled his hat over his eyes, and said, "Reckon it's worth while to shove me over to the other side, Jim McCloskey?"

"What other side?" demanded McCloskey.

Judson scoffed openly. "You ain't making out like you don't know, are you? Who was behind that break of Rufford's last night?"

"There didn't need to be anybody behind it. Bart thinks he has a kick coming because his brother was discharged."

"But there was somebody behind it. Tell me, Mac, did you ever see me too drunk to read my orders and take my signals?"

"No, don't know as I have."

"Well, I never was. And I don't often get too drunk to hear straight, either, even if I do look and act like the biggest fool God ever let live. I was in Cat Biggs's day before yesterday noon, when I ought to have been down here taking 202 east. There were two men in the back room putting their heads together. I don't know whether they knew I was on the other side of the partition or not. If they did, they probably didn't pay any attention to a drivellin' idiot that couldn't wrap his tongue around an order for more whiskey."

"Go on!" snapped McCloskey, almost viciously.

"They were talking about 'fixing' the boss. One of 'em was for the slow and safe way: small bets and a good many of 'em. The other was for pulling a straight flush on Mr. Lidgerwood, right now. Number One said no, that things were moving along all right, and it wasn't worth while to rush. Then something was said about a woman; I didn't catch her name or just what the hurry man said about her, only it was something about Mr. Lidgerwood's bein' in shape to mix up in it. At that Number One flopped over. 'Pull it off whenever you like!' says he, savage-like."

McCloskey sprang from his chair and towered over the smaller man.

"One of those men was Bart Rufford: who was the other one, Judson?"

Judson was apparently unmoved. "You're forgettin' that I was plum' fool drunk, Jim. I didn't see either one of 'em."

"But you heard?"

"Yes, one of 'em was Rufford, as you say, and up to a little bit ago I'd 'a' been ready to swear to the voice of the one you haven't guessed. But now I can't."

"Why can't you do it now?"

"Sit down and I'll tell you. I've been jarred. Everything I've told you so far, I can remember, or it seems as if I can, but right where I broke off a cog slipped. I must 'a' been drunker than I thought I was. Gridley says he was going by and he says I called him in and told him, fool-wise, all the things I was going to do to Mr. Lidgerwood. He says he hushed me up, called me out to the sidewalk, and started me home. Mac, I don't remember a single wheel-turn of all that, and it makes me scary about the other part."

McCloskey relapsed into his swing-chair.

"You said you thought you recognized the other man by his voice. It sounds like a drunken pipe-dream, the whole of it; but who did you think it was?"

Judson rose up, jerked his thumb toward the door of the superintendent's business office, and said, "Mac, if the whiskey didn't fake the whole business for me—the man who was mumblin' with Bart Rufford was—Hallock!"

"Hallock?" said McCloskey; "and you said there was a woman in it? That fits down to the ground, John. Mr. Lidgerwood has found out something about Hallock's family tear-up, or he's likely to find out. That's what that means!"

What more McCloskey said was said to an otherwise empty room. Judson had opened the door and closed it, and was gone.

Summing up the astounding thing afterward, those who could recall the details and piece them together traced Judson thus:

It was ten-forty when he came down from McCloskey's office, and for perhaps twenty minutes he had been seen lounging at the lunch-counter in the station end of the Crow's Nest. At about eleven one witness had seen him striking at the anvil in Hepburn's shop, the town marshal being the town blacksmith in the intervals of official duty.

Still later, he had apparently forgotten the good resolution declared to McCloskey, and all Angels saw him staggering up and down Mesa Avenue, stumbling into and out of the many saloons, and growing, to all appearances, more hopelessly irresponsible with every fresh stumble. This was his condition when he tripped over the doorstep into the "Arcade," and fell full length on the floor of the bar-room. Grimsby, the barkeeper, picked him up and tried to send him home, but with good-natured and maudlin pertinacity he insisted on going on to the gambling-room in the rear.

The room was darkened, as befitted its use, and a lighted lamp hung over the centre of the oval faro table as if the time were midnight instead of midday. Eight men, five of them miners from the Brewster copper mine, and three of them discharged employees of the Red Butte Western, were the bettors; Red-Light himself, in sombrero and shirt-sleeves, was dealing, and Rufford, sitting on a stool at the table's end, was the "lookout."

When Judson reeled in there was a pause, and a movement to put him out. One of the miners covered his table stakes and rose to obey Rufford's nod. But at this conjuncture the railroad men interfered. Judson was a fellow craftsman, and everybody knew that he was harmless in his cups. Let him stay—and play, if he wanted to.

So Judson stayed, and stumbled round the table, losing his money and dribbling foolishness. Now faro is a silent game, and more than once an angry voice commanded the foolish one to choose his place and to shut his mouth. But the ex-engineer seemed quite incapable of doing either. Twice he made the wavering circuit of the oval table, and when he finally gripped an empty chair it was the one nearest to Rufford on the right, and diagonally opposite to the dealer.

What followed seemed to have no connecting sequence for the other players. Too restless to lose more than one bet in the place he had chosen, Judson tried to rise, tangled his feet in the chair, and fell down, laughing uproariously. When he struggled to the perpendicular again, after two or three ineffectual attempts, he was fairly behind Rufford's stool.

One man, who chanced to be looking, saw the "lookout" start and stiffen rigidly in his place, staring straight ahead into vacancy. A moment later the entire circle of witnesses saw him take a revolver from the holster on his hip and lay it upon the table, with another from the breast pocket of his coat to keep it company. Then his hands went quickly behind him, and they all heard the click of the handcuffs.

The man in the sombrero and shirt-sleeves was first to come alive.

"Duck, Bart!" he shouted, whipping a weapon from its convenient shelf under the table's edge. But Judson, trained to the swift handling of many mechanisms in the moment of respite before a wreck or a derailment, was ready for him.

"Bart's afraid he can't duck without dying," he said grimly, screening himself behind his captive. Then to the others, in the same unhasting tone: "Some of you fellows just quiet Sammy down till I get out of here with this peach of mine. I've got the papers, and I know what I'm doin'; if this thing I'm holdin' against Bart's back should happen to go off——"

That ended it, so far as resistance was concerned. Judson backed quickly out through the bar-room, drawing his prisoner backward after him; and a moment later Angels was properly electrified by the sight of Rufford, the Red Desert terror, marching sullenly down to the Crow's Nest, with a fiery-headed little man at his elbow, the little man swinging the weapon which had been made to simulate the cold muzzle of the revolver when he had pressed it into Rufford's back at the gaming-table.

It was nothing more formidable than a short, thick "S"-wrench, of the kind used by locomotive engineers in tightening the nuts of the piston-rod packing glands.

X

The jocosely spectacular arrest of Barton Rufford, with its appeal to the grim humor of the desert, was responsible for a brief lull in the storm of antagonism evoked by Lidgerwood's attempt to bring order out of the chaos reigning in his small kingdom. For a time Angels was a-grin again, and while the plaudits were chiefly for Judson, the figure of the correctly clothed superintendent who was courageous enough to appeal to the law, loomed large in the reflected light of the red-headed engineer's cool daring.

For the space of a week there were no serious disasters, and Lidgerwood, with good help from McCloskey and Benson, continued to dig persistently into the mystery of the wholesale robberies. With Benson's discoveries for a starting-point, the man Flemister was kept under surveillance, and it soon became evident to the three investigators that the owner of the Wire-Silver mine had been profiting liberally at the expense of the railroad company in many ways. That there had been connivance on the part of some one in authority in the railroad service, was also a fact safely assumable; and each added thread of evidence seemed more and more to entangle the chief clerk.

But behind the mystery of the robberies, Lidgerwood began to get glimpses of a deeper mystery involving Flemister and Hallock. Angelic tradition, never very clearly defined and always shot through with prejudice, spoke freely of a former friendship between the two men. Whether the friendship had been broken, or whether, for reasons best known to themselves, they had allowed the impression to go out that it had been broken, Lidgerwood could not determine from the bits of gossip brought in by the trainmaster. But one thing was certain: of all the minor officials in the railway service, Hallock was the one who was best able to forward and to conceal Flemister's thieveries.

It was in the midst of these subterranean investigations that Lidgerwood had a call from the owner of the Wire-Silver. On the Saturday in the week of surcease, Flemister came in on the noon train from the west, and it was McCloskey who ushered him into the superintendent's office. Lidgerwood looked up and saw a small man wearing the khaki of the engineers, with a soft felt hat to match. The snapping black eyes, with the straight brows almost meeting over the nose, suggested Goethe's *Mephistopheles*, and Flemister shaved to fit the part, with curling mustaches and a dagger-pointed imperial. Instantly Lidgerwood began turning the memory pages in an effort to recall where he had seen the man before, but it was not until Flemister began to speak that he remembered his first day in authority, the wreck at Gloria Siding, and the man who had driven up in a buckboard to hold converse with the master-mechanic.

"I've been trying to find time for a month or more to come up and get acquainted with you, Mr. Lidgerwood," the visitor began, when Lidgerwood had waved him to a chair. "I hope you are not going to hold it against me that I haven't done it sooner."

Lidgerwood's smile was meant to be no more than decently hospitable.

"We are not standing much upon ceremony in these days of reorganization," he said. Then, to hold the interview down firmly to a business basis: "What can I do for you, Mr. Flemister?"

"Nothing—nothing on top of earth; it's the other way round. I came to do something for you—or, rather, for one of your subordinates. Hallock tells me that the ghost of the old Mesa Building and

79

Loan Association still refuses to be laid, and he intimates that some of the survivors are trying to make it unpleasant for him by accusing him to you."

"Yes," said Lidgerwood, studying his man shrewdly by the road of the eye, and without prejudice to the listening ear.

"As I understand it, the complaint of the survivors is based upon the fact that they think they ought to have had a cash dividend forthcoming on the closing up of the association's affairs," Flemister went on; and Lidgerwood again said, "Yes."

"As Hallock has probably told you, I had the misfortune to be the president of the company. Perhaps it's only fair to say that it was a losing venture from the first for those of us who put the loaning capital into it. As you probably know, the money in these mutual benefit companies is made on lapses, but when the lapses come all in a bunch——"

"I am not particularly interested in the general subject, Mr. Flemister," Lidgerwood cut in. "As the matter has been presented to me, I understand there was a cash balance shown on the books, and that there was no cash in the treasury to make it good. Since Hallock was the treasurer, I can scarcely do less than I have done. I am merely asking him—and you—to make some sort of an explanation which will satisfy the losers."

"There is only one explanation to be made," said the ex-building-and-loan president, brazenly. "A few of us who were the officers of the company were the heaviest losers, and we felt that we were entitled to the scraps and leavings."

"In other words, you looted the treasury among you," said Lidgerwood coldly. "Is that it, Mr. Flemister?"

The mine-owner laughed easily. "I'm not going to quarrel with you over the word," he returned. "Possibly the proceeding was a little informal, if you measure it by some of the more highly civilized standards."

"I don't care to go into that," was Lidgerwood's comment, "but I cannot evade my responsibility for the one member of your official staff who is still on my pay-roll. How far was Hallock implicated?"

"He was not implicated at all, save in a clerical way."

"You mean that he did not share in the distribution of the money?"

"He did not."

"Then it is only fair that you should set him straight with the others, Mr. Flemister."

The ex-president did not reply at once. He took time to roll a cigarette leisurely, to light it, and to take one or two deep inhalations, before he said: "It's a rather disagreeable thing to do, this digging into old graveyards, don't you think? I can understand why you should wish to be assured of Hallock's non-complicity, and I have assured you of that; but as for these kickers, really I don't know what you can do with them unless you send them to me. And if you do that, I am afraid some of them may come back on hospital stretchers. I haven't any time to fool with them at this late day."

Lidgerwood felt his gorge rising, and a great contempt for Flemister was mingled with a manful desire to pitch him out into the corridor. It was a concession to his unexplainable pity for Hallock that made him temporize.

"As I said before, you needn't go into the ethics of the matter with me, Mr. Flemister," he said. "But in justice to Hallock, I think you ought to make a statement of some kind that I can show to these men who, very naturally, look to me for redress. Will you do that?"

"I'll think about it," returned the mine-owner shortly; but Lidgerwood was not to be put off so easily.

"You must think of it to some good purpose," he insisted. "If you don't, I shall be obliged to put my own construction upon your failure to do so, and to act accordingly."

Flemister's smile showed his teeth.

"You're not threatening me, are you, Mr. Lidgerwood?"

"Oh, no; there is no occasion for threats. But if you don't make me that statement, fully exonerating Hallock, I shall feel at liberty to make one of my own, embodying what you have just told me. And if I am compelled to do this, you must not blame me if I am not able to place the matter in the most favorable light for you."

This time the visitor's smile was a mere baring of the teeth.

"Is it worth your while to make it a personal quarrel with me, Mr. Lidgerwood?" he asked, with a thinly veiled menace in his tone.

"I am not looking for quarrelsome occasions with you or with any one," was the placable rejoinder. "And I hope you are not going to force me to show you up. Is there anything else? If not, I'm afraid I shall have to ask you to excuse me. This is one of my many busy days."

After Flemister had gone, Lidgerwood was almost sorry that he had not struck at once into the matter of the thieveries. But as yet he had no proof upon which to base an open accusation. One thing he did do, however, and that was to summon McCloskey and give instructions pointing to a bit of experimental observation with the mine-owner as the subject.

"He can't get away from here before the evening train, and I should like to know where he goes and what he does with himself," was the form the instructions took. "When we find out who his accomplices are, I shall have something more to say to him."

"I'll have him tagged," promised the trainmaster; and a few minutes later, when the Wire-Silver visitor sauntered up Mesa Avenue in quest of diversion wherewith to fill the hours of waiting for his train, a small man, red-haired, and with a mechanic's cap pulled down over his eyes, kept even step with him from dive to dive.

Judson's report, made to the trainmaster that evening after the westbound train had left, was short and concise.

"He went up and sat in Sammy's game and didn't come out until it was time to make a break for his train. I didn't see him talking to anybody after he left here." This was the wording of the report.

"You are sure of that, are you, John?" questioned McCloskey.

Judson hung his head. "Maybe I ain't as sure as I ought to be. I saw him go into Sammy's, and saw him come out again, and I know he didn't stay in the bar-room. I didn't go in where they keep the tiger. Sammy don't love me any more since I held Bart Rufford up with an S-wrench, and I was afraid I might disturb the game if I went buttin' in to make sure that Flemister was there. But I guess there ain't no doubt about it."

Thus Judson, who was still sober, and who meant to be faithful according to his gifts. He was scarcely blameworthy for not knowing of the existence of a small back room in the rear of the gambling-den; or for the further unknowledge of the fact that the man in search of diversion had passed on into this back room after placing a few bets at the silent game, appearing no more until he had come out through the gambling-room on his way to the train. If Judson had dared to press his espial, he might have been the poorer by the loss of blood, or possibly of his life; but, living to get away with it, he would have been the richer for an important bit of information. For one thing, he would have known that Flemister had not spent the afternoon losing his money across the faro-table; and for another, he might have made sure, by listening to the subdued voices beyond the closed door, that the man he was shadowing was not alone in the back room to which he had retreated.

XI

On the second day following Flemister's visit to Angels, Lidgerwood was called again to Red Butte to another conference with the mine-owners. On his return, early in the afternoon, his special was slowed and stopped at a point a few miles east of the "Y" spur at Silver Switch, and upon looking out he saw that Benson's bridge-builders were once more at work on the wooden trestle spanning the Gloria. Benson himself was in command, but he turned the placing of the string-timbers over to his foreman and climbed to the platform of the superintendent's service-car.

"I won't hold you more than a few minutes," he began, but the superintendent pointed to one of the camp-chairs and sat down, saying: "There's no hurry. We have time orders against 73 at Timanyoni, and we would have to wait there, anyhow. What do you know now?—more than you knew the last time we talked?"

Benson shook his head. "Nothing that would do us any good in a jury trial," he admitted reluctantly. "We are not going to find out anything more until you send somebody up to Flemister's mine with a search-warrant."

Lidgerwood was gazing absently out over the low hills intervening between his point of view and the wooded summit of Little Butte.

"Whom am I to send, Jack?" he asked. "I have just come from Red Butte, and I took occasion to make a few inquiries. Flemister is evidently prepared at all points. From what I learned to-day, I am inclined to believe that the sheriff of Timanyoni County would probably refuse to serve a warrant against him, if we could find a magistrate who would issue one. Nice state of affairs, isn't it?"

"Beautiful," Benson agreed, adding: "But you don't want Flemister half as bad as you want the man who is working with him. Are you still trying to believe that it isn't Hallock?"

"I am still trying to be fair and just. McCloskey says that the two used to be friends—Hallock and Flemister. I don't believe they are now. Hallock didn't want to go to Flemister about that building-and-loan business, and I couldn't make out whether he was afraid, or whether it was just a plain case of dislike."

"It would doubtless be Hallock's policy—and Flemister's, too, for that matter—to make you believe they are not friends. You'll have to admit they are together a great deal."

"I'll admit it if you say so, but I didn't know it before. How do you know it?"

"Hallock is over here every day or two; I have seen him three or four times since that day when he and Flemister were walking down the new spur together and turned back at sight of me," said Benson. "Of course, I don't know what other business Hallock may have over here, but one thing I do know, he has been across the river, digging into the inner consciousness of my old prospector. And that isn't all. After he had got the story of the timber stealing out of the old man, he tried to bribe him not to tell it to any one else; tried the bribe first and a scare afterward—told him that something would happen to him if he didn't keep a still tongue in his head."

Lidgerwood shook his head slowly. "That looks pretty bad. Why should he want to silence the old man?"

"That's just what I've been asking myself. But right on the heels of that, another little mystery developed. Hallock asked the old man if he would be willing to swear in court to the truth of his story. The old man said he would."

"Well?" said Lidgerwood.

"A night or two later the old prospector's shack burned down, and the next morning he found a notice pinned to a tree near one of his sluice-boxes. It was a polite invitation for him to put distance between him and the Timanyoni district. I suppose you can put two and two together, as I did."

Again Lidgerwood said: "It looks pretty bad for Hallock. No one but the thieves themselves could have any possible reason for driving the old man out of the country. Did he go?"

"Not much; he isn't built that way. That same day he went to work building him a new shack; and he swears that the next man who gets near enough to set it afire won't live to get away and brag about it. Two days afterward Hallock showed up again, and the old fellow ran him off with a gun."

Just then the bridge-foreman came up to say that the timbers were in place, and Benson swung off to give Lidgerwood's engineer instructions to run carefully. As the service-car platform came along, Lidgerwood leaned over the railing for a final word with Benson. "Keep in touch with your old man, and tell him to count on us for protection," he said; and Benson nodded acquiescence as the one-car train crept out upon the dismantled bridge.

Having an appointment with Leckhard, of the main line, timed for an early hour the following morning, Lidgerwood gave his conductor instructions to stop at Angels only long enough to get orders for the eastern division.

When the division station was reached, McCloskey met the service-car in accordance with wire instructions sent from Timanyoni, bringing an armful of mail, which Lidgerwood purposed to work through on the run to Copah.

"Nothing new, Mac?" he asked, when the trainmaster came aboard.

"Nothing much, only the operators have notified me that there'll be trouble, *pronto*, if we don't put Hannegan and Dickson back on the wires. The grievance committee intimated pretty broadly that they could swing the trainmen into line if they had to make a fight."

"We put no man back who has been discharged for cause," said the superintendent firmly. "Did you tell them that?"

"I did. I have been saying that so often that it mighty nearly says itself now, when I hear my office door open."

"Well, there is nothing to do but to go on saying it. We shall either make a spoon or spoil a horn. How would you be fixed in the event of a telegraphers' strike?"

"I've been figuring on that. It may seem like tempting the good Lord to say it, but I believe we could hold about half of the men."

"That is decidedly encouraging," said the man who needed to find encouragement where he could. "Two weeks ago, if you had said one in ten, I should have thought you were overestimating. We shall win out yet."

But now McCloskey was shaking his head dubiously. "I don't know. Andy Bradford has been giving me an idea of how the trainmen stand, and he says there is a good deal of strike talk. Williams adds a word about the shop force: he says that Gridley's men are not saying anything, but they'll be likely to go out in a body unless Gridley wakes up at the last minute and takes a club to them."

Lidgerwood's conductor was coming down the platform of the Crow's Nest with his orders in his hand, and McCloskey made ready to swing off. "I can reach you care of Mr. Leckhard, at Copah, I suppose?" he asked.

"Yes. I shall be back some time to-morrow; in the meantime there is nothing to do but to sit tight in the boat. Use my private code if you want to wire me. I don't more than half trust that young fellow, Dix, Callahan's day operator. And, by the way, Mr. Frisbie is sending me a stenographer from Denver. If the young man turns up while I am away, see if you can't get Mrs. Williams to board him."

McCloskey promised and dropped off, and the one-car special presently clanked out over the eastern switches. Lidgerwood went at once to his desk and promptly became deaf and blind to everything but his work. The long desert run had been accomplished, and the service-car train was climbing the Crosswater grades, when Tadasu Matsuwari began to lay the table for dinner. Lidgerwood glanced at his watch, and ran his finger down the line of figures on the framed time-table hanging over his desk.

"Humph!" he muttered; "Acheson's making better time with me than he ever has before. I wonder if Williams has succeeded in talking him over to our side? He is certainly running like a gentleman to-day, at all events."

The superintendent sat down to Tadasu's table and took his time to Tadasu's excellent dinner, indulging himself so far as to smoke a leisurely cigar with his black coffee before plunging again into the sea of work. Not to spoil his improving record, Engineer Acheson continued to make good time, and it was only a little after eleven o'clock when Lidgerwood, looking up from his work at the final slowing of the wheels, saw the masthead lights of the Copah yards.

Taking it for granted that Superintendent Leckhard had long since left his office in the Pacific Southwestern building, Lidgerwood gave orders to have his car placed on the station-spur, and went on with his work. Being at the moment deeply immersed in the voluminous papers of a claim for stock killed, he was quite oblivious of the placement of the car, and of everything else, until the incoming of the fast main-line mail from the east warned him that another hour had passed. When the mail was gone on its way westward, the midnight silence settled down again, with nothing but the minimized crashings of freight cars in the lower shifting-yard to disturb it. The little Japanese had long since made up his bunk in one of the spare state-rooms, the train crew had departed with the engine, and the last mail-wagon had driven away up-town. Lidgerwood had closed his desk and was taking a final pull at the short pipe which was his working companion, when the car door opened silently and he saw an apparition.

Standing in the doorway and groping with her hands held out before her as if she were blind, was a woman. Her gown was the tawdry half-dress of the dance-halls, and the wrap over her bare shoulders was a gaudy imitation in colors of the Spanish mantilla. Her head was without covering, and her hair, which was luxuriant, hung in disorder over her face. One glance at the eyes, fixed and staring, assured Lidgerwood instantly that he had to do with one who was either drink-maddened or demented.

"Where is he?" the intruder asked, in a throaty whisper, staring, not at him, as Lidgerwood was quick to observe, but straight ahead at the portieres cutting off the state-room corridor from the open compartment. And then: "I told you I would come, Rankin; I've been watching years and years for your car to come in. Look—I want you to see what you have made of me, you and that other man."

Lidgerwood sat perfectly still. It was quite evident that the woman did not see him. But his thoughts were busy. Though it was by little more than chance, he knew that Hallock's Christian name was Rankin, and instantly he recalled all that McCloskey had told him about the chief clerk's marital troubles. Was this poor painted wreck the woman who was, or who had been, Hallock's wife? The question had scarcely formulated itself before she began again.

"Why don't you answer me? Where are you?" she demanded, in the same husky whisper; "you needn't hide—I know you are here. *What have you done to that man?* You said you would kill him; you promised me that, Rankin: have you done it?"

Lidgerwood reached up cautiously behind him, and slowly turned off the gas from the bracket desk-lamp. Without wishing to pry deeper than he should into a thing which had all the ear-marks of a tragedy, he could not help feeling that he was on the verge of discoveries which might have an important bearing upon the mysterious problems centring in the chief clerk. And he was afraid the woman would see him.

But he was not permitted to make the discoveries. The woman had taken two or three steps into the car, still groping her way as if the brightly lighted interior were the darkest of caverns, when some one swung over the railing of the observation platform, and Superintendent Leckhard appeared at the open door. Without hesitation he entered and touched the woman on the shoulder. "Hello, Madgie," he said, not ungently, "you here again? It's pretty late for even your kind to be out, isn't it? Better trot away and go to bed, if you've got one to go to; he isn't here."

The woman put her hands to her face, and Lidgerwood saw that she was shaking as if with a sudden chill. Then she turned and darted away like a frightened animal. Leckhard was drawing a chair up to face Lidgerwood.

"Did she give you a turn?" he asked, when Lidgerwood reached up and turned the desk-lamp on full again.

"Not exactly that, though it was certainly startling enough. I had no warning at all; when I looked up, she was standing pretty nearly where she was when you came in. She didn't seem to see me at all, and she was talking crazily all the time to some one else—some one who isn't here."

86

"I know," said Leckhard; "she has done it before."

"Whom is she trying to find?" asked Lidgerwood, wishing to have his suspicion either denied or confirmed.

"Didn't she call him by name?—she usually does. It's your chief clerk, Hallock. She is—or was—his wife. Haven't you heard the ghastly story yet?"

"No; and, Leckhard, I don't know that I care to hear it. It can't possibly concern me."

"It's just as well, I guess," said the main-line superintendent carelessly. "I probably shouldn't get it straight anyway. It's a rather horrible affair, though, I believe. There is another man mixed up in it— the man whom she is always asking if Hallock has killed. Curiously enough, she never names the other man, and there have been a good many guesses. I believe your head boiler-maker, Gridley, has the most votes. He's been seen with her here, now and then—when he's on one of his 'periodicals.' By Jove! Lidgerwood, I don't envy you your job over yonder in the Red Desert a little bit.... But about the consolidation of the yards here: I got a telegram after I wired you, making it necessary for me to go west on main-line Twenty-seven early in the morning, so I stayed up to talk this yard business over with you to-night."

It was well along in the small hours when the roll of blue-print maps was finally laid aside, and Leckhard rose yawning. "We'll carry it out as you propose, and divide the expense between the two divisions," he said in conclusion. "Frisbie has left it to us, and he will approve whatever we agree upon. Will you go up to the hotel with me, or bunk down here?"

Lidgerwood said he would stay with his car; or, better still, now that the business for which he had come to Copah was despatched, he would have the roundhouse night foreman call a Red Butte Western crew and go back to his desert.

"We are in the thick of things over on the jerk-water just now," he explained, "and I don't like to stay away any longer than I have to."

"Having a good bit of trouble with the sure-shots?" asked Leckhard. "What was that story I heard about somebody swiping one of your switching-engines?"

"It was true," said Lidgerwood, adding, "But I think we shall recover the engine—and some other things—presently." He liked Leckhard well enough, but he wished he would go. There are exigencies in which even the comments of a friend and well-wisher are superfluous.

"You have a pretty tough gang to handle over these," the well-wisher went on. "I wouldn't touch a job like yours with a ten-foot pole, unless I could shoot good enough to be sure of hitting a half-dollar nine times out of ten at thirty paces. Somebody was telling me that you have already had trouble with that fellow Rufford."

"Nobody was hurt, and Rufford is in jail," said Lidgerwood, hoping to kill the friendly inquiry before it should run into details.

"Oh, well, it's all in the day's work, I suppose, which reminds me: my day's work to-morrow won't amount to much if I don't go and turn in. Good-night."

When Leckhard was gone, Lidgerwood climbed the stair in the station building to the despatcher's office and gave orders for the return of his car to Angels. Half an hour later the one-car special was retracing its way westward up the valley of the Tumbling Water, and Lidgerwood was trying to go to sleep in the well-appointed little state-room which it was Tadasu Matsuwari's pride to keep spick and span and spotlessly clean. But there were disturbing thoughts, many and varied, to keep him awake, chief among them those which hung upon the dramatic midnight episode with the demented woman for its central figure. Through what dreadful Valley of Humiliation had she come to reach the abysmal depths in which the one cry of her soul was a cry for vengeance? Who was the unnamed man whom Hallock had promised to kill? How much or how little was this tragedy figuring in the trouble storm which was brooding over the Red Desert? And how much or how little would it involve one who was anxious only to see even-handed justice prevail?

These and similar insistent questions kept Lidgerwood awake long after his train had left the crooked pathway marked out by the Tumbling Water, and when he finally fell asleep the laboring engine of the one-car special was storming the approaches to Crosswater Summit.

XII

The freight wreck in the Crosswater Hills, coming a fortnight after Rufford's arrest and deportation to Copah and the county jail, rudely marked the close of the short armistice in the conflict between law and order and the demoralization which seemed to thrive the more lustily in proportion to Lidgerwood's efforts to stamp it out.

Thirty-two boxes, gondolas, and flats, racing down the Crosswater grades in the heart of a flawless, crystalline summer afternoon at the heels of Clay's big ten-wheeler, suddenly left the steel as a unit to heap themselves in chaotic confusion upon the right-of-way, and to round out the disaster at the moment of impact by exploding a shipment of giant powder somewhere in the midst of the debris.

Lidgerwood was on the western division inspecting, with Benson, one of the several tentative routes for a future extension of the Red Butte line to a connection with the Transcontinental at Lemphi beyond the Hophras, when the news of the wreck reached Angels. Wherefore, it was not until the following morning that he was able to leave the head-quarters station, on the second wrecking-train, bringing the big 100-ton crane to reinforce McCloskey, who had been on the ground with the lighter clearing tackle for the better part of the night.

With a slowly smouldering fire to fight, and no water to be had nearer than the tank-cars at La Guayra, the trainmaster had wrought miracles. By ten o'clock the main line was cleared, a temporary siding for a working base had been laid, and McCloskey's men were hard at work picking up what the fire had spared when Lidgerwood arrived.

"Pretty clean sweep this time, eh, Mac?" was the superintendent's greeting, when he had penetrated to the thick of things where McCloskey was toiling and sweating with his men.

"So clean that we get nothing much but scrap-iron out of what's left," growled McCloskey, climbing out of the tangle of crushed cars and bent and twisted iron-work to stand beside Lidgerwood on the main-line embankment. Then to the men who were making the snatch-hitch for the next pull: "A little farther back, boys; farther yet, so she won't overbalance on you; that's about it. Now, *wig* it!"

"You seem to be getting along all right with the outfit you've got," was Lidgerwood's comment. "If you can keep this up we may as well go back to Angels."

"No, don't!" protested the trainmaster. "We can snake out these scrap-heaps after a fashion, but when it comes to resurrecting the 195—did you notice her as you came along? We kept the fire from getting to her, but she's dug herself into the ground like a dog after a woodchuck!"

Lidgerwood nodded. "I looked her over," he said. "If she'd had a little more time and another wheel-turn or two to spare, she might have disappeared entirely—like that switching-engine you can't find. I'm taking it for granted that you haven't found it yet—or have you?"

"No, I haven't!" grated McCloskey, and he said it like a man with a grievance. Then he added: "I gave you all the pointers I could find two weeks ago. Whenever you get ready to put Hallock under the hydraulic press, you'll squeeze what you want to know out of him."

This was coming to be an old subject and a sore one. The trainmaster still insisted that Hallock was the man who was planning the robberies and plotting the downfall of the Lidgerwood management, and he wanted to have the chief clerk systematically shadowed. And it was Lidgerwood's wholly groundless prepossession for Hallock that was still keeping him from turning the matter over to the company's legal department—this in spite of the growing accumulation of evidence all pointing to Hallock's treason. Subjected to a rigid cross-examination, Judson had insisted that a part, at least, of his drunken recollection was real—that part identifying the voices of the two plotters in Cat Biggs's back room as those of Rufford and Hallock. Moreover, it was no longer deniable that the chief clerk was keeping in close touch with the discharged employees, for some purpose best known to himself; and latterly he had been dropping out of his office without notice, disappearing, sometimes, for a day at a time.

Lidgerwood was recalling the last of these disappearances when the second wrecking-train, having backed to the nearest siding to admit of a reversal of its make-up order and the placing of the crane in the lead, came up to go into action. McCloskey shaded his eyes from the sun's glare and looked down the line.

"Hello!" he exclaimed. "Got a new wrecking-boss?"

The superintendent nodded. "I have one in the making. Dawson wanted to come along and try his hand."

"Did Gridley send him?"

"No; Gridley is away somewhere."

"So Fred's your understudy, is he? Well, I've got one, too. I'll show him to you after a while."

They were walking back over the ties toward the half-buried 195. The ten-wheeler was on its side in the ditch, nuzzling the opposite bank of a low cutting. Dawson had already divided his men: half of them to place the huge jack-beams and outriggers of the self-contained steam lifting machine to insure its stability, and the other half to trench under the fallen engine and to adjust the chain slings for the hitch.

"It's a pretty long reach, Fred," said the superintendent. "Going to try it from here?"

"Best place," said the reticent one shortly.

Lidgerwood was looking at his watch.

"Williams will be due here before long with a special from Copah. I don't want to hold him up," he remarked.

"Thirty minutes?" inquired the draftsman, without taking mind or eye off his problem.

"Oh, yes; forty or fifty, maybe."

"All right, I'll be out of the way," was the quiet rejoinder.

"Yes, you will!" was McCloskey's ironical comment, when the draftsman had gone around to the other side of the great crane.

"Let him alone," said Lidgerwood. "It lies in my mind that we are developing a genius, Mac."

"He'll fall down," grumbled the trainmaster. "That crane won't pick up the '95 clear the way she's lying."

"Won't it?" said Lidgerwood. "That's where you are mistaken. It will pick up anything we have on the two divisions. It's the biggest and best there is made. How did you come to get a tool like that on the Red Butte Western?"

McCloskey grinned.

"You don't know Gridley yet. He's a crank on good machinery. That crane was a clean steal."

"What?"

"I mean it. It was ordered for one of the South American railroads, and was on its way to the Coast over the P. S-W. About the time it got as far as Copah, we happened to have a mix-up in our Copah yards, with a ditched engine that Gridley couldn't pick up with the 60-ton crane we had on the ground. So he borrowed this one out of the P. S-W. yards, used it, liked it, and kept it, sending our 60-ton machine on to the South Americans in its place."

"What rank piracy!" Lidgerwood exclaimed. "I don't wonder they call us buccaneers over here. How could he do it without being found out?"

"That puzzled more than two or three of us; but one of the men told me some time afterward how it was done. Gridley had a painter go down in the night and change the lettering—on our old crane and on this new one. It happened that they were both made by the same manufacturing company, and were of substantially the same general pattern. I suppose the P. S-W. yard crew didn't notice particularly that the crane they had lent us out of the through westbound freight had shrunk somewhat in the using. But I'll bet those South Americans are saying pleasant things to the manufacturers yet."

"Doubtless," Lidgerwood agreed, and now he was not smiling. The little side-light on the former Red-Butte-Western methods—and upon Gridley—was sobering.

By this time Dawson had got his big lifter in position, with its huge steel arm overreaching the fallen engine, and was giving his orders quietly, but with clean-cut precision.

"Man that hand-fall and take slack! Pay off, Darby," to the hoister engineer. "That's right; more slack!"

The great tackling-hook, as big around as a man's thigh, settled accurately over the 195.

"There you are!" snapped Dawson. "Now make your hitch, boys, and be lively about it. You've got just about one minute to do it in!"

"Heavens to Betsey!" said McCloskey. "He's going to pick it up at one hitch—and without blocking!"

"Hands off, Mac," said Lidgerwood good-naturedly. "If Fred didn't know this trade before, he's learning it pretty rapidly now."

"That's all right, but if he doesn't break something before he gets through——"

But Dawson was breaking nothing. Having designed locomotives, he knew to the fraction of an inch where the balancing hitch should be made for lifting one. Also machinery, and the breaking strains of it, were as his daily bread. While McCloskey was still prophesying failure, he was giving the word to Darby, the hoister engineer.

"Now then, Billy, try your hitch! Put the strain on a little at a time and often. Steady!—now you've got her—keep her coming!"

Slowly the big freight-puller rose out of its furrow in the gravel, righting itself to the perpendicular as it came. Anticipating the inward swing of it, Dawson was showing his men how to place ties and rails for a short temporary track, and when he gave Darby the stop signal, the hoisting cables were singing like piano strings, and the big engine was swinging bodily in the air in the grip of the crane tackle, poised to a nicety above the steel placed to receive it.

Dawson climbed up to the main-line embankment where Darby could see him, and where he could see all the parts of his problem at once. Then his hands went up to beckon the slacking signals. At the lifting of his finger there was a growling of gears and a backward racing of machinery, a groan of relaxing strains, and a cry of "All gone!" and the 195 stood upright, ready to be hauled out when the temporary track should be extended to a connection with the main line.

"Let's go up to the other end and see how your understudy is making it, Mac," said the gratified superintendent. "It is quite evident that we can't tell this young man anything he doesn't already know about picking up locomotives."

On the way up the track he asked about Clay and Green, the engineer and fireman who were in the wreck.

"They are not badly hurt," said the trainmaster. "They both jumped—on Green's side, luckily. Clay was bruised considerably, and Green says he knows he plowed up fifty yards of gravel with his face before he stopped—and he looked it. They both went home on 201."

Lidgerwood was examining the cross-ties, which were cut and scarred by the flanges of many derailed wheels.

"You have no notion of what did it?" he queried, turning abruptly upon McCloskey.

"Only a guess, and it couldn't be verified in a thousand years. The '95 went off first, and Clay and Green both say it felt as if a rail had turned over on the outside of the curve."

"What did you find when you got here?"

"Chaos and Old Night: a pile of scrap with a hole torn in the middle of it as if by an explosion, and a fire going."

"Of course, you couldn't tell anything about the cause, under such conditions."

"Not much, you'd say; and yet a queer thing happened. The entire train went off so thoroughly that it passed the point where the trouble began before it piled up. I was able to verify Clay's guess—a rail had turned over on the outside of the curve."

"That proves nothing more than poor spike-holds in a few dry-rotted cross-ties," Lidgerwood objected.

"No; there were a number of others farther along also turned over and broken and bent. But the first one was the only freak."

"How was that?"

"Well, it wasn't either broken or bent; but when it turned over it not only unscrewed the nuts of the fish-plate bolts and threw them away—it pulled out every spike on both sides of itself and hid them."

Lidgerwood nodded gravely. "I should say your guess has already verified itself. All it lacks is the name of the man who loosened the fish-plate bolts and pulled the spikes."

"That's about all."

The superintendent's eyes narrowed.

"Who was missing out of the Angels crowd of trouble-makers yesterday, Mac?"

"I hate to say," said the trainmaster. "God knows I don't want to put it all over any man unless it belongs to him, but I'm locoed every time it comes to that kind of a guess. Every bunch of letters I see spells just one name."

"Go on," said Lidgerwood sharply.

"Hallock came somewhere up this way on 202 yesterday."

"I know," was the quick reply. "I sent him out to Navajo to meet Cruikshanks, the cattleman with the long claim for stock injured in the Gap wreck two weeks ago."

"Did he stop at Navajo?" queried the trainmaster.

"I suppose so; at any rate, he saw Cruikshanks."

"Well, I haven't got any more guesses, only a notion or two. This is a pretty stiff up-grade for 202—she passes here at two-fifty—just about an hour before Clay found that loosened rail—and it wouldn't be impossible for a man to drop off as she was climbing this curve."

But now the superintendent was shaking his head.

"It doesn't hold together, Mac; there are too many parts missing. Your hypothesis presupposes that Hallock took a day train out of Angels, rode twelve miles past his destination, jumped off here while the train was in motion, pulled the spikes on this loosened rail, and walked back to Navajo in time to see the cattleman and get in to Angels on the delayed Number 75 this morning. Could he have done all these things without advertising them to everybody?"

"I know," confessed the trainmaster. "It doesn't look reasonable."

"It isn't reasonable," Lidgerwood went on, arguing Hallock's case as if it were his own. "Bradford was 202's conductor; he'd know if Hallock failed to get off at Navajo. Gridley was a passenger on the same train, and he would have known. The agent at Navajo would be a third witness. He was expecting Hallock on that train, and was no doubt holding Cruikshanks. Your guesses prefigure Hallock failing to show up when the train stopped at Navajo, and make it necessary for him to explain to the two men who were waiting for him why he let Bradford carry him by so far that it took him several hours to walk back. You see how incredible it all is?"

"Yes, I see," said McCloskey, and when he spoke again they were several rail-lengths nearer the up-track end of the wreck, and his question went back to Lidgerwood's mention of the expected special.

"You were saying something to Dawson about Williams and a special train; is that Mr. Brewster coming in?"

"Yes. He wired from Copah last night. He has Mr. Ford's car—the *Nadia*."

The trainmaster's face-contortion was expressive of the deepest chagrin.

"Suffering Moses! but this is a nice thing for the president of the road to see as he comes along! Wouldn't the luck we're having make a dog sick?"

Lidgerwood shook his head. "That isn't the worst of it, Mac. Mr. Brewster isn't a railroad man, and he will probably think this is all in the day's work. But he is going to stop at Angels and go over to his copper mine, which means that he will camp right down in the midst of the mix-up. I'd cheerfully give a year's salary to have him stay away a few weeks longer."

McCloskey was not a swearing man in the Red Desert sense of the term, but now his comment was an explosive exclamation naming the conventional place of future punishment. It was the only word he could find adequately to express his feelings.

The superintendent changed the subject.

"Who is your foreman, Mac?" he inquired, as a huge mass of the tangled scrap was seen to rise at the end of the smaller derrick's grapple.

"Judson," said McCloskey shortly. "He asked leave to come along as a laborer, and when I found that he knew more about train-scrapping than I did, I promoted him." There was something like defiance in the trainmaster's tone.

"From the way in which you say it, I infer that you don't expect me to approve," said Lidgerwood judicially.

McCloskey had been without sleep for a good many hours, and his patience was tenuous. The derby hat was tilted to its most contentious angle when he said:

"I can't fight for you when you're right, and not fight against you when I think you are wrong, Mr. Lidgerwood. You can have my head any time you want it."

"You think I should break my word and take Judson back?"

"I think, and the few men who are still with us think, that you ought to give the man who stood in the breach for you a chance to earn bread and meat for his wife and babies," snapped McCloskey, who had gone too far to retreat.

Lidgerwood was frowning when he replied: "You don't see the point involved. I can't reward Judson for what you, yourself, admit was a personal service. I have said that no drunkard shall pull a train on this division. Judson is no less a drink-maniac for the fact that he arrested Rufford when everybody else was afraid to."

McCloskey was mollified a little.

"He says he has quit drinking, and I believe him this time. But this job I've given him isn't pulling trains."

"No; and if you have cooled off enough, you may remember that I haven't yet disapproved your action. I don't disapprove. Give him anything you like where a possible relapse on his part won't involve the lives of other people. Is that what you want me to say?"

"I was hot," said the trainmaster, gruffly apologetic. "We've got none too many friends to stand by us when the pinch comes, and we were losing them every day you held out against Judson."

"I'm still holding out on the original count. Judson can't run an engine for me until he has proved conclusively and beyond question that he has quit the whiskey. Whatever other work you can find for him——"

McCloskey slapped his thigh. "By George! I've got a job right now! Why on top of earth didn't I think of him before? He's the man to keep tab on Hallock."

But now Lidgerwood was frowning again.

"I don't like that, Mac. It's a dirty business to be shadowing a man who has a right to suppose that you are trusting him."

"But, good Lord! Mr. Lidgerwood, haven't you got enough to go on? Hallock is the last man seen around the engine that disappears; he spends a lot of his time swapping grievances with the rebels; and he is out of town and within a few miles of here, as you know, when this wreck happens. If all that isn't enough to earn him a little suspicion——"

"I know; I can't argue the case with you, Mac, But I can't do it."

"You mean you won't do it. I respect your scruples, Mr. Lidgerwood. But it is no longer a personal matter between you and Hallock: the company's interests are involved."

Without suspecting it, the trainmaster had found the weak joint in the superintendent's armor. For the company's sake the personal point of view must be ignored.

"It is such a despicable thing," he protested, as one who yields reluctantly. "And if, after all, Hallock is innocent——"

"That is just the point," insisted McCloskey. "If he is innocent, no harm will be done, and Judson will become a witness for instead of against him."

"Well," said Lidgerwood; and what more he would have said about the conspiracy was cut off by the shrill whistle of a down-coming train. "That's Williams with the special," he announced, when the whistle gave him leave. "Is your flag out?"

"Sure. It's up around the hill, with a safe man to waggle it."

Lidgerwood cast an anxious glance toward Dawson's huge derrick-car, which was still blocking the main line. The hoist tackle was swinging free, and the jack-beams and outriggers were taken in.

"Better send somebody down to tell Dawson to pull up here to your temporary siding, Mac," he suggested; but Dawson was one of those priceless helpers who did not have to be told in detail. He had heard the warning whistle, and already had his train in motion.

By a bit of quick shifting, the main line was cleared before Williams swung cautiously around the hill with the private car. In obedience to Lidgerwood's uplifted finger the brakes were applied, and the *Nadia* came to a full stop, with its observation platform opposite the end of the wrecking-track.

A big man, in a soft hat and loose box dust-coat, with twinkling little eyes and a curling brown beard that covered fully three-fourths of his face, stood at the hand-rail.

"Hello, Howard!" he called down to Lidgerwood. "By George! I'd totally forgotten that you were out here. What are you trying to do? Got so many cars and engines that you have to throw some of them away?"

Lidgerwood climbed up the embankment to the track, and McCloskey carefully let him do it alone. The "Hello, Howard!" had not been thrown away upon the trainmaster.

"It looks a little that way, I must admit, Cousin Ned," said the culprit who had answered so readily to his Christian name. "We tried pretty hard to get it cleaned up before you came along, but we couldn't quite make it."

"Oho! tried to cover it up, did you? Afraid I'd fire you? You needn't be. My job as president merely gets me passes over the road. Ford's your man; he's the fellow you want to be scared of."

"I am," laughed Lidgerwood. The big man's heartiness was always infectious. Then: "Coming over to camp with us awhile? If you are, I hope you carry your commissary along. Angels will starve you, otherwise."

"Don't tell me about that tin-canned tepee village, Howard—I *know*. I've been there before. How are we doing over in the Timanyoni foot-hills? Getting much ore down from the Copperette? Climb up here and tell me all about it. Or, better still, come on across the desert with us. They don't need you here."

The assertion was quite true. With Dawson, the trainmaster, and an understudy Judson for bosses, there was no need of a fourth. Yet intuition, or whatever masculine thing it is that stands for intuition, prompted Lidgerwood to say:

"I don't know as I ought to leave. I've just come out from Angels, you know."

But the president was not to be denied.

"Climb up here and quit trying to find excuses. We'll give you a better luncheon than you'll get out of the dinner-pails; and if you carry yourself handsomely, you may get a dinner invitation after we get in. That ought to tempt any man who has to live in Angels the year round."

Lidgerwood marked the persistent plural of the personal pronoun, and a great fear laid hold upon him. None the less, the president's invitation was a little like the king's—it was, in some sense, a command. Lidgerwood merely asked for a moment's respite, and went down to announce his intention to McCloskey and Dawson. Curiously enough, the draftsman seemed to be trying to ignore the private car. His back was turned upon it, and he was glooming out across the bare hills, with his square jaw set as if the ignoring effort were painful.

"I'm going back to Angels with the president," said the superintendent, speaking to both of them. "You can clean up here without me."

The trainmaster nodded, but Dawson seemed not to have heard. At all events, he made no sign. Lidgerwood turned and ascended the embankment, only to have the sudden reluctance assail him again as he put his foot on the truck of the *Nadia* to mount to the platform. The hesitation was only momentary, this time. Other guests Mr. Brewster might have, without including the one person whom he would circle the globe to avoid.

"Good boy!" said the president, when Lidgerwood swung over the high hand-rail and leaned out to give Williams the starting signal. And when the scene of the wreck was withdrawing into the rearward distance, the president felt for the door-knob, saying: "Let's go inside, where we shan't be obliged to see so much of this God-forsaken country at one time."

One half-minute later the superintendent would have given much to be safely back with McCloskey and Dawson at the vanishing curve of scrap-heaps. In that half-minute Mr. Brewster had opened the car door, and Lidgerwood had followed him across the threshold.

The comfortable lounging-room of the *Nadia* was not empty; nor was it peopled by a group of Mr. Brewster's associates in the copper combine, the alternative upon which Lidgerwood had hopefully hung the "we's" and the "us's."

Seated on a wicker divan drawn out to face one of the wide side-windows were two young women, with a curly-headed, clean-faced young man between them. A little farther along, a rather austere lady, whose pose was of calm superiority to her surroundings, looked up from her magazine to say, as her husband had said: "Why, Howard! are you here?" Just beyond the austere lady, and dozing in his chair, was a white-haired man whose strongly marked features proclaimed him the father of one of the young women on the divan.

And in the farthest corner of the open compartment, facing each other companionably in an "S"-shaped double chair, were two other young people—a man and a woman.... Truly, the heavens had fallen! For the young woman filling half of the *tête-à-tête* chair was that one person whom Lidgerwood would have circled the globe to avoid meeting.

XIII

Taking his cue from certain passages in the book of painful memories, Lidgerwood meant to obey his first impulse, which prompted him to follow Mr. Brewster to the private office state-room in the forward end of the car, disregarding the couple in the *tête-à-tête* contrivance. But the triumphantly beautiful young woman in the nearer half of the crooked-backed seat would by no means sanction any such easy solution of the difficulty.

"Not a word for me, Howard?" she protested, rising and fairly compelling him to stop and speak to her. Then: "For pity's sake! what have you been doing to yourself to make you look so hollow-eyed and anxious?" After which, since Lidgerwood seemed at a loss for an answer to the half-solicitous query, she presented her companion of the "S"-shaped chair. "Possibly you will shake hands a little less abstractedly with Mr. Van Lew. Herbert, this is Mr. Howard Lidgerwood, my cousin, several times removed. He is the tyrant of the Red Butte Western, and I can assure you that he is much more terrible than he looks—aren't you, Howard?"

Lidgerwood shook hands cordially enough with the tall young athlete who, it seemed, would never have done increasing his magnificent stature as he rose up out of his half of the lounging-seat.

"Glad to meet you, Mr. Lidgerwood, I'm sure," said the young man, gripping the given hand until Lidgerwood winced. "Miss Eleanor has been telling me about you—marooned out here in the Red Desert. By Jove! don't you know I believe I'd like to try it awhile myself. It's ages since I've had a chance to kill a man, and they tell me——"

Lidgerwood laughed, recognizing Miss Brewster's romancing gift, or the results of it.

"We shall have to arrange a little round-up of the bad men from Bitter Creek for you, Mr. Van Lew. I hope you brought your armament along—the regulation 45's, and all that."

Miss Brewster laughed derisively.

"Don't let him discourage you, Herbert," she mocked. "Bitter Creek is in Wyoming—or is it in Montana?" this with a quick little eye-stab for Lidgerwood, "and the name of Mr. Lidgerwood's refuge is Angels. Also, papa says there is a hotel there called the 'Celestial.' Do you live at the Celestial, Howard?"

"No, I never properly lived there. I existed there for a few weeks until Mrs. Dawson took pity on me. Mrs. Dawson is from Massachusetts."

"Hear him!" scoffed Miss Eleanor, still mocking. "He says that as if to be 'from Massachusetts' were a patent of nobility. He knows I had the cruel misfortune to be born in Colorado. But tell me, Howard, is Mrs. Dawson a charming young widow?"

"Mrs. Dawson is a very charming middle-aged widow, with a grown son and a daughter," said Lidgerwood, a little stiffly. It seemed entirely unnecessary that she should ridicule him before the athlete.

"And the daughter—is she charming, too? But that says itself, since she must also date 'from Massachusetts.'" Then to Van Lew: "Every one out here in the Red Desert is 'from' somewhere, you know."

"Miss Dawson is quite beneath your definition of charming, I imagine," was Lidgerwood's rather crisp rejoinder; and for the third time he made as if he would go on to join the president in the office state-room.

"You are staying to luncheon with us, aren't you?" asked Miss Brewster. "Or do you just drop in and out again, like the other kind of angels?"

"Your father commands me, and he says I am to stay. And now, if you will excuse me——"

This time he succeeded in getting away, and up to the luncheon hour talked copper and copper prospects to Mr. Brewster in the seclusion of the president's office compartment. The call for the midday meal had been given when Mr. Brewster switched suddenly from copper to silver.

"By the way, there were a few silver strikes over in the Timanyonis about the time of the Red Butte gold excitement," he remarked. "Some of them have grown to be shippers, haven't they?"

"Only two, of any importance," replied the superintendent: "the Ruby, in Ruby Gulch, and Flemister's Wire-Silver, at Little Butte. You couldn't call either of them a bonanza, but they are both shipping fair ore in good quantities."

"Flemister," said the president reflectively. "He's a character. Know him personally, Howard?"

"A little," the superintendent admitted.

"A little is a-plenty. It wouldn't pay you to know him very well," laughed the big man good-naturedly. "He has a somewhat paralyzing way of getting next to you financially. I knew him in the old Leadville days; a born gentleman, and also a born buccaneer. If the men he has held up and robbed were to stand in a row, they'd fill a Denver street."

"He is in his proper longitude out here, then," said Lidgerwood rather grimly. "This is the 'hold-up's heaven.'"

"I'll bet Flemister is doing his share of the looting," laughed the president. "Is he alone in the mine?"

"I don't know that he has any partners. Somebody told me, when I first came over here, that Gridley, our master-mechanic, was in with him; but Gridley says that is a mistake—that he thinks too much of his reputation to be Flemister's partner."

"Hank Gridley," mused the president; "Hank Gridley and 'his reputation'! It would certainly be a pity if that were to get corroded in any way. There is a man who properly belongs to the Stone Age—what you might call an elemental 'scoundrel."

"You surprise me!" exclaimed Lidgerwood. "I didn't like him at first, but I am convinced now that it was only unreasoning prejudice. He appeals to me as being anything but a scoundrel."

"Well, perhaps the word is a bit too savage," admitted Gridley's accuser. "What I meant was that he has capabilities that way, and not much moral restraint. He is the kind of man to wade through fire and blood to gain his object, without the slightest thought of the consequences to others. Ever hear the story of his marriage? No? Remind me of it some time, and I'll tell you. But we were speaking of Flemister. You say the Wire-Silver has turned out pretty well?"

"Very well indeed, I believe. Flemister seems to have money to burn."

"He always has, his own or somebody else's. It makes little difference to him. The way he got the Wire-Silver would have made Black-Beard the pirate turn green with envy. Know anything about the history of the mine?"

Lidgerwood shook his head.

"Well, I do; just happen to. You know how it lies—on the western slope of Little Butte ridge?"

"Yes."

"That is where it lies now. But the original openings were made on the eastern slope of the butte. They didn't pan out very well, and Flemister began to look for a victim to whom he could sell. About that time a man, whose name I can never recall, took up a claim on the western slope of the ridge directly opposite Flemister. This man struck it pretty rich, and Flemister began to bully him on the plea that the new discovery was only a continuation of his own vein straight through the hill. You can guess what happened."

"Fairly well," said Lidgerwood. "Flemister lawed the other man out."

"He did worse than that; he drove straight into the hill, past his own lines, and actually took the money out of the other man's mine to use as a fighting fund. I don't know how the courts sifted it out, finally; I didn't follow it up very closely. But Flemister put the other man to the wall in the end—'put it all over him,' as your man Bradford would say. There was some domestic tragedy involved, too, in which Flemister played the devil with the other man's family; but I don't know any of the details."

"Yet you say Flemister is a born gentleman, as well as a born buccaneer?"

"Well, yes; he behaves himself well enough in decent company. He isn't exactly the kind of man you can turn down short—he has education, good manners, and all that, you know; but if he were hard up I shouldn't let him get within roping distance of my pocket-book, or, if I had given him occasion to dislike me, within easy pistol range."

"Wherein he is neither better nor worse than a good many others who take the sunburn of the Red Desert," was Lidgerwood's comment, and just then the waiter opened the door a second time to say that luncheon was served.

"Don't forget to remind me that I'm to tell you Gridley's story, Howard," said the president, rising out of the depths of his lounging-chair and stripping off the dust-coat, "Reads like a romance—only I fancy it was anything but a romance for poor Lizzie Gridley. Let's go and see what the cook has done for us."

At luncheon Lidgerwood was made known to the other members of the private-car party. The white-haired old man who had been dozing in his chair was Judge Holcombe, Van Lew's uncle and the father of the prettier of the two young women who had been entertaining Jefferis, the curly-headed collegian. Jefferis laughingly disclaimed relationship with anybody; but Miss Carolyn Doty, the less pretty but more talkative of the two young women, confessed that she was a cousin, twice removed, of Mrs. Brewster.

Quite naturally, Lidgerwood sought to pair the younger people when the table gathering was complete, and was not entirely certain of his prefiguring. Eleanor Brewster and Van Lew sat together and were apparently absorbed in each other to the exclusion of all things extraneous. Jefferis had Miss Doty for a companion, and the affliction of her well-balanced tongue seemed to affect neither his appetite nor his enjoyment of what the young woman had to say.

Miriam Holcombe had fallen to Lidgerwood's lot, and at first he thought that her silence was due to the fact that young Jefferis had gotten upon the wrong side of the table. But after she began to talk, he changed his mind.

"Tell me about the wrecked train we passed a little while ago, Mr. Lidgerwood," she began, almost abruptly. "Was any one killed?"

"No; it was a freight, and the crew escaped. It was a rather narrow escape, though, for the engineer, and fireman."

"You were putting it back on the track?" she asked.

"There isn't much of it left to put back, as you may have observed," said Lidgerwood. Then he told her of the explosion and the fire.

She was silent for a few moments, but afterward she went on, half-gropingly he thought.

"Is that part of your work—to get the trains on the track when they run off?"

He laughed. "I suppose it is—or at least, in a certain sense, I'm responsible for it. But I am lucky enough to have a wrecking-boss—two of them, in fact, and both good ones."

She looked up quickly, and he was sure that he surprised something more than a passing interest in the serious eyes—a trouble depth, he would have called it, had their talk been anything more than the ordinary conventional table exchange.

"We saw you go down to speak to two of your men: one who wore his hat pulled down over his eyes and made dreadful faces at you as he talked——"

"That was McCloskey, our trainmaster," he cut in.

"And the other——?"

"Was wrecking-boss Number Two," he told her, "my latest apprentice, and a very promising young subject. This was his first time out under my administration, and he put McCloskey and me out of the running at once."

"What did he do?" she asked, and again he saw the groping wistfulness in her eyes, and wondered at it.

"I couldn't explain it without being unpardonably technical. But perhaps it can best be summed up in saying that he is a fine mechanical engineer with the added gift of knowing how to handle men."

"You are generous, Mr. Lidgerwood, to—to a subordinate. He ought to be very loyal to you."

"He is. And I don't think of him as a subordinate—I shouldn't even if he were on my pay-roll instead of on that of the motive-power department. I am glad to be able to call him my friend, Miss Holcombe."

Again a few moments of silence, during which Lidgerwood was staring gloomily across at Miss Brewster and Van Lew. Then another curiously abrupt question from the young woman at his side.

"His college, Mr. Lidgerwood; do you chance to know where he was graduated?"

At another moment Lidgerwood might have wondered at the young woman's persistence. But now Benson's story of Dawson's terrible misfortune was crowding all purely speculative thoughts out of his mind.

"He took his engineering course in Carnegie, but I believe he did not stay through the four years," he said gravely.

Miss Holcombe was looking down the table, down and across to where her father was sitting, at Mr. Brewster's right. When she spoke again the personal note was gone; and after that the talk, what there was of it, was of the sort that is meant to bridge discomforting gaps.

In the dispersal after the meal, Lidgerwood attached himself to Miss Doty; this in sheer self-defense. The desert passage was still in its earlier stages, and Miss Carolyn's volubility promised to be the less of two evils, the greater being the possibility that Eleanor Brewster might seek to re-open a certain spring of bitterness at which he had been constrained to drink deeply and miserably in the past.

The self-defensive expedient served its purpose admirably. For the better part of the desert run, the president slept in his state-room, Mrs. Brewster and the judge dozed in their respective easy-chairs, and Jefferis and Miriam Holcombe, after roaming for an uneasy half-hour from the rear platform to the cook's galley forward, went up ahead, at one of the stops, to ride—by the superintendent's permission—in the engine cab with Williams. Miss Brewster and Van Lew were absorbed in a book of plays, and their corner of the large, open compartment was the one farthest removed from the double divan which Lidgerwood had chosen for Miss Carolyn and himself.

Later, Van Lew rolled a cigarette and went to the smoking-compartment, which was in the forward end of the car; and when next Lidgerwood broke Miss Doty's eye-hold upon him, Miss Brewster had also disappeared—into her state-room, as he supposed. Taking this as a sign of his release, he gently broke the thread of Miss Carolyn's inquisitiveness, and went out to the rear platform for a breath of fresh air and surcease from the fashery of a neatly balanced tongue.

When it was quite too late to retreat, he found the deep-recessed observation platform of the *Nadia* occupied. Miss Brewster was not in her state-room, as he had mistakenly persuaded himself. She was sitting in one of the two platform camp-chairs, and she was alone.

"I thought you would come, if I only gave you time enough," she said, quite coolly. "Did you find Carolyn very persuasive?"

He ignored the query about Miss Doty, replying only to the first part of her speech.

"I thought you had gone to your state-room. I hadn't the slightest idea that you were out here."

"Otherwise you would not have come? How magnificently churlish you can be, upon occasion, Howard!"

"It doesn't deserve so hard a name," he rejoined patiently. "For the moment I am your father's guest, and when he asked me to go to Angels with him——"

—"He didn't tell you that mamma and Judge Holcombe and Carolyn and Miriam and Herbert and Geof. Jefferis and I were along," she cut in maliciously. "Howard, don't you know you are positively spiteful, at times!"

"No," he denied.

"Don't contradict me, and don't be silly." She pushed the other chair toward him. "Sit down and tell me how you've been enduring the interval. It is more than a year, isn't it?"

"Yes. A year, three months, and eleven days." He had taken the chair beside her because there seemed to be nothing else to do.

"How mathematically exact you are!" she gibed. "To-morrow it will be a year, three months, and twelve days; and the day after to-morrow—mercy me! I should go mad if I had to think back and count up that way every day. But I asked you what you had been doing."

He spread his hands. "Existing, one way and another. There has always been my work."

"'All work and no play makes Jack a dull boy,'" she quoted. "You are excessively dull to-day, Howard. Hasn't it occurred to you?"

"Thank you for expressing it so delicately. It seems to be my misfortune to disappoint you, always."

"Yes," she said, quite unfeelingly. Then, with a swift relapse into pure mockery: "How many times have you fallen in love during the one year, three months, and eleven days?"

His frown was almost a scowl. "Is it worth while to make an unending jest of it, Eleanor?"

"A jest?—of your falling in love? No, my dear cousin, several times removed, no one would dare to jest with you on that subject. But tell me; I am really and truly interested. Will you confess to three times? That isn't so very many, considering the length of the interval."

"No."

"Twice, then? Think hard; there must have been at least two little quickenings of the heartbeats in all that time."

"No."

"Still no? That reduces it to one—the charming Miss Dawson——"

"You might spare her, even if you are not willing to spare me. You know well enough there has never been any one but you, Eleanor; that there never will be any one but you."

The train was passing the western confines of the waterless tract, and a cool breeze from the snowcapped Timanyonis was sweeping across the open platform. It blew strands of the red-brown hair from beneath the closely fitting travelling-hat; blew color into Miss Brewster's cheeks and a daring brightness into the laughing eyes.

"What a pity!" she said in mock sympathy.

"That I can't measure up to your requirements of the perfect man? Yes, it is a thousand pities," he agreed.

"No; that isn't precisely what I meant. The pity is that I seem to you to be unable to appreciate your many excellencies and your—constancy."

"I think you were born to torment me," he rejoined gloomily. "Why did you come out here with your father? You must have known that I was here."

"Not from any line you have ever written," she retorted. "Alicia Ford told me, otherwise I shouldn't have known."

"Still, you came. Why? Were you curious?"

"Why should I be curious, and what about?—the Red Desert? I've seen deserts before."

"I thought you might be curious to know what disposition the Red Desert was making of such a failure as I am," he said evenly. "I can forgive that more easily than I can forgive your bringing of the other man along to be an on-looker."

"Herbert, you mean? He is a good boy, a nice boy—and perfectly harmless. You'll like him immensely when you come to know him better."

"You like him?" he queried.

"How can you ask—when you have just called him 'the other man'?"

Lidgerwood turned in his chair and faced her squarely.

"Eleanor, I had my punishment over a year ago, and I have been hoping you would let it suffice. It was hard enough to lose you without being compelled to stand by and see another man win you. Can't you understand that?"

She did not answer him. Instead, she whipped aside from that phase of the subject to ask a question of her own.

"What ever made you come out here, Howard?"

"To the superintendency of the Red Butte Western? You did."

"I?"

"Yes, you."

"It is ridiculous!"

"It is true."

"Prove it—if you can; but you can't."

"I am proving it day by day, or trying to. I didn't want to come, but you drove me to it."

"I decline to take any such hideous responsibility," she laughed lightly. "There must have been some better reason; Miss Dawson, perhaps."

"Quite likely, barring the small fact that I didn't know there was a Miss Dawson until I had been a month in Angels."

"Oh!" she said half spitefully. And then, with calculated malice, "Howard, if you were only as brave as you are clever!... Why can't you be a man and strike back now and then?"

"Strike back at the woman I love? I'm not quite down to that, I hope, even if I was once too cowardly to strike for her."

"Always *that!* Why won't you let me forget?"

"Because you must not forget. Listen: two weeks ago—only two weeks ago—one of the Angels—er—peacemakers stood up in his place and shot at me. What I did made me understand that I had gained nothing in a year."

"Shot at you?" she echoed, and now he might have discovered a note of real concern in her tone if his ear had been attuned to hear it. "Tell me about it. Who was it? and why did he shoot at you?"

His answer seemed to be indirection itself.

"How long do you expect to stay in Angels and its vicinity?" he asked.

"I don't know. This is partly a pleasure trip for us younger folk. Father was coming out alone, and I—that is, mamma decided to come and make a car-party of it. We may stay two or three weeks, if the others wish it. But you haven't answered me. I want to know who the man was, and why he shot at you."

"Exactly; and you have answered yourself. If you stay two weeks, or two days, in Angels you will doubtless hear all you care to about my troubles. When the town isn't talking about what it is going to do to me, it is gossiping about the dramatic arrest of my would-be assassin."

"You are most provoking!" she declared. "Did you make the arrest?"

"Don't shame me needlessly; of course I didn't. One of our locomotive engineers, a man whom I had discharged for drunkenness, was the hero. It was a most daring thing. The desperado is known in the Red Desert as 'The Killer,' and he has had the entire region terrorized so completely that the town marshal of Angels, a man who has never before shirked his duty, refused to serve the warrant. Judson, the engineer, made the capture—took the 'terror' from his place in a gambling-den, disarmed him, and brought him in. Judson himself was unarmed, and he did the trick with a little steel wrench such as engineers use about a locomotive."

Miss Brewster, being Colorado-born, was deeply interested.

"Now you are no longer dull, Howard!" she exclaimed. "Tell me in words just how Mr. Judson did it."

"It was an old dodge, so old that it seemed new to everybody. As I told you, Judson was discharged for drunkenness. All Angels knows him for a fighter to the finish when he is sober, and for the biggest fool and the most harmless one when he is in liquor. He took advantage of this, reeled into the gambling-place as if he were too drunk to see straight, played the fool till he got behind his man— after which the matter simplified itself. Rufford, the desperado, had no means of knowing that the cold piece of metal Judson was pressing against his back was not the muzzle of a loaded revolver, and he had every reason for supposing that it was; hence, he did all the things Judson told him to do."

Miss Eleanor did not need to vocalize her approval of Judson; the dark eyes were alight with excitement.

"How fine!" she applauded. "Of course, after that, you took Mr. Judson back into the railway service?"

"Indeed, I did nothing of the sort; nor shall I, until he demonstrates that he means what he says about letting the whiskey alone."

"'Until he demonstrates'—don't be so cold-blooded, Howard! Possibly he saved your life."

"Quite probably. But that has nothing to do with his reinstatement as an engineer of passenger-trains. It would be much better for Rufford to kill me than for me to let Judson have the chance to kill a train-load of innocent people."

"And yet, a few moments ago, you called yourself a coward, cousin mine. Could you really face such an alternative without flinching?"

"It doesn't appeal to me as a question involving any special degree of courage," he said slowly. "I am a great coward, Eleanor—not a little one, I hope."

"It doesn't appeal to you?—dear God!" she said. "And I have been calling you ... but would you do it, Howard?"

He smiled at her sudden earnestness.

"How generous your heart is, Eleanor, when you let it speak for itself! If you will promise not to let it change your opinion of me—you shouldn't change it, you know, for I am the same man whom you held up to scorn the day we parted—if you will promise, I'll tell you that for weeks I have gone about with my life in my hands, knowing it. It hasn't required any great amount of courage; it merely comes along in the line of my plain duty to the company—it's one of the things I draw my salary for."

"You haven't told me why this desperado wanted to kill you—why you are in such a deep sea of trouble out here, Howard," she reminded him.

"No; it is a long story, and it would bore you if I had time to tell it. And I haven't time, because that is Williams's whistle for the Angels yard."

He had risen and was helping his companion to her feet when Mrs. Brewster came to the car door to say:

"Oh, you are out here, are you, Howard? I was looking for you to let you know that we dine in the *Nadia* at seven. If your duties will permit——"

Lidgerwood's refusal was apologetic but firm.

"I am very sorry, Cousin Jessica," he protested. "But I left a deskful of stuff when I ran away to the wreck this morning, and really I'm afraid I shall have to beg off."

"Oh, don't be so dreadfully formal!" said the president's wife impatiently. "You are a member of the family, and all you have to do is to say bluntly that you can't come, and then come whenever you can while we are here. Carolyn Doty is dying to ask you a lot more questions about the Red Desert. She confided to me that you were the most interesting talker——"

Miss Eleanor's interruption was calculated to temper the passed-on praise.

"He has been simply boring me to death, mamma, until just a few minutes ago. I shall tell Carolyn that she is too easily pleased."

Mrs. Brewster, being well used to Eleanor's flippancies, paid no attention to her daughter.

"You will come to us whenever you can, Howard; that is understood," she said. And so the social matter rested.

Lidgerwood was half-way down the platform of the Crow's Nest, heading for his office and the neglected desk, when Williams's engine came backing through one of the yard tracks on its way to the roundhouse. At the moment of its passing, a little man with his cap pulled over his eyes dropped from the gangway step and lounged across to the head-quarters building.

It was Judson; and having seen him last toiling away man-fashion at the wreck in the Crosswater Hills, Lidgerwood hailed him.

"Hello, Judson! How did you get here? I thought you were doing a turn with McCloskey."

The small man's grin was ferocious.

"I was, but Mac said he didn't have any further use for me—said I was too much of a runt to be liftin' and pullin' along with growed-up men. I came down with Williams on the '66."

Lidgerwood turned away. He remembered his reluctant consent to McCloskey's proposal touching the espial upon Hallock, and was sorry he had given it. It was too late to recall it now; but neither by word nor look did the superintendent intimate to the discharged engineer that he knew why McCloskey had sent him back to Angels on the engine of the president's special.

XIV

Lidgerwood was not making the conventional excuse when he gave the deskful of work as a reason for not accepting the invitation to dine with the president's party in the *Nadia*. Being the practical as well as the nominal head of the Red Butte line, and the only official with complete authority west of Copah, his daily mail was always heavy, and during his frequent absences the accumulations stored up work for every spare hour he could devote to it.

It was this increasing clerical burden which had led him to ask the general manager for a stenographer, and during one of the later absences the young man had come—a rapid, capable young fellow with the gift of knowing how to make himself indispensable to a superior, coupled with the ability to take care of much of the routine correspondence without specific instructions, and with a disposition to be loyal to his salt.

Climbing the stair to his office on the second floor of the Crow's Nest after the brief exchange of question and answer with Judson, Lidgerwood found his new helper hard at work grinding through the day's train mail.

"Don't scamp your meals, Grady," was his greeting to the stenographer, as he opened his own desk. "This is a pretty busy shop, but it is well to remember that there is always another day coming, and if there isn't, it won't make any difference how much or how little is left undone."

"Colgan wired that you were on Mr. Brewster's special, and I was waiting on the chance that you might want to rush something through when you got in," returned the young Irishman, reaching mechanically for his note-book.

"I shall want to rush a lot of it through after a while, but you'd better go and get your supper now and come back fresh for it," said the superintendent, who was always humane to every one but himself. "Was there anything special in to-day's mail?"

"Only this," turning up a letter marked "Immediate" and bearing the cancellation stamp of the postal car which had passed eastward on Train 202.

Lidgerwood read the marked letter twice before he placed it face down in the "unanswered" basket. It was from Flemister, and it called for a decision which the superintendent was willing to postpone for the moment. After he had read thoughtfully through everything else on the waiting list, he took up the mine-owner's letter again. All things considered, it was a little puzzling. He had not seen Flemister since the day of the rather spiteful conversation, with the building-and-loan theft for a topic, and on that occasion the mine-owner had gone away with threats in his mouth. Yet his letter was distinctly friendly, conveying an offer of neighborly help.

The occasion for the neighborliness arose upon a right-of-way involvement. Acting under instructions from Vice-President Ford, Lidgerwood had already begun to move in the matter of extending the Red Butte Western toward the Nevada gold-fields, and Benson had been running preliminary surveys and making estimates of cost. Of the two more feasible routes, that which left the main line at Little Butte, turning southward up the Wire-Silver gulch, had been favorably reported on by the engineer. The right of way over this route, save for a few miles through an upland valley of cattle ranches, could be acquired from the government, and among the ranch owners only one was disposed to fight the coming of the railroad—for a purely mercenary purpose, Benson declared.

It was about this man, James Grofield, that Flemister wrote. The ranchman, so the letter stated, had passed through Little Butte early in the day, on his way to Red Butte. He would be returning by the accommodation late in the afternoon, and would stop at the Wire-Silver mine, where he had stabled his horses. For some reason he had taken a dislike to Benson, but if Lidgerwood could make it convenient to come over to Little Butte on the evening passenger-train from Angels, the writer of the letter would arrange to keep Grofield over-night, and the right-of-way matter could doubtless be settled satisfactorily.

This was the substance of the mine-owner's letter, and if Lidgerwood hesitated it was partly because he was suspicious of Flemister's sudden friendliness. Then the motive—Flemister's motive—suggested itself, and the suspicion was put to sleep. The Wire-Silver mine was five miles distant from the main line at Little Butte, at the end of a spur; if the extension should be built, it would be a main-line station, with all the advantages accruing therefrom. Flemister was merely putting the personal animosities aside for a good and sufficient business reason.

Lidgerwood looked at his watch. If Grady should not be gone too long, he might be able to work through the pile of correspondence and get away on the evening passenger; and when the stenographer came back the work was attacked with that end in view. But after an hour's rapid dictating, a long-drawn whistle signal announced the incoming of the train he was trying to make and warned him that the race against time had failed.

"It's no use; we'll have to make two bites of it," he said to Grady, and then he left his desk to go downstairs for a breathing moment and the cup of coffee which he meant to substitute for the dinner which the lack of time had made him forego.

Train 205, the train Flemister had suggested that he might take, was just pulling in from the long run across the desert when he reached the foot of the stairs. That it was too late to take this means of reaching Little Butte and the Wire-Silver mine was a small matter; it merely meant that he would be obliged to order out the service-car and go special, if he should finally decide to act upon Flemister's suggestion.

Angels being a meal station, there was a twenty-minute stop for all trains, and the passengers from 205 were crowding the platform and hurrying to the dining-room and lunch-counter when Lidgerwood made his way to the station end of the building. In the men's room, whither he went to order his cup of coffee, there was a mixed throng of travellers, with a sprinkling of trainmen and town idlers, among the latter a number of the lately discharged railroad employees. Lidgerwood marked a group of the trouble-makers withdrawing to a corner of the room as he entered, and while the waiter was serving his coffee, he saw Hallock join the group. It was only a straw, but straws are significant when the wind is blowing from a threatening quarter. Once again Lidgerwood remembered McCloskey's proposal, and his own reluctant assent to it, and now he was not too greatly conscience-stricken when he saw Judson quietly working his way through the crowded room to a point of espial upon the group in the corner.

"Your coffee's getting cold, Mr. Lidgerwood," the man behind the counter warned him, and Lidgerwood whirled around on the pivot stool and turned his back upon the malcontents and their watcher. The keen inner sense, which neither the physiologists nor the psychologists have yet been able to define or to name, apprised him of a threat developing in the distant corner, but he resolutely ignored it, drank his coffee, and presently went his way around the peopled end of the building and back to the office entrance, meaning to go above stairs and put in another hour with Grady before he should decide definitely about making the night run to Little Butte.

His foot was on the threshold of the stairway door when Judson overtook him.

"Mac told me to report to you when I couldn't get at him," the ex-engineman began abruptly. "There's something hatching, but I can't find out what it is. Are you thinking about goin' out on the road anywhere to-night, Mr. Lidgerwood?"

Lidgerwood's decision was taken on the instant.

"Yes; I think I shall go west in my car in an hour or so. Why?"

"There ain't any 'why,' I guess, if you feel like goin'. But what I don't savvy is why them fellows back yonder in the waitin'-room are so dead anxious to find out if you *are* goin'."

As he spoke, a man who had been skulking behind a truck-load of express freight, so near that he could have touched either of them with an out-stretched arm, withdrew silently in the direction of the lunch-room. He was a tall man with stooping shoulders, and his noiseless retreat was cautiously made, yet not quite cautiously enough, since Judson's sharp eyes marked the shuffling figure vanishing in the shadow cast by the over-hanging shelter roof of the station.

"By cripes!—look at that, will you?" he exclaimed, pointing to the retreating figure. "That's Hallock, and he was listening!"

Lidgerwood shook his head.

"No, that isn't Hallock," he denied. And then, with a bit of the man-driving rasp in his voice: "See here, Judson, don't you let McCloskey's prejudices run away with you; make a memorandum of that and paste it in your hat. I know what you have been instructed to do, and I have given my consent, but it is with the understanding that you will be at least as fair as you would be if McCloskey's bias happened to run the other way. I don't want you to make a case against Hallock unless you can get proof positive that he is disloyal to the company and to me; and I'll tell you here and now that I shall be much better pleased if you can bring me the assurance that he is a true man."

"But that *was* Hallock," insisted Judson, "or else it was his livin' double."

"No; follow him and you'll see for yourself. It was more like that Ruby Gulch operator who quit in a quarrel with McCloskey a week or two ago. What is his name?—Sheffield."

Judson hastened down the platform to satisfy himself, and Lidgerwood mounted the stair to his office. Grady was still pounding the keys of the type-writer on the batch of letters given him in the busy hour following his return from supper, and the superintendent turned his back upon the clicking activities and went to stand at the window, from which he could look down upon the platform with the waiting passenger-train drawn up beside it.

Seeing the cheerful lights in the side-tracked *Nadia*, he fell to thinking of Eleanor, opening the door of conscious thought to her and saying to himself that she was never more than a single step beyond the threshold of that door. Looking across to the *Nadia*, he knew now why he had hesitated so long before deciding to go on the night trip to Timanyoni Park. Chilled hearts follow the analogy of cold hands. When the fire is near, a man will go and spread his fingers to the blaze, though he may be never so well assured that they will ache for it afterward.

But with this thought came another and a more manly one—the woman he loved was in Angels, and she would doubtless remain in Angels or its immediate vicinity for some time; that was unpreventable; but he could still resolve that there should not be a repetition of the old tragedy of the moth and the candle. It was well that at the very outset a duty call had come to enable him to break the spell of her nearness, and it was also well that he had decided not to disregard it.

The train conductor's "All aboard!" shouted on the platform just below his window, drew his attention from the *Nadia* and the distracting thought of Eleanor's nearness. Train 205 was ready to resume its westward flight, and the locomotive bell was clanging musically. A half-grown moon, hanging low in the black dome of the night, yellowed the glow of the platform incandescents. The last few passengers were hurrying up the steps of the cars, and the conductor was swinging his lantern in the starting signal for the engineer.

At the critical moment, when the train was fairly in motion, Lidgerwood saw Hallock—it was unmistakably Hallock this time—spring from the shadow of a baggage-truck and whip up to the step of the smoker, and a scant half-second later he saw Judson race across the wide platform and throw himself like a self-propelled projectile against and through the closing doors of the vestibule at the forward end of the sleeper.

Judson's dash and his capture of the out-going train were easily accounted for: he had seen Hallock. But where was Hallock going? Lidgerwood was still asking himself the question half-abstractedly when he crossed to his desk and touched the buzzer-push which summoned an operator from the despatcher's room.

"Wire Mr. Pennington Flemister, care of Goodloe, at Little Butte, that I am coming out with my car, and should be with him by eleven o'clock. Then call up the yard office and tell Matthews to let me have the car and engine by eight-thirty, sharp," he directed.

The operator made a note of the order and went out, and the superintendent settled himself in his desk-chair for another hour's hard work with the stenographer. At twenty-five minutes past eight he heard the wheel-grindings of the up-coming service-car, and the weary short-hand man snapped a rubber band upon the notes of the final letter.

"That's all for to-night, Grady, and it's quite enough," was the superintendent's word of release. "I'm sorry to have to work you so late, but I'd like to have those letters written out and mailed before you lock up. Are you good for it?"

"I'm good for anything you say, Mr. Lidgerwood," was the response of the one who was loyal to his salt, and the superintendent put on his light coat and went out and down the stair.

At the outer door he turned up the long platform, instead of down, and walked quickly to the *Nadia*, persuading himself that he must, in common decency, tell the president that he was going away; persuading himself that it was this, and not at all the desire to warm his hands at the ungrateful fire of Eleanor's mockery, that was making him turn his back for the moment upon the waiting special train.

XV

The president's private car was side-tracked on the short spur at the eastern end of the Crow's Nest, and when Lidgerwood reached it he found the observation platform fully occupied. The night was no more than pleasantly cool, and the half-grown moon, which was already dipping to its early extinguishment behind the upreared bulk of the Timanyonis, struck out stark etchings in silver and blackest shadow upon a ground of fallow dun and vanishing grays. On such nights the mountain desert hides its forbidding face, and the potent spell of the silent wilderness had drawn the young people of the *Nadia's* party to the out-door trysting-place.

"Hello, Mr. Lidgerwood, is that you?" called Van Lew, when the superintendent came across to the spur track. "I thought you said this was a bad man's country. We have been out here for a solid hour, and nobody has shot up the town or even whooped a single lonesome war-whoop; in fact, I think your village with the heavenly name has gone ingloriously to bed. We're defrauded."

"It does go to bed pretty early—that part of it which doesn't stay up pretty late," laughed Lidgerwood. Then he came closer and spoke to Miss Brewster. "I am going west in my car, and I don't know just when I shall return. Please tell your father that everything we have here is entirely at his service. If you don't see what you want, you are to ask for it."

"Will there be any one to ask when you are gone?" she inquired, neither sorrowing nor rejoicing, so far as he could determine.

"Oh, yes; McCloskey, my trainmaster, will be in from the wreck before morning, and he will turn flip-flaps trying to make things pleasant for you, if you will give him the chance."

She made the adorable little grimace which always carried him swiftly back to a certain summer of ecstatic memories; to a time when her keenest retort had been no more than a playful love-thrust and there had been no bitterness in her mockery.

"Will he make dreadful faces at me, as he did at you this morning when you went down among the smashed cars at the wreck to speak to him?" she asked.

"So you were looking out of the window, too, were you? You are a close observer and a good guesser. That was Mac, and—yes, he will probably make faces at you. He can't help it any more than he can help breathing."

Miss Brewster was running her fingers along the hand-rail as if it were the key-board of a piano. "You say you don't know how long you will be away?" she asked.

"No; but probably not more than the night. I was only providing for the unexpected, which some people say is what always happens."

"Will your run take you as far as the Timanyoni Canyon?"

"Yes; through it, and some little distance beyond."

"You have just said that we are to ask for what we want. Did you mean it?"

"Surely," he replied unguardedly.

"Then we may as well begin at once," she said coolly; and turning quickly to the others: "O all you people; listen a minute, will you? Hush, Carolyn! What do you say to a moonlight ride through one of the grandest canyons in the West in Mr. Lidgerwood's car? It will be something to talk about as long as you live. Don't all speak at once, please."

But they did. There was an instant and enthusiastic chorus of approval, winding up rather dolefully, however, with Miss Doty's, "But your mother will never consent to it, Eleanor!"

"Mr. Lidgerwood will never consent, you mean," put in Miriam Holcombe quietly.

Lidgerwood said what he might without being too crudely inhospitable. His car was entirely at the service of the president's party, of course, but it was not very commodious compared with the *Nadia*. Moreover, he was going on a business trip, and at the end of it he would have to leave them for an hour or two, or maybe longer. Moreover, again, if they got tired they would have to sleep as they could, though possibly his state-room in the service-car might be made to accommodate the three young women. All this he said, hoping and believing that Mrs. Brewster would not only refuse to go herself but would promptly veto an unchaperoned excursion.

But this was one time when his distantly related kinswoman disappointed him. Mrs. Brewster, cajoled by her daughter, yielded a reluctant consent, going to the car door to tell Lidgerwood that she would hold him responsible for the safe return of the trippers.

"See, now, how fatally easy it is for one to promise more—oh, so very much more!—than one has any idea of performing," murmured the president's daughter, dropping out to walk beside the victim when the party trooped down the long platform of the Crow's Nest to the service-car. And when he did not reply: "Please don't be grumpy."

"It was the maddest notion!" he protested. "Whatever made you suggest it?"

"More churlishness?" she said reproachfully. And then, with ironical sentiment: "There was a time when you would have moved heaven and earth for a chance to take me somewhere with you, Howard."

"To be with you; yes, that is true. But——"

Her rippling laugh was too sweet to be shrill; none the less it held in it a little flick of the whip of malice.

"Listen," she said. "I did it out of pure hatefulness. You showed so plainly this afternoon that you wished to be quit of me—of the entire party—that I couldn't resist the temptation to pay you back with good, liberal interest. Possibly you will think twice before you snub me again, Howard, dear."

Quickly he stopped and faced her. The others were a few steps in advance; were already boarding the service-car.

"One word, Eleanor—and for Heaven's sake let us make it final. There are some things that I can endure and some others that I cannot—will not. I love you; what you said to me the last time we were together made no difference; nothing you can ever say will make any difference. You must take that fact into consideration while you are here and we are obliged to meet."

"Well?" she said, and there was nothing in her tone to indicate that she felt more than a passing interest in his declaration.

"That is all," he ended shortly. "I am, as I told you this afternoon, the same man that I was a year ago last spring, as deeply infatuated and, unhappily, just as far below your ideal of what your lover should be. In justice to me, in justice to Van Lew—"

"I think your conductor is waiting to speak to you," she broke in sweetly, and he gave it up, putting her on the car and turning to confront the man with the green-shaded lantern who proved to be Bradford.

"Any special orders, Mr. Lidgerwood?" inquired the reformed cattle-herder, looking stiff and uncomfortable in his new service uniform—one of Lidgerwood's earliest requirements for men on duty in the train service.

"Yes. Run without stop to Little Butte, unless the despatcher calls you down. Time yourself to make Little Butte by eleven o'clock, or a little later. Who is on the engine?"

"Williams."

"Williams? How does it come that he is doubling out with me? He has just made the run over the Desert Division with the president's car."

"So have I, for that matter," said Bradford calmly; "but we both got a hurry call about fifteen minutes ago."

Lidgerwood held his watch to the light of the green-shaded lantern. If he meant to keep the wire appointment with Flemister, there was no time to call out another crew.

"I don't like to ask you and Williams to double out of your turn, especially when I know of no necessity for it. But I'm in a rush. Can you two stand it?"

"Sure," said the ex-cow-man. Then he ventured a word of his own. "I'll ride up ahead with Williams—you're pretty full up, back here in the car, anyway—and then you'll know that two of your own men are keepin' tab on the run. With the wrecks we're enjoying——"

Lidgerwood was impatient of mysteries.

"What do you mean, Andy?" he broke in. "Anything new?"

"Oh, nothing you could put your finger on. Same old rag-chewin' going on up at Cat Biggs's and the other waterin' troughs about how you've got to be done up, if it costs money."

"That isn't new," objected Lidgerwood irritably.

"Tumble-weeds," said Bradford, "rollin' round over the short-grass. But they show which way the wind's comin' from, and give you the jumps when you wouldn't have 'em natural. Williams had a spell of 'em a few minutes ago when he went over to take the 266 out o' the roundhouse and found one of the back-shop men down under her tinkerin' with her trucks."

"What's that?" was the sharp query.

"That's all there was to it," Bradford went on imperturbably. "Williams asked the shopman politely what in hell he was doing under there, and the fellow crawled out and said he was just lookin' her over to see if she was all right for the night run. Now, you wouldn't think there was any tumble-weed in that to give a man the jumps, but Williams had 'em, all the same. Says he to me, tellin' me about it just now: 'That's all right, Andy, but how in blue blazes did he, or anybody else except Matthews and the caller, know that the 266 was goin' out? that's what I'd like to know.' And I had to pass it up."

Lidgerwood asked a single question.

"Did Williams find that anything had been tampered with?"

"Nothing that you could shoot up the back-shop man for. One of the truck safety-chains—the one on the left side, back—was loose. But it couldn't have hurt anything if it had been taken off. We ain't runnin' on safety-chains these days."

"Safety-chain loose, you say?—so if the truck should jump and swing it would keep on swinging? You tell Williams when you go up ahead that I want that machinist's name."

"H'm," said Bradford; "reckon it was meant to do that?"

"God only knows what isn't meant, these times, Andy. Hold on a minute before you give Williams the word to go." Then he turned to young Jefferis, who had come out on the car platform to light a cigarette. "Will you ask Miss Brewster to step out here for a moment?"

Eleanor came at the summons, and Jefferis gave the superintendent a clear field by dropping off to ask Bradford for a match.

"You sent for me, Howard?" said the president's daughter, and honey could not have matched her tone for sweetness.

"Yes. I shall have to anticipate the Angels gossips a little by telling you that we are in the midst of a pretty bitter labor fight. That is why people go gunning for me. I can't take you and your friends over the road to-night."

"Why not?" she inquired.

"Because it may not be entirely safe."

"Nonsense!" she flashed back. "What could happen to us on a little excursion like this?"

"I don't know, but I wish you would reconsider and go back to the *Nadia*."

"I shall do nothing of the sort," she said, wilfully. And then, with totally unnecessary cruelty, she added: "Is it a return of the old malady? Are you afraid again, Howard?"

The taunt was too much. Wheeling suddenly, Lidgerwood snapped out a summons to Jefferis: "Get aboard, Mr. Jefferis; we are going."

At the word Bradford ran forward, swinging his lantern, and a moment later the special train shot away from the Crow's Nest platform and out over the yard switches, and began to bore its way into the westward night.

XVI

Forty-two miles south-west of Angels, at a point where all further progress seems definitely barred by the huge barrier of the great mountain range, the Red Butte Western, having picked its devious way to an apparent *cul-de-sac* among the foot-hills and hogbacks, plunges abruptly into the echoing canyon of the Eastern Timanyoni.

For forty added miles the river chasm, throughout its length a narrow, tortuous crevice, with sheer and towering cliffs for its walls, affords a precarious footing for the railway embankment, leading the double line of steel with almost sentient reluctance, as it seems, through the mighty mountain barrier. At its western extremity the canyon forms the gate-way to a shut-in valley of upheaved hills and inferior mountains isolated by wide stretches of rolling grassland. To the eastward and westward of the great valley rise the sentinel peaks of the two enclosing mountain ranges; and across the shut-in area the river plunges from pool to pool, twisting and turning as the craggy and densely forested lesser heights constrain it.

Red Butte, the centre of the evanescent mining excitement which was originally responsible for the building of the railroad, lies high-pitched among the shouldering spurs of the western boundary range. Seeking the route promising the fewest cuts and fills and the easiest grades, Chandler, the construction chief of the building company, had followed the south bank of the river to a point a short distance beyond the stream-fronting cliffs of the landmark hill known as Little Butte; and at the station of the same name he had built his bridge across the Timanyoni and swung his line in a great curve for the northward climb among the hogbacks to the gold-mining district in which Red Butte was the principal camp.

Elsewhere than in a land of sky-piercing peaks and continent-cresting highlands, Little Butte would have been called a true mountain. On the engineering maps of the Red Butte Western its outline appears as a roughly described triangle with five-mile sides, the three angles of the figure marked respectively by Silver Switch, Little Butte station and bridge, and the Wire-Silver mine.

Between Silver Switch and the bridge station, the main line of the railroad follows the base of the triangle, with the precipitous bluffs of the big hill on the left and the torrenting flood of the Timanyoni on the right. Along the eastern side of the triangle, and leaving the main track at Silver Switch, ran the spur which had formerly served the Wire-Silver when the working opening of the mine had been on the eastern slope of the ridge-like hill. For some years previous to the summer of overturnings this spur had been disused, though its track, ending among a group of the old mine buildings five miles away, was still in commission.

Along the western side of the triangle, with Little Butte station for its point of divergence from the main line, ran the new spur, built to accommodate Flemister after he had dug through the hill, ousted the rightful owner of the true Wire-Silver vein, and had transferred his labor hamlet and his plant—or the major part of both—to the western slope of the butte, at this point no more than a narrow ridge separating the eastern and western gulches.

Train 205, with ex-engineer Judson apparently sound asleep in one of the rearward seats of the day coach, was on time when it swung out of the lower canyon portal and raced around the curves and down the grades in its crossing of Timanyoni Park. At Point-of-Rocks Judson came awake sufficiently to put his face to the window, with a shading hand to cut off the car lights; but having thus located the train's placement in the Park-crossing race, he put his knees up against the back of the adjoining seat, pulled his cap over his eyes, and to all outward appearances went to sleep again. Four or five miles farther along, however, there came a gentle grinding of brake-shoes upon the chilled wheel-treads that aroused him quickly. Another flattening of his nose against the window-pane showed him the familiar bulk of Little Butte looming black in the moonlight, and a moment later he had let himself silently into the rear vestibule of the day coach, and was as silently opening the folding doors of the vestibule itself.

Hanging off by the hand-rails, he saw the engine's headlight pick up the switch-stand of the old spur. The train was unmistakably slowing now, and he made ready to jump if the need should arise, picking his place at the track side as the train lights showed him the ground. As the speed was checked, Judson saw what he was expecting to see. Precisely at the instant of the switch passing, a man dropped from the forward step of the smoker and walked swiftly away up the disused track of the old spur. Judson's turn came a moment later, and when his end of the day coach flicked past the switch-stand he, too, dropped to the ground, and, waiting only until he could follow without being detected, set out after the tall figure, which was by that time scarcely more than an indistinct and retreating blur in the moonlight.

The chase led directly up the old spur, but it did not continue quite to the five-mile-distant end of it. A few hundred yards short of the stockade enclosing the old buildings the shadowy figure took to the forest and began to climb the ridge, going straight up, as nearly as Judson could determine. The ex-engineer followed, still keeping his distance. From the first bench above the valley level he looked back and down into the stockade enclosure. All of the old buildings were dark, but one of the two new and unpainted ones was brilliantly lighted, and there were sounds familiar enough to Judson to mark it as the Wire-Silver power-house. Notwithstanding his interest in the chase, Judson was curious enough to stand a moment listening to the sharply defined exhausts of the high-speeded steam-engine driving the generators.

"Say!" he ejaculated, under his breath, "if that engine ain't a dead match for the old 216 pullin' a grade, I don't want a cent! Double cylinder, set on the quarter, and *choo-chooin'* like it ought to have a pair o' steel rails under it. If I had time I'd go down yonder and break a winder in that power-shack; blamed if I wouldn't!"

But, unhappily, there was no time to spare; as it was, he had lingered too long, and when he came out upon the crest of the narrow ridge and attained a point of view from which he could look down upon the buildings clustering at the foot of the western slope, he had lost the scent. The tall man had disappeared as completely and suddenly as if the earth had opened and swallowed him.

This, in Judson's prefiguring, was a small matter. The tall man, whom the ex-engineer had unmistakably recognized at the moment of train-forsaking as Rankin Hallock, was doubtless on his way to Flemister's head-quarters at the foot of the western slope. Why he should take the roundabout route up the old spur and across the mountain, when he might have gone on the train to Little Butte station and so have saved the added distance and the hard climb, was a question which Judson answered briefly: for some reason of his own, Hallock did not wish to be seen going openly to the

Wire-Silver head-quarters. Hence the drop from the train at Silver Switch and the long tramp up the gulch and over the ridge.

Forecasting it thus, Judson lost no time on the summit of mysterious disappearances. Choosing the shortest path he could find which promised to lead him down to the mining hamlet at the foot of the westward-fronting slope, he set his feet in it and went stumbling down the steep declivity, bringing up, finally, on a little bench just above the mine workings. Here he stopped to get his breath and his bearings. From his halting-place the mine head-quarters building lay just below him, at the right of the tunnel entrance to the mine. It was a long log building of one story, with warehouse doors in the nearer gable and lighted windows to mark the location of the offices at the opposite end.

Making a détour to dodge the electric-lighted tunnel mouth, Judson carefully reconnoitred the office end of the head-quarters building. There was a door, with steps giving upon the down-hill side, and there were two windows, both of which were blank to the eye by reason of the drawn-down shades. Two persons, at least, were in the lighted room; Judson could hear their voices, but the thick log walls muffled the sounds to an indistinct murmur. On the mountain-facing side of the building, which was in shadow, the ex-engineer searched painstakingly for some open chink or cranny between the logs, but there was no avenue of observation either for the eye or the ear. Just as he had made up his mind to risk the moonlight on the other side of the head-quarters, a sound like the moving of chairs on a bare floor made him dodge quickly behind the bole of a great mountain pine which had been left standing at the back of the building. The huge tree was directly opposite one of the windows, and when Judson looked again the figure of a man sitting in a chair was sharply silhouetted on the drawn window-shade.

Judson stared, rubbed his eyes, and stared again. It had never occurred to him before that the face of a man, viewed in blank profile, could differ so strikingly from the same face as seen eye to eye. That the man whose shadow was projected upon the window-shade was Rankin Hallock, he could not doubt. The bearded chin, the puffy lips, the prominent nose were all faithfully outlined in the exaggerated shadowgraph. But the hat was worn at an unfamiliar angle, and there was something in the erect, bulking figure that was still more unfamiliar. Judson backed away and stared again, muttering to himself. If he had not traced Hallock almost to the door of Flemister's quarters, there might have been room for the thin edge of the doubt wedge. The unfamiliar pose and the rakish tilt of the soft hat were not among the chief clerk's remembered characteristics; but making due allowance for the distortion of the magnified facial outline, the profile was Hallock's.

Having definitely settled for himself the question of identity, Judson renewed his search for some eavesdropping point of vantage. Risking the moonlight, he twice made the circuit of the occupied end of the building. There was a line of light showing under the ill-fitting door, and with the top step of the down-hill flight for a perching-place one might lay an ear to the crack and overhear. But door and steps were sharply struck out in the moonlight, and they faced the mining hamlet where the men of the day shift were still stirring.

Judson knew the temper of the Timanyoni miners. To be seen crouching on the boss's doorstep would be to take the chance of making a target of himself for the first loiterer of the day shift who happened to look his way. Dismissing the risky expedient, he made a third circuit from moon-glare to shadow, this time upon hands and knees. To the lowly come the rewards of humility. Framed level upon stout log pillars on the down-hill side, the head-quarters warehouse and office sheltered a space beneath its floor which was roughly boarded up with slabs from the log-sawing. Slab by slab the ex-engineer sought for his rat-hole, trying each one softly in its turn. When there remained but three more to be tugged at, the loosened one was found. Judson swung it cautiously aside and wriggled through the narrow aperture left by its removal. A crawling minute later he was crouching beneath the loosely jointed floor of the lighted room, and the avenue of the ear had broadened into a fair highway.

Almost at once he was able to verify his guess that there were only two men in the room above. At all events, there were only two speakers. They were talking in low tones, and Judson had no difficulty in identifying the rather high-pitched voice of the owner of the Wire-Silver mine. The man whose profile he had seen on the window-shade had the voice which belonged to the outlined features, but the listener under the floor had a vague impression that he was trying to disguise it. Judson knew nothing about the letter in which Flemister had promised to arrange for a meeting between Lidgerwood and the ranchman Grofield. What he did know was that he had followed Hallock almost to the door of Flemister's office, and that he had seen a shadowed face on the office window-shade which could be no other than the face of the chief clerk. It was in spite of all this that the impression that the second speaker was trying to disguise his voice persisted. But the ex-engineer of fast passenger-trains was able to banish the impression after the first few minutes of eavesdropping.

Judson had scarcely found his breathing space between the floor timbers, and had not yet overheard enough to give him the drift of the low-toned talk, when the bell of the private-line telephone rang in the room above. It was Flemister who answered the bell-ringer.

"Hello! Yes; this is Flemister.... Yes, I say; *this* is Flemister; you're talking to him.... What's that?—a message about Mr. Lidgerwood?... All right; fire away."

"Who is it?" came the inquiry, in the grating voice which fitted, and yet did not fit, the man whom Judson had followed from his boarding of the train at Angels to Silver Switch, and from the gulch of the old spur to his disappearance on the wooded slope of Little Butte ridge.

The listener heard the click of the telephone ear-piece replacement.

"It's Goodloe, talking from his station office at Little Butte," replied the mine owner. "The despatcher has just called him up to say that Lidgerwood left Angels in his service-car, running special, at eight-forty, which would figure it here at about eleven, or a little later."

"Who is running it?" inquired the other man rather anxiously, Judson decided.

"Williams and Bradford. A fool for luck, every time. We might have had to *écraser* a couple of our friends."

The French was beyond Judson, but the mine-owner's tone supplied the missing meaning, and the listener under the floor had a sensation like that which might be produced by a cold wind blowing up the nape of his neck.

126

"There is no such thing as luck," rasped the other voice. "My time was damned short—after I found out that Lidgerwood wasn't coming on the passenger. But I managed to send word to Matthews and Lester, telling them to make sure of Williams and Bradford. We could spare both of them, if we have to."

"Good!" said Flemister. "Then you had some such alternative in mind as that I have just been proposing?"

"No," was the crusty rejoinder. "I was merely providing for the hundredth chance. I don't like your alternative."

"Why don't you?"

"Well, for one thing, it's needlessly bloody. We don't have to go at this thing like a bull at a gate. I've had my finger on the pulse of things ever since Lidgerwood took hold. The dope is working all right in a purely natural way. In the ordinary run of things, it will be only a few days or weeks before Lidgerwood will throw up his hands and quit, and when he goes out, I go in. That's straight goods this time."

"You thought it was before," sneered Flemister, "and you got beautifully left." Then: "You're talking long on 'naturals' and the 'ordinary run of things,' but I notice you schemed with Bart Rufford to put him out of the fight with a pistol bullet!"

Judson felt a sudden easing of strains. He had told McCloskey that he would be willing to swear to the voice of the man whom he had overheard plotting with Rufford in Cat Biggs's back room. Afterward, after he had sufficiently remembered that a whiskey certainty might easily lead up to a sober perjury, he had admitted the possible doubt. But now Flemister's taunt made assurance doubly sure. Moreover, the arch-plotter was not denying the fact of the conspiracy with "The Killer." "Rufford is a blood-thirsty devil—like yourself," the other man was saying calmly. "As I have told you before, I've discovered Lidgerwood's weakness—he can't call a sudden bluff. Rufford's play—the play I told him to make—was to get the drop on him, scare him up good, and chase him out of town—out of the country. He overran his orders—and went to jail for it."

"Well?" said the mine-owner.

"Your scheme, as you outlined it to me in your cipher wire this afternoon, was built on this same weakness of Lidgerwood's, and I agreed to it. As I understood it, you were to toll him up here with some lie about meeting Grofield, and then one of us was to put a pistol in his face and bluff him into throwing up his job. As I say, I agreed to it. He'll have to go when the fight with the men gets hot enough; but he might hold on too long for our comfort."

"Well?" said Flemister again, this time more impatiently, Judson thought.

"He queered your lay-out by carefully omitting to come on the passenger, and now you propose to fall back upon Rufford's method. I don't approve."

Again the mine-owner said "Why don't you?" and the other voice took up the question argumentatively.

"First, because it is unnecessary, as I have explained. Lidgerwood is officially dead, right now. When the grievance committees tell him what has been decided upon, he will put on his hat and go back to wherever it was that he came from."

"And secondly?" suggested Flemister, still with the nagging sneer in his tone.

There was a little pause, and Judson listened until the effort grew positively painful.

"The secondly is a weakness of mine, you'll say, Flemister. I want his job; partly because it belongs to me, but chiefly because if I don't get it a bunch of us will wind up breaking stone for the State. But I haven't anything against the man himself. He trusts me; he has defended me when others have tried to put him wise; he has been damned white to me, Flemister."

"Is that all?" queried the mine-owner, in the tone of the prosecuting attorney who gives the criminal his full length of the rope with which to hang himself.

"All of that part of it—and you are saying to yourself that it is a good deal more than enough. Perhaps it is; but there is still another reason for thinking twice before burning all the bridges behind us. Lidgerwood is Ford's man; if he throws up his job of his own accord, I may be able to swing Ford into line to name me as his successor. On the other hand, if Lidgerwood is snuffed out and there is the faintest suspicion of foul play.... Flemister, I'm telling you right here and now that that man Ford will neither eat nor sleep until he has set the dogs on us!"

There was another pause, and Judson shifted his weight cautiously from one elbow to the other. Then Flemister began, without heat and equally without compunction. The ex-engineer shivered, as if the measured words had been so many drops of ice-water dribbling through the cracks in the floor to fall upon his spine.

"You say it is unnecessary; that Lidgerwood will be pushed out by the labor fight. My answer to that is that you don't know him quite as well as you think you do. If he's allowed to live, he'll stay—unless somebody takes him unawares and scares him off, as I meant to do to-night when I wired you. If he continues to live, and stay, you know what will happen, sooner or later. He'll find you out for the double-faced cur that you are—and after that, the fireworks."

At this the other voice took its turn at the savage sneering.

"You can't put it all over me that way, Flemister; you can't, and, by God, you sha'n't! You're in the hole just as deep as I am, foot for foot!"

"Oh, no, my friend," said the cooler voice. "I haven't been stealing in car-load lots from the company that hires me; I have merely been buying a little disused scrap from you. You may say that I have planned a few of the adverse happenings which have been running the loss-and-damage account of the road up into the pictures during the past few weeks—possibly I have; but you are the man who has been carrying out the plans, and you are the man the courts will recognize. But we're wasting time sitting here jawing at each other like a pair of old women. It's up to us to obliterate Lidgerwood; after which it will be up to you to get his job and cover up your tracks as you can. If he lives, he'll dig; and if he digs, he'll turn up things that neither of us can stand for. See how he hangs onto that building-and-loan ghost. He'll tree somebody on that before he's through, you mark my words! And it runs in my mind that the somebody will be you."

"But this trap scheme of yours," protested the other man; "it's a frost, I tell you! You say the night passenger from Red Butte is late. I know it's late, now; but Cranford's running it, and it is all down-hill from Red Butte to the bridge. Cranford will make up his thirty minutes, and that will put his train right here in the thick of things. Call it off for to-night, Flemister. Meet Lidgerwood when he comes and tell him an easy lie about your not being able to hold Grofield for the right-of-way talk."

Judson heard the creak and snap of a swing-chair suddenly righted, and the floor dust jarred through the cracks upon him when the mine-owner sprang to his feet.

"Call it off and let you drop out of it? Not by a thousand miles, my cautious friend! Want to stay here and keep your feet warm while I go and do it? Not on your tintype, you yapping hound! I'm about ready to freeze you, anyway, for the second time—mark that, will you?—for the second time. No, keep your hands where I can see 'em, or I'll knife you right where you sit! You can bully and browbeat a lot of railroad buckies when you're playing the boss act, *but I know you*! You come with me or I'll give the whole snap away to Vice-President Ford. I'll tell him how you built a street of houses in Red Butte out of company material and with company labor. I'll prove to him that you've scrapped first one thing and then another—condemned them so you might sell them for your own pocket. I'll——"

"Shut up!" shouted the other man hoarsely. And then, after a moment that Judson felt was crammed to the bursting point with murderous possibilities: "Get your tools and come on. We'll see who's got the yellows before we're through with this!"

XVII

There are moments when the primal instincts assert themselves with a sort of blind ferocity, and to Judson, jammed under the floor timbers of Flemister's head-quarters office, came one of these moments when he heard the two men in the room above moving to depart, and found himself caught between the timbers so that he could not retreat.

What had happened he was unable, in the first fierce struggle for freedom, fully to determine. It was as if a living hand had reached down to pin him fast in the tunnel-like space. Then he discovered that a huge splinter on one of the joists was thrust like a great barb into his coat. Ordinarily cool and collected in the face of emergencies, the ex-engineer lost his head for a second or so and fought like a trapped animal. Then the frenzy fit passed and the quick wit reasserted itself. Extending his arms over his head and digging his toes into the dry earth for a purchase, he backed, crab-wise, out of the entangled coat, freed the coat, and made for the narrow exit in a sweating panic of excitement.

Notwithstanding the excitement, however, the recovered wit was taking note of the movements of the men who were leaving the room overhead. They were not going out by the direct way—out of the door facing the moonlight and the mining hamlet. They were passing out through the store-room in the rear. Also, there were other foot-falls—cautious treadings, these—as of some third person hastening to be first at the more distant door of egress.

Judson was out of his dodge-hole and flitting from pine to pine on the upper hill-side in time to see a man leap from the loading platform at the warehouse end of the building and run for the sheltering shadows of the timbering at the mine entrance. Following closely upon the heels of their mysterious file leader came the two whose footsteps Judson had been timing, and these, too, crossed quickly to the tunnel mouth of the mine and disappeared within it.

Judson pursued swiftly and without a moment's hesitation. Happily for him, the tunnel was lighted at intervals by electric incandescents, their tiny filaments glowing mistily against the wet and glistening tunnel roof. Going softly, he caught a glimpse of the two men as they passed under one of the lights in the receding tunnel depths, and a moment later he could have sworn that a third, doubtless the man who had leaped from the loading platform to run and hide in the shadows at the mine mouth, passed the same light, going in the same direction.

A hundred yards deeper into the mountain there was a confirming repetition of the flash-light picture for the ex-engineer. The two men, walking rapidly now, one a step in advance of the other, passed under another of the overhead light bulbs, and this time Judson, watching for the third man, saw him quite plainly. The sight gave him a start. The third man was tall, and he wore a soft hat drawn low over his face.

"Well, I'll be jiggered!" muttered the trailer, pulling his cap down to his ears and quickening his pace. "If I didn't know better, I'd swear that was Hallock again—or Hallock's shadder follerin' him at a good long range!"

The chase was growing decidedly mysterious. The two men in the lead could be no others than Flemister and the chief clerk, presumably on their way to the carrying out of whatever plot they had agreed upon, with Lidgerwood for the potential victim. But since this plot evidently turned upon the nearing approach of Lidgerwood's special train, why were they plunging on blindly into the labyrinthine depths of the Wire-Silver mine? This was an even half of the mystery, and the other half was quite as puzzling. Who was the third man? Was he a confederate in the plot, or was he also following to spy upon the conspirators?

Judson was puzzled, but he did not let his bewilderment tangle the feet of his principal purpose, which was to keep Flemister and his reluctant accomplice in sight. This purpose was presently defeated in a most singular manner. At the end of one of the longer tunnel levels, a black and dripping cavern, lighted only by a single incandescent shining like a star imprisoned in the dismal depths, the ex-engineer saw what appeared to be a wooden bulkhead built across the passage and effectively blocking it. When the two men came to this bulkhead they passed through it and disappeared, and the shock of the confined air in the tunnel told of a door slammed behind them.

Judson broke into a stumbling run, and then stopped short in increasing bewilderment. At the slamming of the door the third man had darted forward out of the shadows to fling himself upon the wooden barrier, beating upon it with his fists and cursing like a madman. Judson saw, understood, and acted, all with the instinctive instantaneousness born of his trade of engine-driving. The two men in advance were merely taking the short cut through the mountain to the old workings on the eastern slope, and the door in the bulkhead, which was doubtless one of the airlocks in the ventilating system of the mine, had fastened itself automatically after Flemister had released it.

Judson was a hundred yards down the tunnel, racing like a trained sprinter for the western exit, before he thought to ask himself why the third man was playing the madman before the locked door. But that was a matter negligible to him; his affair was to get out of the mine with the loss of the fewest possible seconds of time—to win out, to climb the ridge, and to descend the eastern slope to the old workings before the two plotters should disappear beyond the hope of rediscovery.

He did his best, flying down the long tunnel reaches with little regard for the precarious footing, tripping over the cross-ties of the miniature tramway and colliding with the walls, now and then, between the widely separated electric bulbs. Far below, in the deeper levels, he could hear the drumming chatter of the power-drills and the purring of the compressed air, but the upper gangway was deserted, and it was not until he was stumbling through the timbered portal that a watchman rose up out of the shadows to confront and halt him. There was no time to spare for soft words or skilful evasions. With a savage upper-cut that caught the watchman on the point of the jaw and sent him crashing among the picks and shovels of the mine-mouth tool-room, Judson darted out into the moonlight. But as yet the fierce race was only fairly begun. Without stopping to look for a path, the ex-engineer flung himself at the steep hill-side, running, falling, clambering on hands and knees, bursting by main strength through the tangled thickets of young pines, and hurling himself blindly over loose-lying bowlders and the trunks of fallen trees. When, after what seemed like an eternity of lung-bursting struggles, he came out upon the bare summit of the ridge, his tongue was like a dry stick in his mouth, refusing to shape the curses that his soul was heaping upon the alcohol which had made him a wind-broken, gasping weakling in the prime of his manhood.

For, after all the agonizing strivings, he was too late. It was a rough quarter-mile down to the shadowy group of buildings whence the humming of the dynamo and the quick exhausts of the high-speeded steam-engine rose on the still night air. Judson knew that the last lap was not in his trembling muscles or in the thumping heart and the wind-broken lungs. Moreover, the path, if any there were, was either to the right or the left of the point to which he had attained; fronting him there was a steep cliff, trifling enough as to real heights and depths, but an all-sufficient barrier for a spent runner.

The ex-engineer crawled cautiously to the edge of the barrier cliff, rubbed the sweat out of his smarting eyes, and peered down into the half-lighted shadows of the stockaded enclosure. It was not very long before he made them out—two indistinct figures moving about among the disused and dilapidated ore sheds clustering at the track end of the old spur. Now and again a light glowed for an instant and died out, like the momentary brilliance of a gigantic fire-fly, by which the watcher on the cliff's summit knew that the two were guiding their movements by the help of an electric flash-lamp.

What they were doing did not long remain a mystery. Judson heard a distance-diminished sound, like the grinding of rusty wheels upon iron rails, and presently a shadowy thing glided out of one of the ore sheds and took its place upon the track of the old spur. Followed a series of clankings still more familiar to the watcher—the *ting* of metal upon metal, as of crow-bars and other tools cast carelessly, one upon the other, in the loading of the shadowy vehicle. Making a telescope of his hands to shut out the glare from the lighted windows of the power-house, Judson could dimly discern the two figures mounting to their places on the deck of the thing which he now knew to be a hand-car. A moment later, to the musical *click-click* of wheels passing over rail-joints, the little car shot through the gate-way in the stockade and sped away down the spur, the two indistinct figures bowing alternately to each other like a pair of grotesque automatons.

Winded and leg-weary as he was, Judson's first impulse prompted him to seek for the path to the end that he might dash down the hill and give chase. But if he would have yielded, another pursuer was before him to show him the futility of that expedient. While the clicking of the hand-car wheels was still faintly audible, a man—the door-hammering madman, Judson thought it must be—materialized suddenly from somewhere in the under-shadows to run down the track after the disappearing conspirators. The engineer saw the racing foot-pursuer left behind so quickly that his own hope of overtaking the car died almost before it had taken shape.

"That puts it up to me again," he groaned, rising stiffly. Then he faced once more toward the western valley and the point of the great triangle, where the lights of Little Butte station and bridge twinkled uncertainly in the distance. "If I can get down yonder to Goodloe's wire in time to catch the super's special before it passes Timanyoni"—he went on, only to drop his jaw and gasp when he held the face of his watch up to the moonlight. Then, brokenly, "My God! I couldn't begin to do it unless I had wings: he said eleven o'clock, and it's ten-ten right now!"

There was the beginning of a frenzied outburst of despairing curses upbubbling to Judson's lips when he realized his utter helplessness and the consequences menacing the superintendent's special. True, he did not know what the consequences were to be, but he had overheard enough to be sure that Lidgerwood's life was threatened. Then, at the climax of despairing helplessness he remembered that there was a telephone in the mine-owner's office—a telephone that connected with Goodloe's station at Little Butte. Here was a last slender chance of getting a warning to Goodloe, and through him, by means of the railroad wire, to the superintendent's special. Instantly Judson forgot his weariness, and raced away down the western slope of the mountain, prepared to fight his way to the telephone if the entire night shift of the Wire-Silver should try to stop him.

It cost ten of the precious fifty minutes to retrace his steps down the mountain-side, and five more, were lost in dodging the mine watchman, who, having recovered from the effects of Judson's savage blow, was prowling about the mine buildings, revolver in hand, in search of his mysterious assailant. After the watchman was out of the way, five other minutes went to the cautious prying open of the window least likely to attract attention—the window upon whose drawn shade the convincing profile had been projected. Judson's lips were dry and his hands were shaking again when he crept through the opening, and dropped into the unfamiliar interior, where the darkness was but thinly diluted by the moonlight filtering through the small, dingy squares of the opposite window. To have the courage of a house-breaker, one must be a burglar in fact; and the ex-engineer knew how swiftly and certainly he would pay the penalty if any one had seen him climbing in at the forced window, or should chance to discover him now that he was in.

But there was a stronger motive than fear, fear for himself, to set him groping for the telephone. The precious minutes were flying, and he knew that by this time the two men on the hand-car must have reached the main line at Silver Switch. Whatever helpful chain of events might be set in motion by communicating with Goodloe, must be linked up quickly.

He found the telephone without difficulty. It was an old-fashioned set, with a crank and bell for ringing up the call at the other end of the line. A single turn of the crank told him that it was cut off somewhere, doubtless by a switch in the office wiring. In a fresh fever of excitement he began a search for the switch, tracing with his fingers the wires which led from the instrument and following where they ran around the end of the room on the wainscoting. In the corner farthest from his window of ingress he found the switch and felt it out. It was a simple cut-out, designed to connect either the office instrument or the mine telephones with the main wire, as might be desired. Under the switch stood a corner cupboard, and in feeling for the wire connections on top of the cupboard, Judson found his fingers running lightly over the bounding surfaces of an object with which he was, unhappily, only too familiar—a long-necked bottle with the seal blown in the glass. The corner cupboard was evidently Flemister's sideboard.

Almost before he knew what he was doing, Judson had grasped the bottle and had removed the cork. Here was renewed strength and courage, and a swift clearing of the brain, to be had for the taking. At the drawing of the cork the fine bouquet of the liquor seemed instantly to fill the room with its subtle and intoxicating essence. With the smell of the whiskey in his nostrils he had the bottle half-way to his lips before he realized that the demon of appetite had sprung upon him out of the darkness, taking him naked and unawares. Twice he put the bottle down, only to take it up again. His lips were parched; his tongue rattled in his mouth, and within there were cravings like the fires of hell, threatening torments unutterable if they should not be assuaged.

"God have mercy!" he mumbled, and then, in a voice which the rising fires had scorched to a hoarse whisper: "If I drink, I'm damned to all eternity; and if I don't take just one swallow, I'll never be able to talk so as to make Goodloe understand me!"

It was the supreme test of the man. Somewhere, deep down in the soul-abyss of the tempted one, a thing stirred, took shape, and arose to help him to fight the devil of appetite. Slowly the fierce thirst burned itself out. The invisible hand at his throat relaxed its cruel grip, and a fine dew of perspiration broke out thickly on his forehead. At the sweating instant the newly arisen soul-captain within him whispered, "Now, John Judson—once for all!" and staggering to the open window he flung the tempting bottle afar among the scattered bowlders, waiting until he had heard the tinkling crash of broken glass before he turned back to his appointed task.

His hands were no longer trembling when he once more wound the crank of the telephone and held the receiver to his ear. There was an answering skirl of the bell, and then a voice said: "Hello! This is Goodloe: what's wanted?"

Judson wasted no time in explanations. "This is Judson—John Judson. Get Timanyoni on your wire, quick, and catch Mr. Lidgerwood's special. Tell Bradford and Williams to run slow, looking for trouble. Do you get that?"

A confused medley of rumblings and clankings crashed in over the wire, and in the midst of the interruption Judson heard Goodloe put down the receiver. In a flash he knew what was happening at Little Butte station. The delayed passenger-train from the west had arrived, and the agent was obliged to break off and attend to his duties.

Anxiously Judson twirled the crank, again and yet again. Since Goodloe had not cut off the connection, the mingled clamor of the station came to the listening ear; the incessant clicking of the telegraph instruments on Goodloe's table, the trundling roar of a baggage-truck on the station platform, the cacophonous screech of the passenger-engine's pop-valve. With the *phut* of the closing safety-valve came the conductor's cry of "All aboard!" and then the long-drawn sobs of the big engine as Cranford started the train. Judson knew that in all human probability the superintendent's special had already passed Timanyoni, the last chance for a telegraphic warning; and here was the passenger slipping away, also without warning.

Goodloe came back to the telephone when the train clatter had died away, and took up the broken conversation.

"Are you there yet, John?" he called. And when Judson's yelp answered him: "All right; now, what was it you were trying to tell me about the special?"

Judson did not swear; the seconds were too vitally precious. He merely repeated his warning, with a hoarse prayer for haste.

There was another pause, a break in the clicking of Goodloe's telegraph instruments, and then the agent's voice came back over the wire: "Can't reach the special. It passed Timanyoni ten minutes ago."

Judson's heart was in his mouth, and he had to swallow twice before he could go on.

"Where does it meet the passenger?" he demanded.

"You can search me," replied the Little Butte agent, who was not of those who go out of their way to borrow trouble. Then, suddenly: "Hold the 'phone a minute; the despatcher's calling me, right now."

There was a third trying interval of waiting for the man in the darkened room at the Wire-Silver head-quarters; an interval shot through with pricklings of feverish impatience, mingled with a lively sense of the risk he was running; and then Goodloe called again.

"Trouble," he said shortly. "Angels didn't know that Cranford had made up so much time. Now he tries to give me an order to hold the passenger—after it's gone by. So long. I'm going to take a lantern and mog along up the track to see where they come together."

Judson hung up the receiver, reset the wire switch to leave it as he had found it, climbed out through the open window and replaced the sash; all this methodically, as one who sets the death chamber in order after the sheet has been drawn over the face of the corpse. Then he stumbled down the hill to the gulch bottom and started out to walk along the new spur toward Little Butte station, limping painfully and feeling mechanically in his pocket for his pipe, which had apparently been lost in some one of the many swift and strenuous scene-shiftings.

XVIII

Like that of other railroad officials, whose duties constrain them to spend much time in transit, Lidgerwood's desk-work went with him up and down and around and about on the two divisions, and before leaving his office in the Crow's Nest to go down to the waiting special, he had thrust a bunch of letters and papers into his pocket to be ground through the business-mill on the run to Little Butte.

It was his surreptitious transference of the rubber-banded bunch of letters to the oblivion of the closed service-car desk, observed by Miss Brewster, that gave the president's daughter an opportunity to make partial amends for having turned his business trip into a car-party. Before the special was well out of the Angels yard she was commanding silence, and laying down the law for the others, particularizing Carolyn Doty, though only by way of a transfixing eye.

"Listen a moment, all of you," she called. "We mustn't forget that this isn't a planned excursion for us; it's a business trip for Mr. Lidgerwood, and we are here by our own invitation. We must make ourselves small, accordingly, and not bother him. *Savez vous?*"

Van Lew laughed, spread his long arms, and swept them all out toward the rear platform. But Miss Eleanor escaped at the door and went back to Lidgerwood.

"There, now!" she whispered, "don't ever say that I can't do the really handsome thing when I try. Can you manage to work at all, with these chatterers on the car?"

She was steadying herself against the swing of the car, with one shapely hand on the edge of the desk, and he covered it with one of his own.

"Yes, I can work," he asserted. "The one thing impossible is not to love you, Eleanor. It's hard enough when you are unkind; you mustn't make it harder by being what you used always to be to me."

"What a lover you are when you forget to be self-conscious!" she said softly; none the less she freed the imprisoned hand with a hasty little jerk. Then she went on with playful austerity: "Now you are to do exactly what you were meaning to do when you didn't know we were coming with you. I'll make them all stay away from you just as long as I can."

She kept her promise so well that for an industrious hour Lidgerwood scarcely realized that he was not alone. For the greater part of the interval the sight-seers were out on the rear platform, listening to Miss Brewster's stories of the Red Desert. When she had repeated all she had ever heard, she began to invent; and she was in the midst of one of the most blood-curdling of the inventions when Lidgerwood, having worked through his bunch of papers, opened the door and joined the platform party. Miss Brewster's animation died out and her voice trailed away into—"and that's all; I don't know the rest of it."

Lidgerwood's laugh was as hearty as Van Lew's or the collegian's.

"Please go on," he teased. Then quoting her: "'And after they had shot up all the peaceable people in the town, they fell to killing each other, and'—Don't let me spoil the dramatic conclusion."

"You are the dramatic conclusion to that story," retorted Miss Brewster, reproachfully. Whereupon she immediately wrenched the conversation aside into a new channel by asking how far it was to the canyon portal.

"Only a mile or two now," was Lidgerwood's rejoinder. "Williams has been making good time." And two minutes later the one-car train, with the foaming torrent of the Timanyoni for its pathfinder, plunged between the narrow walls of the upper canyon, and the race down the grade of the crooked water-trail through the heart of the mountains began.

There was little chance for speech, even if the overawing grandeurs of the stupendous crevice, seen in their most impressive presentment as alternating vistas of stark, moonlighted crags and gulches and depths of blackest shadow, had encouraged it. The hiss and whistle of the air-brakes, the harsh, sustained note of the shrieking wheel-flanges shearing the inner edges of the railheads on the curves, and the stuttering roar of the 266's safety-valve were continuous; a deafening medley of sounds multiplied a hundred-fold by the demoniac laughter of the echoes.

Miss Carolyn clung to the platform hand-rail, and once Lidgerwood thought he surprised Van Lew with his arm about her; thought it, and immediately concluded that he was mistaken. Miriam Holcombe had the opposite corner of the platform, and Jefferis was making it his business to see to it that she was not entirely crushed by the grandeurs.

Miss Brewster, steadying herself by the knob of the closed door, was not overawed; she had seen Rocky Mountain canyons at their best and their worst, many times before. But excitement, and the relaxing of the conventional leash that accompanies it, roused the spirit of daring mockery which was never wholly beyond call in Miss Brewster's mental processes. With her lips to Lidgerwood's ear she said: "Tell me, Howard; how soon should a chaperon begin to make a diversion? I'm only an apprentice, you know. Does it occur to you that these young persons need to be shocked into a better appreciation of the conventions?"

There was a small Pintsch globe in the hollow of the "umbrella roof," with its single burner turned down to a mere pea of light. Lidgerwood's answer was to reach up and flood the platform with a sudden glow of artificial radiance. The chorus of protest was immediate and reproachful.

"Oh, Mr. Lidgerwood! don't spoil the perfect moonlight that way!" cried Miss Doty, and the others echoed the beseeching.

"You'll get used to it in a minute," asserted Lidgerwood, in good-natured sarcasm. "It is so dark here in the canyon that I'm afraid some of you might fall overboard or get hit by the rocks, or something."

"The idea!" scoffed Miss Carolyn. Then, petulantly, to Van Lew: "We may as well go in. There is nothing more to be seen out here."

Lidgerwood looked to Eleanor for his cue, or at least for a whiff of moral support. But she turned traitor.

"You can do the meanest things in the name of solicitude, Howard," she began; but before she could finish he had reached up and turned the gas off with a snap, saying, "All right; anything to please the children." After which, however, he spoke authoritatively to Van Lew and Jefferis. "Don't let your responsibilities lean out over the railing, you two. There are places below here where the rocks barely give a train room to pass."

"*I'm* not leaning out," said Miss Brewster, as if she resented his care-taking. Then, for his ear alone: "But I shall if I want to."

"Not while I am here to prevent you."

"But you couldn't prevent me, you know."

"Yes, I could."

"How?"

The special was rushing through the darkest of the high-walled clefts in the lower part of the canyon. "This way," he said, his love suddenly breaking bounds, and he took her in his arms.

She freed herself quickly, breathless and indignantly reproachful.

"I am ashamed for you!" she panted. And then, with carefully calculated malice: "What if Herbert had been looking?"

"I shouldn't care if all the world had been looking," was the stubborn rejoinder. Then, passionately: "Tell me one thing before we go any farther, Eleanor: have you given him the right to call me out?"

"How can you doubt it?" she said; but now she was laughing at him again.

There was safety only in flight, and he fled; back to his desk and the work thereon. He was wading dismally through a thick mass of correspondence, relating to a cattleman's claim for stock killed, and thinking of nothing so little as the type-written words, when the roar of the echoing canyon walls died away, and the train came to a stand at Timanyoni, the first telegraph station in the shut-in valley between the mountain ranges. A minute or two later the wheels began to revolve again, and Bradford came in.

"More maverick railroading," he said disgustedly. "Timanyoni had his red light out, and when I asked for orders he said he hadn't any—thought maybe we'd want to ask for 'em ourselves, being as we was running wild."

"So he thoughtfully stopped us to give us the chance!" snapped Lidgerwood in wrathful scorn. "What did you do?"

"Oh, as long as he had done it, I had him call up the Angels despatcher to find out where we were at. We're on 204's time, you know—ought to have met her here."

"Why didn't we?" asked the superintendent, taking the time-card from its pigeon-hole and glancing at Train 204's schedule.

"She was late out of Red Butte; broke something and had to stop and tie it up; lost a half-hour makin' her get-away."

"Then we reach Little Butte before 204 gets there—is that it?"

"That's about the way the night despatcher has it ciphered out. He gave the Timanyoni plug operator hot stuff for holdin' us up."

Lidgerwood shook his head. The artless simplicity of Red-Butte-Western methods, or unmethods, was dying hard, inexcusably hard.

"Does the night despatcher happen to know just where 204 is, at this present moment?" he inquired with gentle irony.

Bradford laughed.

"I'd be willing to bet a piebald pinto against a no-account yaller dog that he don't. But I reckon he won't be likely to let her get past Little Butte, comin' this way, when he has let us get by Timanyoni goin' t'other way."

"That's all right, Andy; that is the way you would have a right to figure it out if you were running a special on a normally healthy railroad—you'd be justified in running to your next telegraph station, regardless. But the Red Butte Western is an abnormally unhealthy railroad, and you'd better feel your way—pretty carefully, too. From Point-of-Rocks you can see well down toward Little Butte. Tell Williams to watch for 204's headlight, and if he sees it, to take the siding at Silver Switch, the old Wire-Silver spur."

Bradford nodded, and when Lidgerwood reimmersed himself in the cattleman's claim papers, went forward to share Williams's watch in the cab of the 266.

Twenty minutes farther on, the train slowed again, made a momentary stop, and began to screech and grind heavily around a sharp curve. Lidgerwood looked out of the window at his right. The moon had gone behind a huge hill, a lantern was pricking a point in the shadows some little distance from the track, and the tumultuous river was no longer sweeping parallel with the embankment. He shut his desk and went to the rear platform, projecting himself into the group of sight-seers just as the train stopped for the second time.

"Where are we now?" asked Miss Brewster, looking up at the dark mass of the hill whose forested ramparts loomed black in the near foreground.

"At Silver Switch," replied Lidgerwood; and when the bobbing lantern came nearer he called to the bearer of it. "What is it, Bradford?"

"The passenger, I reckon," was the answer. "Williams thought he saw it as we came around Point-o'-Rocks, and he was afraid the despatcher had got balled up some and let 'em get past Little Butte without a meet-order."

For a moment the group on the railed platform was silent, and in the little interval a low, humming sound made itself felt rather than heard; a shuddering murmur, coming from all points of the compass at once, as it seemed, and filling the still night air with its vibrations.

"Williams was right!" rejoined the superintended sharply. "She's coming!" And even as he spoke, the white glare of an electric headlight burst into full view on the shelf-like cutting along the northern face of the great hill, pricking out the smallest details of the waiting special, the closed switch, and the gleaming lines of the rails.

With this powerful spot-light to project its cone of dazzling brilliance upon the scene, the watchers on the railed platform of the superintendent's service-car saw every detail in the swift outworking of the tragic spectacle for which the hill-facing curve was the stage-setting.

When the oncoming passenger-train was within three or four hundred yards of the spur track switch and racing toward it at full speed, a man, who seemed to the onlookers to rise up out of the ground in the train's path, ran down the track to meet the uprushing headlight, waving his arms frantically in the stop signal. For an instant that seemed an age, the passenger engineer made no sign. Then came a short, sharp whistle-scream, a spewing of sparks from rail-head and tire at the clip of the emergency brakes, a crash as of the ripping asunder of the mechanical soul and body, and a wrecked train lay tilted at an angle of forty-five degrees against the bank of the hill-side cutting.

It was a moment for action rather than for words, and when he cleared the platform hand-rail and dropped, running, Lidgerwood was only the fraction of a second ahead of Van Lew and Jefferis. With Bradford swinging his lantern for Williams and his fireman to come on, the four men were at the wreck before the cries of fright and agony had broken out upon the awful stillness following the crash.

There was quick work and heart-breaking to be done, and, for the first few critical minutes, a terrible lack of hands to do it. Cranford, the engineer, was still in his cab, pinned down by the coal which had shifted forward at the shock of the sudden stop. In the wreck of the tender, the iron-work of which was rammed into shapeless crumplings by the upreared trucks of the baggage-car, lay the fireman, past human help, as a hasty side-swing of Bradford's lantern showed.

The baggage-car, riding high upon the crushed tender, was body-whole, but the smoker, day-coach, and sleeper were all more or less shattered, with the smoking-car already beginning to blaze from the broken lamps. It was a crisis to call out the best in any gift of leadership, and Lidgerwood's genius for swift and effective organization came out strong under the hammer-blow of the occasion.

"Stay here with Bradford and Jefferis, and get that engineer out!" he called to Van Lew. Then, with arms outspread, he charged down upon the train's company, escaping as it could through the broken windows of the cars. "This way, every man of you!" he yelled, his shout dominating the clamor of cries, crashing glass, and hissing steam. "The fire's what we've got to fight! Line up down to the river, and pass water in anything you can get hold of! Here, Groner"—to the train conductor, who was picking himself up out of the ditch into which the shock had thrown him—"send somebody to the Pullman for blankets. Jump for it, man, before this fire gets headway!"

Luckily, there were by this time plenty of willing hands to help. The Timanyoni is a man's country, and there were few women in the train's passenger list. Quickly a line was formed to the near-by margin of the river, and water, in hats, in buckets improvised out of pieces of tin torn from the wrecked car-roofs, in saturated coats, cushion covers, and Pullman blankets, hissed upon the fire, beat it down, and presently extinguished it.

Then the work of extricating the imprisoned ones began, light for it being obtained by the backing of Williams's engine to the main line above the switch so that the headlight played upon the scene.

Lidgerwood was fairly in the thick of the rescue work when Miss Brewster, walking down the track from the service-car and bringing the two young women who were afraid to be left behind, launched herself and her companions into the midst of the nerve-racking horror.

"Give us something to do," she commanded, when he would have sent them back; and he changed his mind and set them at work binding up wounds and caring for the injured quite as if they had been trained nurses sent from heaven at the opportune moment.

In a very little time the length and breadth of the disaster were fully known, and its consequences alleviated, so far as they might be with the means at hand. There were three killed outright in the smoker, two in the half-filled day-coach, and none in the sleeper; six in all, including the fireman pinned beneath the wreck of the tender. Cranford, the engineer, was dug out of his coal-covered grave by Van Lew and Jefferis, badly burned and bruised, but still living; and there were a score of other woundings, more or less dreadful.

Red Butte was the nearest point from which a relief-train could be sent, and Lidgerwood promptly cut the telegraph wire, connected his pocket set of instruments, and sent in the call for help. That done he transferred the pocket relay to the other end of the cut wire, and called up the night despatcher at Angels. Fortunately, McCloskey and Dawson were just in with the two wrecking-trains from the Crosswater Hills, and the superintendent ordered Dawson to come out immediately with his train and a fresh crew, if it could be obtained.

Dawson took the wire and replied in person. His crew was good for another tussle, he said, and his train was still in readiness. He would start west at once, or the moment the despatcher could clear for him, and would be at Silver Switch as soon as the intervening miles would permit.

Eleanor Brewster and her guests were grouped beside Lidgerwood when he disconnected the pocket set from the cut wire, and temporarily repaired the break. The service-car had been turned into a make-shift hospital for the wounded, and the car-party was homeless.

"We are all waiting to say how sorry we are that we insisted on coming and thus adding to your responsibilities, Howard," said the president's daughter, and now there was no trace of mockery in her voice.

His answer was entirely sympathetic and grateful.

"I'm only sorry that you have been obliged to see and take part in such a frightful horror, that's all. As for your being in the way—it's quite the other thing. Cranford owes his life to Mr. Van Lew and

Jefferis; and as for you three," including Eleanor and the two young women, "your work is beyond any praise of mine. I'm anxious now merely because I don't know what to do with you while we wait for the relief-train to come."

"Ignore us completely," said Eleanor promptly. "We are going over to that little level place by the side-track and make us a camp-fire. We were just waiting to be comfortably forgiven for having burdened you with a pleasure party at such a time."

"We couldn't foresee this, any of us," he made haste to say. "Now, if you'll do what you suggested—go and build a fire to wait by?—I hope it won't be very long."

Freed of the more crushing responsibilities, Lidgerwood found Bradford and Groner, and with the two conductors went down the track to the point of derailment to make the technical investigation of causes.

Ordinarily, the mere fact of a destructive derailment leaves little to be discovered when the cause is sought afterward. But, singularly enough, the curved track was torn up only on the side toward the hill; the outer rail was still in place, and the cross-ties, deeply bedded in the hard gravel of the cutting, showed only the surface mutilation of the grinding wheels.

"Broken flange under the 215, I'll bet," said Groner, holding his lantern down to the gashed ties. But Bradford denied it.

"No," he contradicted: "Cranford was able to talk a little after we toted him back to the service-car. He says it was a broken rail; says he saw it and saw the man that was flaggin' him down, all in good time to give her the air before he hit it."

"What man was that?" asked Groner, whose point of view had not been that of an onlooker.

Lidgerwood answered for himself and Bradford.

"That is one of the things we'd like to know, Groner. Just before the smash a man, whom none of us recognized, ran down the track and tried to give Cranford the stop signal."

They had been walking on down the line, looking for the actual point of derailment. When it was found, it proved Cranford's assertion—in part. There was a gap in the rail on the river side of the line, but it was not a fracture. At one of the joints the fish-plates were missing, and the rail-ends were sprung apart sidewise sufficiently to let the wheel flanges pass through. Groner went down on his hands and knees with the lantern held low, and made another discovery.

"This ain't no happen-so, Mr. Lidgerwood," he said, when he got up. "The spikes are pulled!"

Lidgerwood said nothing. There are discoveries which are beyond speech. But he stooped to examine for himself. Groner was right. For a distance of eight or ten feet the rail had been loosened, and the spikes were gone out of the corresponding cross-ties. After it was loosened, the rail had been sprung aside, and the bit of rock inserted between the parted ends to keep them from springing together was still in place.

Lidgerwood's eyes were bloodshot when he rose and said:

"I'd like to ask you two men, as men, what devil out of hell would set a trap like this for a train-load of unoffending passengers?"

Bradford's slow drawl dispelled a little of the mystery.

"It wasn't meant for Groner and his passenger-wagons, I reckon. In the natural run of things, it was the 266 and the service-car that ought to've hit this thing first—204 bein' supposed to be a half-hour off her schedule. It was aimed for us, all right enough. And it wasn't meant to throw us into the hill, neither. If we'd hit it goin' west, we'd be in the river. That's why it was sprung out instead of in."

Lidgerwood's right hand, balled into a fist, smote the air, and his outburst was a fierce imprecation. In the midst of it Groner said, "Listen!" and a moment later a man, walking rapidly up the track from the direction of Little Butte station, came into the small circle of lantern-light. Groner threw the light on the new-comer, revealing a haggard face—the face of the owner of the Wire-Silver mine.

"Heavens and earth, Mr. Lidgerwood—this is awful!" he exclaimed. "I heard of it by 'phone, and hurried over to do what I could. My men of the night-shift are on the way, walking up the track, and the entire Wire-Silver outfit is at your disposal."

"I am afraid you are a little late, Mr. Flemister," was Lidgerwood's rejoinder, unreasoning antagonism making the words sound crisp and ungrateful. "Half an hour ago——"

"Yes, certainly; Goodloe should have 'phoned me, if he knew," cut in the mine-owner. "Anybody hurt?"

"Half of the number involved, and six dead," said the superintendent soberly; then the four of them walked slowly and in silence up the track toward the two camp-fires, where the unhurt survivors and the service-car's guests were fighting the chill of the high-mountain midnight.

XIX

Lidgerwood was unpleasantly surprised to find that the president's daughter knew the man whom her father had tersely characterized as "a born gentleman and a born buccaneer," but the fact remained. When he came with Flemister into the circle of light cast by the smaller of the two fires, Miss Brewster not only welcomed the mine-owner; she immediately introduced him to her friends, and made room for him on the flat stone which served her for a seat.

Lidgerwood sat on a tie-end a little apart, morosely observant. It is the curse of the self-conscious soul to find itself often at the meeting-point of comparisons. The superintendent knew Flemister a little, as he had admitted to the president; and he also knew that some of his evil qualities were of the sort which appeal, by the law of opposites, to the normal woman, the woman who would condemn evil in the abstract, perhaps, only to be irresistibly drawn by some of its purely masculine manifestations. The cynical assertion that the worst of men can win the love of the best of women is something both more and less than a mere contradiction of terms; and since Eleanor Brewster's manly ideal was apparently builded upon physical courage as its pedestal, Flemister, in his dare-devil character, was quite likely to be the man to embody it.

But just now the "gentleman buccaneer" was not living up to the full measure of his reputation in the dare-devil field, as Lidgerwood was not slow to observe. His replies to Miss Brewster and the others were not always coherent, and his face, seen in the flickering firelight, was almost ghastly. True, the talk was low-toned and fragmentary; desultory enough to require little of any member of the group sitting around the smouldering fire on the spur embankment. Death, in any form, insists upon its rights, of silence and of respect, and the six motionless figures lying under the spread Pullman-car sheets on the other side of the spur track were not to be ignored.

Yet Lidgerwood fancied that of the group circling the fire, Flemister was the one whose eyes turned oftenest toward the sheeted figures across the track; sometimes in morbid starings, but now and again with the haggard side-glance of fear. Why was the mine-owner afraid? Lidgerwood analyzed the query shrewdly. Was he implicated in the matter of the loosened rail? Remembering that the trap had been set, not for the passenger train, but for the special, the superintendent dismissed the charge against Flemister. Thus far he had done little to incur the mine-owner's enmity—at least, nothing to call for cold-blooded murder in reprisal. Yet the man was acting very curiously. Much of the time he scarcely appeared to hear what Miss Brewster was saying to him. Moreover, he had lied. Lidgerwood recalled his glib explanation at the meeting beside the displaced rail. Flemister claimed to have had the news of the disaster by 'phone: where had he been when the 'phone message found him? Not at his mine, Lidgerwood decided, since he could not have walked from the Wire-Silver to the wreck in an hour. It was all very puzzling, and what little suppositional evidence there was, was conflicting. Lidgerwood put the query aside finally, but with a mental reservation. Later he would go into this newest mystery and probe it to the bottom. Judson would doubtless have a report to make, and this might help in the probing.

Fortunately, the waiting interval was not greatly prolonged; fortunately, since for the three young women the reaction was come and the full horror of the disaster was beginning to make itself felt. Lidgerwood contrived the necessary diversion when the relief-train from Red Butte shot around the curve of the hillside cutting.

"Van Lew, suppose you and Jefferis take the women out of the way for a few minutes, while we are making the transfer," he suggested quietly. "There are enough of us to do the work, and we can spare you."

This left Flemister unaccounted for, but with a very palpable effort he shook himself free from the spell of whatever had been shackling him.

"That's right," he assented briskly. "I was just going to suggest that." Then, indicating the men pouring out of the relief train: "I see that my buckies have come up on your train to lend a hand; command us just the same as if we belonged to you. That is what we are here for."

Van Lew and the collegian walked the three young women a little way up the old spur while the wrecked train's company, the living, the injured, and the dead, were transferring down the line to the relief-train to be taken back to Red Butte. Flemister helped with the other helpers, but Lidgerwood had an uncomfortable feeling that the man was always at his elbow; he was certainly there when the last of the wounded had been carried around the wreck, and the relief-train was ready to back away to Little Butte, where it could be turned upon the mine-spur "Y." It was while the conductor of the train was gathering his volunteers for departure that Flemister said what he had apparently been waiting for a chance to say.

"I can't help feeling indirectly responsible for this, Mr. Lidgerwood," he began, with something like a return of his habitual self-possession. "If I hadn't asked you to come over here to-night——"

Lidgerwood interrupted sharply: "What possible difference would that have made, Mr. Flemister?"

It was not a special weakness of Flemister's to say the damaging thing under pressure of the untoward and unanticipated event; it is rather a common failing of human nature. In a flash he appeared to realize that he had admitted too much.

"Why—I understood that it was the unexpected sight of your special standing on the 'Y' that made the passenger engineer lose his head," he countered lamely, evidently striving to recover himself and to efface the damaging admission.

It chanced that they were standing directly opposite the break in the track where the rail ends were still held apart by the small stone. Lidgerwood pointed to the loosened rail, plainly visible under the volleying play of the two opposing headlights.

"There is the cause of the disaster, Mr. Flemister," he said hotly; "a trap set, not for the passenger-train, but for my special. Somebody set it; somebody who knew almost to a minute when we should reach it. Mr. Flemister, let me tell you something: I don't care any more for my own life than a sane man ought to care, but the murdering devil who pulled the spikes on that rail reached out, unconsciously perhaps, but none the less certainly, after a life that I would safe-guard at the price of my own. Because he did that, I'll spend the last dollar of the fortune my father left me, if needful, in finding that man and hanging him!"

It was the needed flick of the whip for the shaken nerve of the mine-owner.

"Ah," said he, "I am sure every one will applaud that determination, Mr. Lidgerwood; applaud it, and help you to see it through." And then, quite as calmly: "I suppose you will go back from here with your special, won't you? You can't get down to Little Butte until the track is repaired, and the wreck cleared. Your going back will make no difference in the right-of-way matter; I can arrange for a meeting with Grofield at any time—in Angels, if you prefer."

"Yes," said Lidgerwood absently, "I am going back from here."

"Then I guess I may as well ride down to my jumping-off place with my men; you don't need us any longer. Make my adieux to Miss Brewster and the young ladies, will you, please?"

Lidgerwood stood at the break in the track for some minutes after the retreating relief-train had disappeared around the steep shoulder of the great hill; was still standing there when Bradford, having once more side-tracked the service-car on the abandoned mine spur, came down to ask for orders.

"We'll hold the siding until Dawson shows up with the wrecking-train," was the superintendent's reply, "He ought to be here before long. Where are Miss Brewster and her friends?"

"They are all up at the bonfire. I'm having the Jap launder the car a little before they move in."

There was another interval of delay, and Lidgerwood held aloof from the group at the fire, pacing a slow sentry beat up and down beside the ditched train, and pausing at either turn to listen for the signal of Dawson's coming. It sounded at length: a series of shrill whistle-shrieks, distance-softened, and presently the drumming of hasting wheels.

The draftsman was on the engine of the wrecking-train, and he dropped off to join the superintendent.

"Not so bad for my part of it, this time," was his comment, when he had looked the wreck over. Then he asked the inevitable question: "What did it?"

Lidgerwood beckoned him down the line and showed him the sprung rail. Dawson examined it carefully before he rose up to say: "Why didn't they spring it the other way, if they wanted to make a thorough job of it? That would have put the train into the river."

Lidgerwood's reply was as laconic as the query. "Because the trap was set for my car, going west; not for the passenger, going east."

"Of course," said the draftsman, as one properly disgusted with his own lack of perspicacity. Then, after another and more searching scrutiny, in which the headlight glare of his own engine was helped out by the burning of half a dozen matches: "Whoever did that, knew his business."

"How do you know?"

"Little things. A regular spike-puller claw-bar was used—the marks of its heel are still in the ties; the place was chosen to the exact rail-length—just where your engine would begin to hug the outside of the curve. Then the rail is sprung aside barely enough to let the wheel flanges through, and not enough to attract an engineer's attention unless he happened to be looking directly at it, and in a good light."

The superintendent nodded. "What is your inference?" he asked.

"Only what I say; that the man knew his business. He is no ordinary hobo; he is more likely in your class, or mine."

Lidgerwood ground his heel into the gravel, and with the feeling that he was wasting precious time of Dawson's which should go into the track-clearing, asked another question.

"Fred, tell me; you've known John Judson longer than I have: do you trust him—when he's sober?"

"Yes." The answer was unqualified.

"I think I do, but he talks too much. He is over here, somewhere, to-night, shadowing the man who may have done this. He—and the man—came down on 205 this evening. I saw them both board the train at Angels as it was pulling out."

Dawson looked up quickly, and for once the reticence which was his customary shield was dropped.

"You're trusting me, now, Mr. Lidgerwood: who was the man? Gridley?"

"Gridley? No. Why, Dawson, he is the last man I should suspect!"

"All right; if you think so."

"Don't you think so?"

It was the draftsman's turn to hesitate.

"I'm prejudiced," he confessed at length. "I know Gridley; he is a worse man than a good many people think he is—and not so bad as some others believe him to be. If he thought you, or Benson, were getting in his way—up at the house, you know——"

Lidgerwood smiled.

"You don't want him for a brother-in-law; is that it, Fred?"

"I'd cheerfully help to put my sister in her coffin, if that were the alternative," said Dawson quite calmly.

"Well," said the superintendent, "he can easily prove an alibi, so far as this wreck is concerned. He went east on 202 yesterday. You knew that, didn't you?"

"Yes, I knew it, but——"

"But what?"

"It doesn't count," said the draftsman, briefly. Then: "Who was the other man, the man who came west on 205?"

"I hate to say it, Fred, but it was Hallock. We saw the wreck, all of us, from the back platform of my car. Williams had just pulled us out on the old spur. Just before Cranford shut off and jammed on his air-brakes, a man ran down the track, swinging his arms like a madman. Of course, there wasn't the time or any chance for me to identify him, and I saw him only for the second or two intervening, and with his back toward us. But the back looked like Hallock's; I'm afraid it was Hallock's."

"But why should he weaken at the last moment and try to stop the train?" queried Dawson.

"You forget that it was the special, and not the passenger, that was to be wrecked."

"Sure," said the draftsman.

"I've told you this, Fred, because, if the man we saw were Hallock, he'll probably turn up while you are at work; Hallock, with Judson at his heels. You'll know what to do in that event?"

"I guess so: keep a sharp eye on Hallock, and make Judson hold his tongue. I'll do both."

"That's all," said the superintendent. "Now I'll have Bradford pull us up on the spur to give you room to get your baby crane ahead; then you can pull down and let us out."

The shifting took some few minutes, and more than a little skill. While it was in progress Lidgerwood was in the service-car, trying to persuade the young women to go to his state-room for a little rest and sleep on the return run. In the midst of the argument, the door opened and Dawson came in. From the instant of his entrance it was plain that he had expected to find the superintendent alone; that he was visibly and painfully embarrassed.

Lidgerwood excused himself and went quickly to the embarrassed one, who was still anchoring himself to the door-knob. "What is it, Fred?" he asked.

"Judson: he has just turned up, walking from Little Butte, he says, with a pretty badly bruised ankle. He is loaded to the muzzle with news of some sort, and he wants to know if you'll take him with you to An—" The draftsman, facing the group under the Pintsch globe at the other end of the open compartment, stopped suddenly and his big jaw grew rigid. Then he said, in an awed whisper, "God! let me get out of here!"

"Tell Judson to come aboard," said Lidgerwood; and the draftsman was twisting at the door-knob when Miriam Holcombe came swiftly down the compartment.

"Wait, Fred," she said gently. "I have come all the way out here to ask my question, and you mustn't try to stop me: are you going to keep on letting it make us both desolate—for always?" She seemed not to see or to care that Lidgerwood made a listening third.

Dawson's face had grown suddenly haggard, and he, too, ignored the superintendent.

"How can you say that to me, Miriam?" he returned almost gruffly. "Day and night I am paying, paying, and the debt never grows less. If it wasn't for my mother and Faith ... but I must go on paying. I killed your brother——"

"No," she denied, "that was an accident for which you were no more to blame than he was: but you are killing me."

Lidgerwood stood by, man-like, because he did not know enough to vanish. But Miss Brewster suddenly swept down the compartment to drag him out of the way of those who did not need him.

"You'd spoil it all, if you could, wouldn't you?" she whispered, in a fine feminine rage; "and after I have moved heaven and earth to get Miriam to come out here for this one special blessed moment! Go and drive the others into a corner, and keep them there."

Lidgerwood obeyed, quite meekly; and when he looked again, Dawson had gone, and Miss Holcombe was sobbing comfortably in Eleanor's arms.

Judson boarded the service-car when it was pulled up to the switch; and after Lidgerwood had disposed of his passengers for the run back to Angels, he listened to the ex-engineer's report, sitting quietly while Judson told him of the plot and of the plotters. At the close he said gravely: "You are sure it was Hallock who got off of the night train at Silver Switch and went up the old spur?"

It was a test question, and the engineer did not answer it off-hand.

"I'd say yes in a holy minute if there wasn't so blamed much else tied on to it, Mr. Lidgerwood. I was sure, at the time, that it was Hallock; and besides, I heard him talking to Flemister afterward, and I saw his mug shadowed out on the window curtain, just as I've been telling you. All I can say crosswise, is that I didn't get to see him face to face anywhere; in the gulch, or in the office, or in the mine, or any place else."

"Yet you are convinced, in your own mind?"

"I am."

"You say you saw him and Flemister get on the hand-car and pump themselves down the old spur; of course, you couldn't identify either of them from the top of the ridge?"

"That's a guess," admitted the ex-engineer frankly. "All I could see was that there were two men on the car. But it fits in pretty good: I hear 'em plannin' what-all they're going to do; foller 'em a good bit more'n half-way through the mine tunnel; hike back and hump myself over the hill, and get there in time to see two men—*some* two men—rushin' out the hand-car to go somewhere. That ain't court evidence, maybe, but I've seen more'n one jury that'd hang both of 'em on it."

"But the third man, Judson; the man you saw beating with his fists on the bulkhead air-lock: who was he?" persisted Lidgerwood.

"Now you've got me guessin' again. If I hadn't been dead certain that I saw Hallock go on ahead with Flemister—but I did see him; saw 'em both go through the little door, one after the other, and heard it

150

slam before the other dub turned up. No," reading the question in the superintendent's eye, "not a drop, Mr. Lidgerwood; I ain't touched not, tasted not, n'r handled not—'r leastwise, not to drink any," and here he told the bottle episode which had ended in the smashing of Flemister's sideboard supply.

Lidgerwood nodded approvingly when the modest narrative reached the bottle-smashing point.

"That was fine, John," he said, using the exengineer's Christian name for the first time in the long interview. "If you've got it in you to do such a thing as that, at such a time, there is good hope for you. Let's settle this question once for all: all I ask is that you prove up on your good intentions. Show me that you have quit, not for a day or a week, but for all time, and I shall be only too glad to see you pulling passenger-trains again. But to get back to this crime of to-night: when you left Flemister's office, after telephoning Goodloe, you walked down to Little Butte station?"

"Yes; walked and run. There was nobody there but the bridge watchman. Goodloe had come on up the track to find out what had happened."

"And you didn't see Flemister or Hallock again?"

"No."

"Flemister told us he got the news by 'phone, and when he said it the wreck was no more than an hour old. He couldn't have walked down from the mine in that time. Where could he have got the message, and from whom?"

Judson was shaking his head.

"He didn't need any message—and he didn't get any. I'd put it up this way: after that rail-joint was sprung open, they'd go back up the old spur on the hand-car, wouldn't they? And on the way they'd be pretty sure to hear Cranford when he whistled for Little Butte. That'd let 'em know what was due to happen, right then and there. After that, it'd be easy enough. All Flemister had to do was to rout out his miners over his own telephones, jump onto the hand-car again, and come back in time to show up to you."

Lidgerwood was frowning thoughtfully.

"Then both of them must have come back; or, no—that must have been your third man who tried to flag Cranford down. Judson, I've got to know who that third man is. He has complicated things so that I don't dare move, even against Flemister, until I know more. We are not at the ultimate bottom of this thing yet."

"We're far enough to put the handcuffs onto Mr. Pennington Flemister any time you say," asserted Judson. "There was one little thing that I forgot to put in the report: when you get ready to take that missing switch-engine back, you'll find it *choo-chooin'* away up yonder in Flemister's new power-house that he's built out of boards made from Mr. Benson's bridge-timbers."

"Is that so? Did you see the engine?" queried the superintendent quickly.

"No, but I might as well have. She's there, all right, and they didn't care enough to even muffle her exhaust."

Lidgerwood took a slender gold-banded cigar from his desk-box, and passed the box to the ex-engineer.

"We'll get Mr. Pennington Flemister—and before he is very many hours older," he said definitely. And then: "I wish we were a little more certain of the other man."

Judson bit the end from his cigar, but he forbore to light it. The Red Desert had not entirely effaced his sense of the respect due to a superintendent riding in his own private car.

"It's a queer sort of a mix-up, Mr. Lidgerwood," he said, fingering the cigar tenderly. "Knowin' what's what, as some of us do, you'd say them two'd never get together, unless it was to cut each other's throats."

Lidgerwood nodded. "I've heard there was bad blood between them: it was about that building-and-loan business, wasn't it?"

"Shucks! no; that was only a drop in the bucket," said Judson, surprised out of his attitude of rank-and-file deference. "Hallock was the original owner of the Wire-Silver. Didn't you know that?"

"No."

"He was, and Flemister beat him out of it—lock, stock, and barrel: just simply reached out an' took it. Then, when he'd done that, he reached out and took Hallock's wife—just to make it a clean sweep, was the way he bragged about it."

"Heavens and earth!" ejaculated the listener. Then some of the hidden things began to define themselves in the light of this astounding revelation: Hallock's unwillingness to go to Flemister for the proof of his innocence in the building-and-loan matter; his veiled warning that evil, and only evil, would come upon all concerned if Lidgerwood should insist; the invasion of the service-car at Copah by the poor demented creature whose cry was still for vengeance upon her betrayer. Truly, Flemister had many crimes to answer for. But the revelation made Hallock's attitude all the more mysterious. It was unaccountable save upon one hypothesis—that Flemister was able to so play upon the man's weaknesses as to make him a mere tool in his hands. But Judson was going on to elucidate.

"First off, we all thought Hallock'd kill Flemister. Rankin was never much of a bragger or much of a talker, but he let out a few hints, and, accordin' to Red Desert rulin's, Flemister wasn't much better than a dead man, right then. But it blew over, some way, and now——"

"Now he is Flemister's accomplice in a hanging matter, you would say. I'm afraid you are right, Judson," was the superintendent's comment; and with this the subject was dropped.

The early dawn of the summer morning was graying over the desert when the special drew into the Angels yard. Lidgerwood had the yard crew place the service-car on the same siding with the *Nadia*, and near enough so that his guests, upon rising, could pass across the platforms.

That done, and he saw to the doing of it himself, he climbed the stair in the Crow's Nest, meaning to snatch a little sleep before the labors and hazards of a new day should claim him. But McCloskey, the dour-faced, was waiting for him in the upper corridor—with news that would not wait.

"The trouble-makers have sent us their ultimatum at last," he said gruffly. "We cancel the new 'Book of Rules' and reinstate all the men that have been discharged, or a strike will be declared and every wheel on the line will stop at midnight to-night."

Weary to the point of mental stagnation, Lidgerwood still had resilience enough left to rise to the new grapple.

"Is the strike authorized by the labor union leaders?" he asked.

McCloskey shook his head. "I've been burning the wires to find out. It isn't; the Brotherhoods won't stand for it, and our men are pulling it off by their lonesome. But it'll materialize, just the same. The strikers are in the majority, and they'll scare the well-affected minority to a standstill. Business will stop at twelve o'clock to-night."

"Not entirely," said the superintendent, with anger rising. "The mails will be carried, and perishable freight will continue moving. Get every man you can enlist on our side, and buy up all the guns you can find and serve them out; we'll prepare to fight with whatever weapons the other side may force us to use. Does President Brewster know anything about this?"

"I guess not. They had all gone to bed in the *Nadia* when the grievance committee came up."

"That's good; he needn't know it. He is going over to the Copperette, and we must arrange to get him and his party out of town at once. That will eliminate the women. See to engaging the buckboards for them, and call me when the president's party is ready to leave. I'm going to rest up a little before we lock horns with these pirates, and you'd better do the same after you get things shaped up for to-night's hustle."

"I'm needing it, all right," admitted the trainmaster. And then; "Was this passenger wreck another of the 'assisted' ones?"

"It was. Two men broke a rail-joint on Little Butte side-cutting for my special—and caught the delayed passenger instead. Flemister was one of the two."

"And the other?" said McCloskey.

Lidgerwood did not name the other.

"We'll get the other man in good time, and if there is any law in this God-forsaken desert we'll hang both of them. Have you unloaded it all? If you have, I'll turn in."

"All but one little item, and maybe you'll rest better if I don't tell you that right now."

"Give it a name," said Lidgerwood crisply.

"Bart Rufford has broken jail, and he is here, in Angels."

McCloskey was watching his chief's face, and he was sorry to see the sudden pallor make it colorless. But the superintendent's voice was quite steady when he said:

"Find Judson, and tell him to look out for himself. Rufford won't forgive the episode of the 'S'-wrench. That's all—I'm going to bed."

XX

Though Lidgerwood had been up for the better part of two nights, and the day intervening, it was apparent to at least one member of the head-quarters force that he did not go to bed immediately after the arrival of the service-car from the west; the proof being a freshly typed telegram which Operator Dix found impaled upon his sending-hook when he came on duty in the despatcher's office at seven o'clock in the morning.

The message was addressed to Leckhard, superintendent of the Pannikin Division of the Pacific Southwestern system, at Copah. It was in cipher, and it contained two uncodified words—"Fort" and "McCook," which small circumstance set Dix to thinking—Fort McCook being the army post, twelve miles as the crow flies, down the Pannikin from Copah.

Now Dix was not one of the rebels. On the contrary, he was one of the few loyal telegraphers who had promised McCloskey to stand by the Lidgerwood management in case the rebellion grew into an organized attempt to tie up the road. But the young man had, for his chief weakness, a prying curiosity which had led him, in times past, to experiment with the private office code until he had finally discovered the key to it.

Hence, a little while after the sending of the Leckhard message, Callahan, the train despatcher, hearing an emphatic "Gee whiz!" from Dix's' corner, looked up from his train-sheet to say, "What hit you, brother?"

"Nothing," said Dix shortly, but Callahan observed that he was hastily folding and pocketing the top sheet of the pad upon which he had been writing. Dix went off duty at eleven, his second trick beginning at three in the afternoon. It was between three and four when McCloskey, having strengthened his defenses in every way he could devise, rapped at the door of his chief's sleeping-room. Fifteen minutes later Lidgerwood joined the trainmaster in the private office.

"I couldn't let you sleep any longer," McCloskey began apologetically, "and I don't know but you'll give me what-for as it is. Things are thickening up pretty fast."

"Put me in touch," was the command.

"All right. I'll begin at the front end. Along about ten o'clock this morning Davidson, the manager of the Copperette, came down to see Mr. Brewster. He gave the president a long song and dance about the tough trail and the poor accommodations for a pleasure-party up at the mine, and the upshot of it was that Mr. Brewster went out to the mine with him alone, leaving the party in the *Nadia* here."

Lidgerwood said "Damn!" and let it go at that for the moment. The thing was done, and it could not be undone. McCloskey went on with his report, his hat tilted to the bridge of his nose.

"Taking it for granted that you mean to fight this thing to a cold finish, I've done everything I could think of. Thanks to Williams and Bradford, and a few others like them, we can count on a good third of the trainmen; and I've got about the same proportion of the operators in line for us. Taking advantage of the twenty-four-hour notice the strikers gave us, I've scattered these men of ours east and west on the day trains to the points where the trouble will hit us at twelve o'clock to-night."

"Good!" said Lidgerwood briefly. "How will you handle it?"

"It will handle itself, barring too many broken heads. At midnight, in every important office where a striker throws down his pen and grounds his wire, one of our men will walk in and keep the ball rolling. And on every train in transit at that time, manned by men we're not sure of, there will be a relief crew of some sort, deadheading over the road and ready to fall in line and keep it coming when the other fellows fall out."

Again the superintendent nodded his approval. The trainmaster was showing himself at his loyal best.

"That brings us down to Angels and the present, Mac. How do we stand here?"

"That's what I'd give all my old shoes to know," said McCloskey, his homely face emphasizing his perplexity. "They say the shopmen are against us, and if that's so we're outnumbered here, six to one. I can't find out anything for certain. Gridley is still away, and Dawson hasn't got back, and nobody else knows anything about the shop force."

"You say Dawson isn't in? He didn't have more than five or six hours' work on that wreck. What is the matter?"

"He had a bit of bad luck. He got the main line cleared early this morning, but in shifting his train and the 'cripples' on the abandoned spur, a culvert broke and let the big crane off. He has been all day getting it on again, but he'll be in before dark—so Goodloe says."

"And how about Benson?" queried Lidgerwood.

"He's on 203. I caught him on the other side of Crosswater, and took the liberty of signing your name to a wire calling him in."

"That was right. With this private-car party on our hands, we may need every man we can depend upon. I wish Gridley were here. He could handle the shop outfit. I'm rather surprised that he should be away. He must have known that the volcano was about ready to spout."

"Gridley's a law to himself," said the trainmaster. "Sometimes I think he's all right, and at other times I catch myself wondering if he wouldn't tread on me like I was a cockroach, if I happened to be in his way."

Having had exactly the same feeling, and quite without reason, Lidgerwood generously defended the absent master-mechanic.

"That is prejudice, Mac, and you mustn't give it room. Gridley's all right. We mustn't forget that his department, thus far, is the only one that hasn't given us trouble and doesn't seem likely to give us trouble. I wish I could say as much for the force here in the Crows' Nest."

"With a single exception, you can—to-day," said McCloskey quickly. "I've cleaned house. There is only one man under this roof at this minute who won't fight for you at the drop of the hat."

"And that one is——?"

The trainmaster jerked his head toward the outer office. "It's the man out there—or who was out there when I came through; the one you and I haven't been agreeing on."

"Hallock? Is he here?"

"Sure; he's been here since early this morning."

"But how—" Lidgerwood's thought went swiftly backward over the events of the preceding night. Judson's story had left Hallock somewhere in the vicinity of the Wire-Silver mine and the wreck at some time about midnight, or a little past, and there had been no train in from that time on until the regular passenger, reaching Angels at noon. It was McCloskey who relieved the strain of bewilderment.

"How did he get here? you were going to say. You brought him from somewhere down the road on your special. He rode on the engine with Williams."

Lidgerwood pushed his chair back and got up. It was high time for a reckoning of some sort with the chief clerk.

"Is there anything else, Mac?" he asked, closing his desk.

"Yes; one more thing. The grievance committee is in session up at the Celestial. Tryon, who is heading it, sent word down a little while ago that the men would wreck every dollar's worth of company property in Angels if you didn't countermand your wire of this morning to Superintendent Leckhard."

"I haven't wired Leckhard."

"They say you did; and when I asked 'em what about it, they said you'd know."

The superintendent's hand was on the knob of the corridor door.

"Look it up in Callahan's office," he said. "If any message has gone to Leckhard to-day, I didn't write it."

When he closed the door of his private office behind him, Lidgerwood's purpose was to go immediately to the *Nadia* to warn the members of the pleasure-party, and to convince them, if possible, of the advisability of a prompt retreat to Copah. But there was another matter which was even more urgent. After the events of the night, it had not been unreasonable to suppose that Hallock would scarcely be foolhardy enough to come back and take his place as if nothing had happened. Since he had come back, there was only one thing to be done, and the safety of all demanded it.

Lidgerwood left the Crow's Nest and walked quickly uptown. Contrary to his expectations, he found the avenue quiet and almost deserted, though there was a little knot of loungers on the porch of the Celestial, and Biggs's bar-room, and Red-Light Sammy's, were full to overflowing. Crossing to the corner opposite the hotel, the superintendent entered the open door of Schleisinger's "Emporium." At the moment there was a dearth of trade, and the round-faced little German who had weathered all the Angelic storms was discovered shaving himself before a triangular bit of looking-glass, stuck up on the packing-box which served him by turns as a desk and a dressing-case.

"How you vas, Mr. Litchervood?" was his greeting, offered while the razor was on the upward sweep. "Don'd tell me you vas come aboud some more of dose chustice businesses. Me, I make oud no more of dem warrants, *nichts*. Dot *teufel* Rufford iss come back again, alretty, and——"

Lidgerwood broke the refusal in the midst.

"You are an officer of the law, Schleisinger—more is the pity, both for you and the law—and you must do your duty. I have come to swear out another warrant. Get your blank and fill it in."

The German shopkeeper put down his razor with only one side of his face shaven. "Oh, *mein Gott!*" was his protest; but he rummaged in the catch-all packing-box and found the pad of blank warrants. Lidgerwood dictated slowly, in charity for the trembling fingers that held the pen. Knowing his own weakness, he could sympathize with others. When it came to the filling in of Hallock's name, Schleisinger stopped, open-mouthed.

"*Donnerwetter!*" he gasped, "you don'd mean dot, Mr. Litchervood; you don'd neffer mean dot?"

"I am sorry to say that I do; sorrier than you or any one else can possibly be."

"Bud—bud——"

"I know what you would say," interrupted Lidgerwood hastily. "You are afraid of Hallock's friends—as you were afraid of Rufford and his friends. But you must do your sworn duty."

"*Nein, nein*, dot ain'd it," was the earnest denial. "Bud—bud nobody vould serve a warrant on Mr. Hallock, Mr. Litchervood! I——"

"I'll find some one to serve it," said the complainant curtly, and Schleisinger made no further objections.

With the warrant in his pocket, a magistrate's order calling for the arrest and detention of Rankin Hallock on the double charge of train-wrecking and murder, Lidgerwood left Schleisinger's, meaning to go back to the Crow's Nest and have McCloskey put the warrant in Judson's hands. But there was a thing to come between; a thing not wholly unlooked for, but none the less destructive of whatever small hope of regeneration the victim of unreadiness had been cherishing.

When the superintendent recrossed to the Celestial corner, Mesa Avenue was still practically deserted, though the group on the hotel porch had increased its numbers. Three doors below, in front of Biggs's, a bunch of saddled cow-ponies gave notice of a fresh accession to the bar-room crowd which was now overflowing upon the steps and the plank sidewalk. Lidgerwood's thoughts shuttled swiftly. He argued that a brave man would neither hurry nor loiter in passing the danger nucleus, and he strove with what determination there was in him to keep even step with the reasoned-out resolution.

But once more his weakness tricked him. When the determined stride had brought him fairly opposite Biggs's door, a man stepped out of the sidewalk group and calmly pushed him to a stand with the flat of his hand. It was Rufford, and he was saying quite coolly: "Hold up a minute, pardner; I'm going to cut your heart out and feed it to that pup o Schleisinger's that's follerin' you. He looks mighty hungry."

With reason assuring him that the gambler was merely making a grand-stand play for the benefit of the bar-room crowd wedging itself in Biggs's doorway, Lidgerwood's lips went dry, and he knew that the haunting terror was slipping its humiliating mask over his face. But before he could say or do any fear-prompted thing a diversion came. At the halting moment a small man, red-haired, and with his cap pulled down over his eyes, had separated himself from the group of loungers on the Celestial porch to make a swift détour through the hotel bar, around the rear of Biggs's, and so to the street and the sidewalk in front. As once before, and under somewhat less hazardous conditions, he came up behind Rufford, and again the gambler felt the pressure of cold metal against his spine.

"It ain't an S-wrench this time, Bart," he said gently, and the crowd on Biggs's doorstep roared its appreciation of the joke. Then: "Keep your hands right where they are, and side-step out o' Mr. Lidgerwood's way—that's business." And when the superintendent had gone on: "That's all for the present, Bart. After I get a little more time and ain't so danged busy I'll borrow another pair o' clamps from Hepburn and take you back to Copah. So long."

By all the laws of Angelic procedure, Judson should have been promptly shot in the back when he turned and walked swiftly down the avenue to overtake the superintendent. But for once the onlookers were disappointed. Rufford was calmly relighting his cigar, and when he had sufficiently cursed the bar-room audience for not being game enough to stop the interference, he kicked Schleisinger's dog, and turned his back upon Biggs's and its company.

It was a bit of common human perverseness that kept Lidgerwood from thanking Judson when the engineer overtook him at the corner of the plaza. Uppermost in his thoughts at the moment was the keen sense of humiliation arising upon the conviction that the plucky little man had surprised his secret and would despise him accordingly. Hence his first word to Judson was the word of authority.

"Go back to Schleisinger and have him swear you in as a deputy constable," he directed tersely. "When you are sworn in, come down here and serve this," and he gave Judson the warrant for Hallock's arrest.

The engineer glanced at the name in the body of the warrant and nodded.

"So you've made up your mind?" he said.

Lidgerwood was frowning abstractedly up at the windows of Hallock's office in the head-quarters building.

"I don't know," he said, half hesitantly. "But he is implicated in that murderous business of last night—that we both know—and now he is back here. McCloskey told you that, didn't he?"

Judson nodded again, and Lidgerwood went on, irresistibly impelled to justify his own action.

"It would be something worse than folly to leave him at liberty when we are on the ragged edge of a fight. Arrest him wherever you can find him, and take him over to Copah on the first train that serves. He'll have to clear himself, if he can; that's all."

When Judson, with his huge cow-boy pistol sagging at his hip, had turned back to do the first part of his errand, Lidgerwood went on around the Crow's Nest and presented himself at the door of the *Nadia*. Happily, for his purpose, he found only Mrs. Brewster and Judge Holcombe in possession, the young people having gone to climb one of the bare mesa hills behind the town for an unobstructed view of the Timanyonis.

The superintendent left Judge Holcombe out of the proposal which he urged earnestly upon Mrs. Brewster. Telling her briefly of the threatened strike and its promise of violence and rioting, he tried to show her that the presence of the private-car party was a menace, alike to its own members and to him. The run to Copah could be made on a special schedule and the party might be well outside of the danger zone before the armistice expired. Would she not defer to his judgment and let him send the *Nadia* back to safety while there was yet time?

Mrs. Brewster, the placid, let him say his say without interruption. But when he finished, the placidity became active opposition. The president's wife would not listen for a moment to an expedient which did not—could not—include the president himself.

"I know, Howard, you're nervous—you can't help being nervous," she said, cutting him to the quick when nothing was farther from her intention. "But you haven't stopped to think what you're asking. If there is any real danger for us—which I can't believe—that is all the more reason why we shouldn't run away and leave your cousin Ned behind. I wouldn't think of it for an instant, and neither would any of the others."

Being hurt again in his tenderest part by the quite unconscious gibe, Lidgerwood did not press his proposal further.

"I merely wished to state the case and to give you a chance to get out and away from the trouble while we could get you out," he said, a little stiffly. Then: "It is barely possible that the others may agree with me instead of with you: will you tell them about it when they come back to the car, and send word to my office after you have decided in open council what you wish to do? Only don't let it be very late; a delay of two or three hours may make it impossible for us to get the *Nadia* over the Desert Division."

Mrs. Brewster promised, and the superintendent went upstairs to his office. A glance into Hallock's room in passing showed him the chief clerk's box-like desk untenanted, and he wondered if Judson would find his man somewhere in the town. He hoped so. It would be better for all concerned if the arrest could be made without too many witnesses. True, Hallock had few friends in the railroad service, at least among those who professed loyalty to the management, but with explosives lying about everywhere underfoot, one could not be too careful of matches and fire.

The superintendent had scarcely closed the door upon his entrance into his own room when it was opened again with McCloskey's hand on the latch. The trainmaster came to report that a careful search of Callahan's files had not disclosed any message to Leckhard. Also, he added that Dix, who should have come on duty at three o'clock, was still absent.

"What do you make out of that?" queried Lidgerwood.

McCloskey's scowl was grotesquely horrible.

"Bullying or bribery," he said shortly. "They've got Dix hid away uptown somewhere. But there was a message, all right, and with your name signed to it. Callahan saw it on Dix's hook this morning before the boy came down. It was in code, your private code."

"Call up the Copah offices and have it repeated back," ordered the superintendent. "Let's find out what somebody has been signing my name to."

McCloskey shook his grizzled head. "You won't mind if I say that I beat you to it, this time, will you? I got Orton, a little while ago, on the Copah wire and pumped him. He says there was a code message, and that Dix sent it. But when I asked him to repeat it back here, he said he couldn't—that Mr. Leckhard had taken it with him somewhere down the main line."

Lidgerwood's exclamation was profane. The perversity of things, animate and inanimate, was beginning to wear upon him.

"Go and tell Callahan to keep after Orton until he gets word that Mr. Leckhard has returned. Then have him get Leckhard himself at the other end of the wire and call me," he directed. "Since there is only one man besides myself in Angels who knows the private-office code, I'd like to know what that message said."

McCloskey nodded. "You mean Hallock?"

"Yes."

The trainmaster was half-way to the door when he turned suddenly to say: "You can fire me if you want to, Mr. Lidgerwood, but I've got to say my say. You're going to let that yellow dog run loose until he bites you."

"No, I am not."

"By gravies! I'd have him safe under lock and key before the shindy begins to-night, if it was my job."

Lidgerwood had turned to his desk and was opening it.

"He will be," he announced quietly. "I have sworn out a warrant for his arrest, and Judson has it and is looking for his man."

McCloskey smote fist into palm and gritted out an oath of congratulation. "That's where you hit the proper nail on the head!" he exclaimed. "He's the king-pin of the whole machine, and if you can pull him out, the machine will fall to pieces. What charge did you put in the warrant? I only hope it's big enough to hold him."

"Train-wrecking and murder," said Lidgerwood, without looking around; and a moment later McCloskey went out, treading softly as one who finds himself a trespasser on forbidden ground.

The afternoon sun was poising for its plunge behind the western barrier range and Lidgerwood had sent Grady, the stenographer, up to the cottage on the second mesa to tell Mrs. Dawson that he would not be up for dinner, when the door opened to admit Miss Brewster.

"'And the way into my parlor is up a winding stair,'" she quoted blithely and quite as if the air were not thick with threatening possibilities. "So this is where you live, is it? What a dreary, bleak, blank place!"

"It was, a moment ago; but it isn't, now," he said, and his soberness made the saying something more than a bit of commonplace gallantry. Then he gave her his swing-chair as the only comfortable one in the bare room, adding, "I hope you have come to tell me that your mother has changed her mind."

"Indeed I haven't! What do you take us for, Howard?"

"For an exceedingly rash party of pleasure-hunters—if you have decided to stay here through what is likely to happen before to-morrow morning. Besides, you are making it desperately hard for me."

She laughed lightly. "If you can't be afraid for yourself, you'll be afraid for other people, won't you? It seems to be one of your necessities."

He let the taunt go unanswered.

"I can't believe that you know what you are facing, any of you, Eleanor. I'll tell you what I told your mother: there will be battle, murder, and sudden death let loose here in Angels before to-morrow morning. And it is so utterly unnecessary for any of you to be involved."

She rose and stood before him, putting a comradely hand on his shoulder, and looking him fairly in the eyes.

"There was a ring of sincerity in that, Howard. Do you really mean that there is likely to be violence?"

"I do; it is almost certain to come. The trouble has been brewing for a long time—ever since I came here, in fact. And there is nothing we can do to prevent it. All we can do is to meet it when it does come, and fight it out."

"'We,' you say; who else besides yourself, Howard?" she asked.

"A little handful of loyal ones."

"Then you will be outnumbered?"

"Six to one here in town if the shopmen go out. They have already threatened to burn the company's buildings if I don't comply with their demands, and I know the temper of the outfit well enough to give it full credit for any violence it promises. Won't you go and persuade the others to consent to run for it, Eleanor? It is simply the height of folly for you to hold the *Nadia* here. If I could have had ten words with your father this morning before he went out to the mine, you would all have been in Copah, long ago. Even now, if I could get word to him, I'm sure he would order the car out at once."

She nodded.

"Perhaps he would; quite likely he would—and he would stay here himself." Then, suddenly: "You may send the *Nadia* back to Copah on one condition—that you go with it."

At first he thought it was a deliberate insult; the cruelest indignity she had ever put upon him. Knowing his weakness, she was good-natured enough, or solicitous enough, to try to get him out of harm's way. Then the steadfast look in her eyes made him uncertain.

"If I thought you could say that, realizing what it means—" he began, and then he looked away.

"Well?" she prompted, and the hand slipped from his shoulder.

His eyes were coming back to hers. "If I thought you meant that," he repeated; "if I believed that you could despise me so utterly as to think for a moment that I would deliberately turn my back upon my responsibilities here—go away and hunt safety for myself, leaving the men who have stood by me to whatever——"

"You are making it a matter of duty," she interrupted quite gravely. "I suppose that is right and proper. But isn't your first duty to yourself and to those who—" She paused, and then went on in the same steady tone: "I have been hearing some things to-day—some of the things you said I would hear. You are well hated in the Red Desert, Howard—hated so fiercely that this quarrel with your men will be almost a personal one."

"I know," he said.

"They will kill you, if you stay here and let them do it."

"Quite possibly."

"Howard! Do you tell me you can stay here and face all this without flinching?"

"Oh, no; I didn't say that."

"But you are facing it!"

He smiled.

"As I told you yesterday—that is one of the things for which I draw my salary. Don't mistake me; there is nothing heroic about it—the heroics are due to come to-night. That is another thing, Eleanor—another reason why I want you to go away. When the real pinch comes, I shall probably disgrace myself and everybody remotely connected with me. I'd a good bit rather be torn into little pieces, privately, than have you here to be made ashamed—again."

She turned away.

"Tell me, in so many words, what you think will be done to-night—what are you expecting?"

163

"I told you a few moments ago, in the words of the Prayer Book: battle, and murder, and sudden death. A strike has been planned, and it will fail. Five minutes after the first strike-abandoned train arrives, the town will go mad."

She had come close to him again.

"Mother won't go and leave father; that is settled. You must do the best you can, with us for a handicap. What will you do with us, Howard?"

"I have been thinking about that. The farther you can get away from the shops and the yard, which will be the storm-centre, the safer you will be. I can have the *Nadia* set out on the Copperette switch, which is a good half-mile below the town, with Van Lew and Jefferis to stand guard——"

"They will both be here, with you," she interrupted.

"Then the alternative is to place the car as near as possible to this building, which will be defended. If there is a riot, you can all come up here and be out of the way of chance pistol-shots, at least."

"Ugh!" she shivered. "Is this really civilized America?"

"It's America—without much of the civilization. Now, will you go and tell the others what to expect, and send Van Lew to me? I want to tell him just what to do and how to do it, while there is time and an undisturbed chance."

XXI

Miss Brewster evidently obeyed her instructions precisely, since Van Lew came almost immediately to tap on the door of the superintendent's private room.

"Miss Eleanor said you wanted to see me," he began, when Lidgerwood had admitted him; adding: "I was just about to chase out to see what had become of her."

The frank confession of solicitude was not thrown away upon Lidgerwood, and it cost him an effort to put the athlete on a plane of brotherly equality as a comrade in arms. But he compassed it.

"Yes, I asked her to send you up," he replied. Then: "I suppose you know what we are confronting, Mr. Van Lew?"

"Mrs. Brewster told us as soon as we came back from the hills. Is it likely to be serious?"

"Yes. I wish I could have persuaded Mrs. Brewster to order the *Nadia* out of it. But she has refused to go and leave Mr. Brewster behind."

"I know," said Van Lew; "we have all refused."

"So Miss Brewster has just told me," frowned Lidgerwood. "That being the case, we must make the best of it. How are you fixed for arms in the president's car?"

"I have a hunting rifle—a forty-four magazine; and Jefferis has a small armory of revolvers—boy-like."

"Good! The defense of the car, if a riot materializes, will fall upon you two. Judge Holcombe can't be counted in. I'll give you all the help I can spare, but you'll have to furnish the brains. I suppose I don't need to tell you not to take any chances?"

Van Lew shook his head and smiled.

"Not while the dear girl whom, God willing, I'm going to marry, is a member of our car-party. I'm more likely to be over-cautious than reckless, Mr. Lidgerwood."

Here, in terms unmistakable, was a deep grave in which to bury any poor phantom of hope which might have survived, but Lidgerwood did not advertise the funeral.

"She is altogether worthy of the most that you can do for her, and the best that you can give her, Mr. Van Lew," he said gravely. Then he passed quickly to the more vital matter. "The *Nadia* will be placed on the short spur track at this end of the building, close in, where you can step from the rear platform of the car to the station platform. I'll try to keep watch for you, but you must also keep watch for yourself. If any firing begins, get your people out quietly and bring them up here. Of course, none of you will have anything worse than a stray bullet to fear, but the side walls of the *Nadia* would offer no protection against that."

Van Lew nodded understandingly.

"Call it settled," he said. "Shall I use my own judgment as to the proper moment to make the break, or will you pass us the word?"

Lidgerwood took time to consider. Conditions might arise under which the Crow's Nest would be the most unsafe place in Angels to which to flee for shelter.

"Perhaps you would better sit tight until I give the word," he directed, after the reflective pause. Then, in a lighter vein: "All of these careful prefigurings may be entirely beside the mark, Mr. Van Lew; I hope the event may prove that they were. And until the thing actually hits us, we may as well keep up appearances. Don't let the women worry any more than they have to."

"You can trust me for that," laughed the athlete, and he went his way to begin the keeping up of appearances.

At seven o'clock, just as Lidgerwood was finishing the luncheon which had been sent up to his office from the station kitchen, Train 203 pulled in from the east; and a little later Dawson's belated wrecking-train trailed up from the west, bringing the "cripples" from the Little Butte disaster. Not to leave anything undone, Lidgerwood summoned McCloskey by a touch of the buzzer-push connecting with the trainmaster's office.

"No word from Judson yet?" he asked, when McCloskey's homely face appeared in the doorway.

"No, not yet," was the reply.

"Let me know when you hear from him; and in the meantime I wish you would go downstairs and see if Gridley came in on 203. If he did, bring him and Benson up here and we'll hold a council of war. If you see Dawson, send him home to his mother and sister. He can report to me later, if he finds it safe to leave his womankind."

The door of the outer office had barely closed behind McCloskey when that opening into the corridor swung upon its hinges to admit the master-mechanic. He was dusty and travel-stained, but nothing seemed to stale his genial good-humor.

"Well, well, Mr. Lidgerwood! so the hoboes have asked to see your hand, at last, have they?" he began sympathetically. "I heard of it over in Copah, just in good time to let me catch 203. You're not going to let them make you show down, are you?"

"No," said Lidgerwood.

"That's right; that's precisely the way to stack it up. Of course, you know you can count on me. I've got a beautiful lot of pirates over in the shops, but we'll try to hold them level." Then, in the same even tone: "They tell me we went into the hole again last night, over at Little Butte. Pretty bad?"

"Very bad; six killed outright, and as many more to bury later on, I am told by the Red Butte doctors."

"Heavens and earth! The men are calling it a broken rail; was it?"

"A loosened rail," corrected Lidgerwood.

The master-mechanic's eyes narrowed.

"Natural?" he asked.

"No, artificial."

Gridley swore savagely.

"This thing's got to stop, Lidgerwood! Sift it, sift it to the bottom! Whom do you suspect?"

It was a plain truth, though an unintentionally misleading one, that the superintendent put into his reply.

"I don't suspect any one, Gridley," he began, and he was going on to say that suspicion had grown to certainty, when the latch of the door opening from the outer office clicked again and McCloskey came in with Benson. The master-mechanic excused himself abruptly when he saw who the trainmaster's follower was.

"I'll go and get something to eat," he said hurriedly; "after which I'll pick up a few men whom we can depend upon and garrison the shops. Send over for me if you need me."

Benson looked hard at the door which was still quivering under Gridley's outgoing slam. And when the master-mechanic's tread was no longer audible in the upper corridor, the young engineer turned to the man at the desk to say: "What tickled the boss machinist, Lidgerwood?"

"I don't know. Why?"

Benson looked at McCloskey.

"Just as we came in, he was standing over you with a look in his eyes as if he were about to murder you, and couldn't quite make up his mind as to the simplest way of doing it. Then the look changed to his usual cast-iron smile in the flirt of a flea's hind leg—at some joke you were telling, I took it."

Being careful and troubled about many things, Lidgerwood missed the point of Benson's remark; could not remember, when he tried, just what it was that he had been saying to Gridley when the interruption came. But the matter was easily dismissed. Having his two chief lieutenants before him, the superintendent seized the opportunity to outline the plan of campaign for the night. McCloskey was to stay by the wires, with Callahan to share his watch. Dawson, when he should come down, was to pick up a few of the loyal enginemen and guard the roundhouse. Benson was to take charge of the yards, keeping his eye on the *Nadia*. At the first indication of an outbreak, he was to pass the word to Van Lew, who would immediately transfer the private-car party to the second-floor offices in the head-quarters building.

"That is all," was Lidgerwood's summing up, when he had made his dispositions like a careful commander-in-chief; "all but one thing. Mac, have you seen anything of Hallock?"

"Not since the middle of the afternoon," was the prompt reply.

"And Judson has not yet reported?"

"No."

"Well—this is for you, Benson—Mac already knows it: Judson is out looking for Hallock. He has a warrant for Hallock's arrest."

Benson's eyes narrowed.

"Then you have found the ringleader at last, have you?" he asked.

"I am sorry to say that there doesn't seem to be any doubt of Hallock's guilt. The arrest will be made quietly. Judson understands that. There is another man that we've got to have, and there is no time just now to go after him."

"Who is the other man?" asked Benson.

"It is Flemister; the man who has the stolen switching-engine boxed up in a power-house built out of planks sawed from your Gloria bridge-timbers."

"I told you so!" exclaimed the young engineer. "By Jove! I'll never forgive you if you don't send him to the rock-pile for that, Lidgerwood!"

"I have promised to hang him," said the superintendent soberly—"him and the man who has been working with him."

"And that's Rankin Hallock!" cut in the trainmaster vindictively, and his scowl was grotesquely hideous. "Can you hang them, Mr. Lidgerwood?"

"Yes. Flemister, and a man whom Judson has identified as Hallock, were the two who ditched 204 at Silver Switch last night. The charge in Judson's warrant reads,'train-wrecking and murder.'"

The trainmaster smote the desk with his fist.

"I'll add one more strand to the rope—Hallock's rope," he gritted ferociously. "You remember what I told you about that loosened rail that caused the wreck in the Crosswater Hills? You said Hallock had gone to Navajo to see Cruikshanks; he did go to Navajo, but he got there just exactly four hours after 202 had gone on past Navajo, and he came on foot, walking down the track from the Hills!"

"Where did you get that?" asked Lidgerwood quickly.

"From the agent at Navajo. I wasn't satisfied with the way it shaped up, and I did a little investigating on my own hook."

"Pass him up," said Benson briefly, "and let's go over this lay-out for to-night again. I shall be out of touch down in the yards, and I want to get it straight in my head."

Lidgerwood went carefully over the details again, and again cautioned Benson about the *Nadia* and its party. From that the talk ran upon the ill luck which had projected the pleasure-party into the thick of things; upon Mrs. Brewster's obstinacy—which Lidgerwood most inconsistently defended—

and upon the probability of the president's return from the Copperette—also in the thick of things, and it was close upon eight o'clock when the two lieutenants went to their respective posts.

It was fully an hour farther along, and the tense strain of suspense was beginning to tell upon the man who sat thoughtful and alone in the second-floor office of the Crow's Nest, when Benson ran up to report the situation in the yards.

"Everything quiet so far," was the news he brought. "We've got the Nadia on the east spur, where the folks can slip out and make their get-away, if they have to. There are several little squads of the discharged men hanging around, but not many more than usual. The east and west yards are clear, and the three sections of the midnight freight are crewed and ready to pull out when the time comes. The folkses are playing dummy whist in the Nadia; and Gridley is holding the fort at the shops with the toughest-looking lot of myrmidons you ever laid your eyes on."

Once again Lidgerwood was making tiny squares on his desk blotter.

"I'm thankful that the news of the strike got to Copah in time to bring Gridley over on 203," he said.

Benson's boyish eyes opened to their widest angle.

"Did he say he came in on Two-three?" he asked.

"He did."

"Well, that's odd—devilish odd! I was on that train, and I rambled it from one end to the other—which is a bad habit I have when I'm trying to kill travel-time. Gridley isn't a man to be easily overlooked. Reckon he was riding on the brake-beams? He was dirty enough to make the guess good. Hello, Fred"—this to Dawson, who had at that moment let himself in through the deserted outer office—"we were just talking about your boss, and wondering how he got here from Copah on Two-three without my seeing him."

"He didn't come from Copah," said the draftsman briefly. "He came in with me from the west, on the wrecking-train. He was in Red Butte, and he had an engine bring him down to Silver Switch, where he caught us just as we were pulling out."

XXII

Engineer John Judson, disappearing at the moment when the superintendent had sent him back to bully Schleisinger into appointing him constable, from the ken of those who were most anxious to hear from him, was late in reporting. But when he finally climbed the stair of the Crow's Nest to tap at Lidgerwood's door, he brought the first authentic news from the camp of the enemy.

When McCloskey had come at a push of the call-button, Lidgerwood snapped the night-latch on the corridor door.

"Let us have it, Judson," he said, when the trainmaster had dragged his chair into the circle of light described by the green cone shade of the desk lamp. "We have been wondering what had become of you."

Summarized, Judson's story was the report of an intelligent scout. Since he was classed with the discharged men, he had been able to find out some of the enemy's moves in the game of coercion. The strikers had transferred their head-quarters from the Celestial to Cat Biggs's place, where the committees, jealously safeguarded, were now sitting "in permanence" in the back room. Judson had not been admitted to the committee-room; but the thronged bar-room was public, and the liquor which was flowing freely had loosened many tongues.

From the bar-room talk Judson had gathered that the strikers knew nothing as yet of McCloskey's plan to keep the trains moving and the wires alive. Hence—unless the free-flowing whiskey should precipitate matters—there would probably be no open outbreak before midnight. As an offset to this, however, the engineer had overheard enough to convince him that the Copah wire had been tapped; that Dix, the day operator, had been either bribed or intimidated, and was now under guard at the strikers' head-quarters, and that some important message had been intercepted which was, in Judson's phrase, "raising sand" in the camp of the disaffected. This recurrence of the mysterious message, of which no trace could be found in the head-quarters record, opened a fresh field of discussion, and it was McCloskey who put his finger upon the only plausible conclusion.

"It is Hallock again," he rasped. "He is the only man who could have used the private code. Dix probably picked out the cipher; he's got a weakness for such things. Hallock's carrying double. He has fixed up some trouble-making message, or faked one, and signed your name to it, and then schemed to let it leak out through Dix."

"It's making the trouble, all right," was Judson's comment. "When I left Biggs's a few minutes ago, Tryon was calling for volunteers to come down here and steal an engine. From what he said, I took it they were aimin' to go over into the desert to tear up the track and stop somebody or something coming this way from Copah—all on account of that make-believe message that you didn't send."

Thus far Judson's report had dealt with facts. But there were other things deducible. He insisted that the strength of the insurrection did not lie in the dissatisfied employees of the Red Butte Western, or even in the ex-employees; it was rather in the lawless element of the town which lived and fattened upon the earnings of the railroad men—the saloon-keepers, the gamblers, the "tin-horns" of every stripe. Moreover, it was certain that some one high in authority in the railroad service was furnishing

171

the brains. There was a chief to whom all the malcontents deferred, and who figured in the bar-room talk as the "boss," or "the big boss."

"And that same 'big boss' is sitting up yonder in Cat Biggs's back room, right now, givin' his orders and tellin' 'em what to do," was Judson's crowning guess, and since Hallock had not been visible since the early afternoon, for the three men sitting under the superintendent's desk lamp, Judson's inference stood as a fact assured. It was Hallock who had fomented the trouble; it was Hallock who was now directing it.

"I suppose you didn't see anything of Grady, my stenographer?" inquired Lidgerwood, when Judson had made an end.

The engineer shook his head. "Reckon they've got him cooped up along with Dix?"

"I hope not. But he has disappeared. I sent him up to Mrs. Dawson's with a message late this afternoon, and he hasn't shown up since."

"Of course, they've got him," said McCloskey, sourly. "Does he know anything that he can tell?"

"Nothing that can make any difference now. They are probably holding him to hamper me. The boy's loyal."

"Yes," growled McCloskey, "and he's Irish."

"Well, my old mother is Irish, too, for the matter of that," snapped Judson. "If you don't like the Irish, you'll be finding a chip on my shoulder any day in the week, except to-day, Jim McCloskey!"

Lidgerwood smiled. It brought a small relaxing of strains to hear these two resurrecting the ancient race feud in the midst of the trouble storm. And when the trainmaster returned to his post in the wire office, and Judson had been sent back to Biggs's to renew his search for the hidden ring-leader, it was the memory of the little race tiff that cleared the superintendent's brain for the grapple with the newly defined situation.

Judson's report was grave enough, but it brought a good hope that the crucial moment might be postponed until many of the men would be too far gone in liquor to take any active part. Lidgerwood took the precautions made advisable by Tryon's threat to steal an engine, sending word to Benson to double his guards on the locomotives in the yard, and to Dawson to block the turn-table so that none might be taken from the roundhouse.

Afterward he went out to look over the field in person. Everything was quiet; almost suspiciously so. Gridley was found alone in his office at the shops, smoking a cigar, with his chair tilted to a comfortable angle and his feet on the desk. His guards, he said, were posted in and around the shops, and he hoped they were not asleep. Thus far, there had been little enough to keep them awake.

Lidgerwood, passing out through the door opening upon the electric-lighted yard, surprised a man in the act of turning the knob to enter. It was the merest incident, and he would not have remarked it if the door, closing behind Gridley's visitor, had not bisected a violent outburst of profanity, vocalizing itself in the harsh tones of the master-mechanic, as thus: "You —— —— chuckle-headed fool!

Haven't you any better sense than to come—" At this point the closing door cut the sentence of objurgation, and Lidgerwood continued his round of inspection, trying vainly to recall the identity of the chance-met man whose face, half hidden under the drooping brim of a worn campaign-hat, was vaguely familiar. The recollection came at length, with the impact of a blow. The "chuckle-headed fool" of Gridley's malediction was Richard Rufford, the "Killer's" younger brother.

Lidgerwood said nothing of this incident to Dawson, whom he found patrolling the roundhouse. Here, as at the shops and in the yard, everything was quiet and orderly. The crews for the three sections of the midnight freight were all out, guarding their trains and engines, and Dawson had only Bradford and the roundhouse night-men for company.

"Nothing stirring, Fred?" inquired the superintendent.

"Less than nothing; it's almost too quiet," was the sober reply. And then: "I see you haven't sent the *Nadia* out; wouldn't it be a good scheme to get a couple of buckboards and have the women and Judge Holcombe driven up to our place on the mesa? The trouble, when it comes, will come this way."

Lidgerwood shook his head.

"My stake in the *Nadia* is precisely the same size as yours, Fred, and I don't want to risk the buckboard business. We'll do a better thing than that, if we have to let the president's party make a run for it. Get your smartest passenger flyer out on the table, head it east, and when I send for it, rush it over to couple on to the *Nadia*—with Williams for engineer. Has Benson had any trouble in the yard?"

"There has been nobody to make any. Tryon came down a few minutes ago, considerably more than half-seas over, and said he was ready to take his engine and the first section of the east-bound midnight—which would have been his regular run. But he went back uptown peaceably when Benson told him he was down and out."

Lidgerwood did not extend his round to include Benson's post at the yard office, which was below the coal chutes. Instead, he went over to the Nadia, thinking pointedly of the two added mysteries: the fact that Gridley had told a deliberate lie to account for his appearance in Angels, and the other and more recent fact that the master-mechanic was conferring, even in terms of profanity, with Rufford's brother, who was not, and never had been, in his department.

Under the "umbrella roof" of the *Nadia's* rear platform the young people of the party were sitting out the early half of the perfect summer night, the card-tables having been abandoned when Benson had brought word of the tacit armistice. There was an unoccupied camp-chair, and Miss Brewster pointed it out to the superintendent.

"Climb over and sit with us, Howard," she said, hospitably. "You know you haven't a thing in the world to do."

Lidgerwood swung himself over the railing, and took the proffered chair.

"You are right; I haven't very much to do just now," he admitted.

"Has your strike materialized yet?" she asked.

"No; it isn't due until midnight."

"I don't believe there is going to be any."

"Don't you? I wish I might share your incredulity—with reason."

Miss Doty and the others were talking about the curious blending of the moonlight with the masthead electrics, and the two in the shadowed corner of the deep platform were temporarily ignored. Miss Brewster took advantage of the momentary isolation to say, "Confess that you were a little bit over-wrought this afternoon when you wanted to send us away: weren't you?"

"I only hope that the outcome will prove that I was," he rejoined patiently.

"You still believe there will be trouble?"

"Yes."

"Then I'm afraid you are still overwrought," she countered lightly. "Why, the very atmosphere of this beautiful night breathes peace."

Before he could reply, a man came up to the platform railing, touched his cap, and said, "Is Mr. Lidgerwood here?"

Lidgerwood answered in person, crossing to the railing to hear Judson's latest report, which was given in hoarse whispers. Miss Brewster could distinguish no word of it, but she heard Lidgerwood's reply. "Tell Benson and Dawson, and say that the engine I ordered had better be sent up at once."

When Lidgerwood had resumed his chair he was promptly put upon the question rack of Miss Eleanor's curiosity.

"Was that one of your scouts?" she asked.

"Yes."

"Did he come to tell you that there wasn't going to be any strike?"

"No."

"How lucidly communicative you are! Can't you see that I am fairly stifling with curiosity?"

"I'm sorry, but you shall not have the chance to say that I was overwrought twice in the same half-day."

"Howard! Don't be little and spiteful. I'll eat humble pie and call myself hard names, if you insist; only—gracious goodness! is that engine going to smash into our car?"

The anxious query hinged itself upon the approach of a big, eight-wheeled passenger flyer which was thundering down the yard on the track occupied by the *Nadia*. Within half a car-length of collision, the air-brake hissed, the siderods clanked and chattered, and the shuddering monster rolled gently backward to a touch coupling with the president's car.

Eleanor's hand was on her cousin's arm. "Howard, what does this mean?" she demanded.

"Nothing, just at present; it is merely a precaution."

"You are not going to take us away from Angels?"

"Not now; not at all, unless your safety demands it." Then he rose and spoke to the others. "I'm sorry to have to shut off your moon-vista with that noisy beast, but it may be necessary to move the car, later on. Don't get out of touch with the *Nadia*, any of you, please."

He had vaulted the hand-rail and was saying good-night, when Eleanor left her chair and entered the car. He was not greatly surprised to find her waiting for him at the steps of the forward vestibule when he had gone so far on his way to his office.

"One moment," she pleaded. "I'll be good, Howard; and I know that there *is* danger. Be very careful of yourself, won't you, for my sake."

He stopped short, and his arms went out to her. Then his self-control returned and his rejoinder was almost bitter.

"Eleanor, you must not! you tempt me past endurance! Go back to Van—to the others, and, whatever happens, don't let any one leave the car."

"I'll do anything you say, only you *must* tell me where you are going," she insisted.

"Certainly; I am going up to my office—where you found me this afternoon. I shall be there from this on, if you wish to send any word. I'll see that you have a messenger. Good-by."

He left her before her sympathetic mood should unman him, his soul crying out at the kindness which cut so much more deeply than her mockery. At the top of the corridor stair McCloskey was waiting for him.

"Judson has told you what's due to happen?" queried the trainmaster.

"He told me to look for swift trouble; that somebody had betrayed your strike-breaking scheme."

"He says they'll try to keep the east-bound freights from going out."

"That would be a small matter. But we mustn't lose the moral effect of taking the first trick in the game. Are the sections all in line on the long siding?"

"Yes."

"Good. We'll start them a little ahead of time; and let them kill back to schedule after they get out on the road. Send Bogard down with their clearance orders, and 'phone Benson at the yard office to couple them up into one train, engine to the caboose in front, and send them out solid. When they have cleared the danger limit, they can split up and take the proper time intervals—ten minutes apart."

"Call it done," said the trainmaster, and he went to carry out the order. Two minutes later Bogard, the night-relief operator off duty, darted out of the despatcher's room with the clearance-cards for the three sections. Lidgerwood stopped him in mid-flight.

"One second, Robert: when you have done your errand, come back to the president's car, ask for Miss Brewster, and say that I sent you. Then stay within call and be ready to do whatever she wants you to do."

Bogard did the first part of his errand swiftly, and he was taking the duplicate signatures of the engineer and conductor of the third and last section when Benson came up to put the solid-train order into effect. The couplings were made deftly and without unnecessary stir. Then Benson stepped back and gave the starting signal, twirling his lantern in rapid circles. Synchronized as perfectly as if a single throttle-lever controlled them all, the three heavy freight-pullers hissed, strained, belched fire, and the long train began to move out.

It was Lidgerwood's challenge to the outlaws, and as if the blasts of the three tearing exhausts had been the signal it was awaiting, the strike storm broke with the suddenness and fury of a tropical hurricane. From a hundred hiding-places in the car-strewn yard, men came running, some to swarm thickly upon the moving engines and cabooses, others swinging by the drawheads to cut the air-brake hose.

Benson was swept aside and overpowered before he could strike a blow. Bogard, speeding across to take his post beside the *Nadia*, was struck down before he could get clear of the pouring hornet swarm. Shots were fired; shrill yells arose. Into the midst of the clamor the great siren whistle at the shops boomed out the fire alarm, and almost at the the same instant a red glow, capped by a rolling nimbus of sooty oil smoke, rose to beacon the destruction already begun in the shop yards. And while the roar of the siren was still jarring upon the windless night air, the electric-light circuits were cut out, leaving the yards and the Crow's Nest in darkness, and the frantic battle for the trains to be lighted only by the moon and the lurid glow of destruction spreading slowly under its black canopy of smoke.

In the Crow's Nest the sudden coup of the strikers had the effect which its originator had doubtless counted upon. It was some minutes after the lights were cut off, and the irruption had swept past the captured and disabled trains to the shops, before Lidgerwood could get his small garrison together and send it, with McCloskey for its leader, to reinforce the shop guard, which was presumably fighting desperately for the control of the power plant and the fire pumps.

Only McCloskey's protest and his own anxiety for the safety of the *Nadia's* company, kept Lidgerwood from leading the little relief column of loyal trainmen and head-quarters clerks in person. The lust of battle was in his blood, and for the time the shrinking palsy of physical fear held aloof.

When the sally of the trainmaster and his forlorn-hope squad had left the office-story of the head-quarters building almost deserted, it was the force of mere mechanical habit that sent Lidgerwood back to his room to close his desk before going down to order the *Nadia* out of the zone of immediate danger. There was a chair in his way, and in the darkness and in his haste he stumbled over it. When he recovered himself, two men, with handkerchief masks over their faces, were entering from the corridor, and as he turned at the sound of their footsteps, they sprang upon him.

For the first rememberable time in his life, Howard Lidgerwood met the challenge of violence joyfully, with every muscle and nerve singing the battle-song, and a huge willingness to slay or be slain arming him for the hand-to-hand struggle. Twice he drove the lighter of the two to the wall with well-planted blows, and once he got a deadly wrestler's hold on the tall man and would have killed him if the free accomplice had not torn his locked fingers apart by main strength. But it was two against one; and when it was over, the conflagration light reddening the southern windows sufficed for the knotting of the piece of hemp lashing with which the two masked garroters were binding their victim in his chair.

Meanwhile, the pandemonium raging at the shops was beginning to surge backward into the railway yard. Some one had fired a box-car, and the upblaze centred a fresh fury of destruction. Up at the head of the three-sectioned freight train a mad mob was cutting the leading locomotive free.

Dawson, crouching in the roundhouse door directly opposite, knew all that Judson could tell him, and he instantly divined the purpose of the engine thieves. They were preparing to send the freight engine eastward on the Desert Division main line to collide with and wreck whatever coming thing it was that they feared.

The threatened deed wrought itself out before the draftsman could even attempt to prevent it. A man sprang to the footboard of the freed locomotive, jerked the throttle open, stayed at the levers long enough to hook up to the most effective cut-off for speed, and jumped for his life.

Dawson was deliberate, but not slow-witted. While the abandoned engine was, as yet, only gathering speed for the eastward dash, he was dodging the straggling rioters in the yard, racing purposefully for the only available locomotive, ready and headed to chase the runaway—namely, the big eight-wheeler coupled to the president's car. He set the switch to the main line as he passed it, but there was no time to uncouple the engine from the private car, even if he had been willing to leave the woman he loved, and those with her, helpless in the midst of the rioting.

So there was no more than a gasped-out word to Williams as he climbed to the cab before the eight-wheeler, with the *Nadia* in tow, shot away from the Crow's Nest platform. And it was not until the car was growling angrily over the yard-limit switches that Van Lew burst into the central compartment like a man demented, to demand excitedly of the three women who were clinging, terror-stricken, to Judge Holcombe:

"Who has seen Miss Eleanor? Where is Miss Eleanor?"

XXIII

Only Miss Brewster herself could have answered the question of her whereabouts at the exact moment of Van Lew's asking. She was left behind, standing aghast in the midst of tumults, on the platform of the Crow's Nest. Terrified, like the others, at the sudden outburst of violence, she had ventured from the car to look for Lidgerwood's messenger, and in the moment of frightened bewilderment the *Nadia* had been whisked away.

Naturally, her first impulse was to fly, and the only refuge that offered was the superintendent's office on the second floor. The stairway door was only a little distance down the platform, and she was presently groping her way up the stair, praying that she might not find the offices as dark and deserted as the lower story of the building seemed to be.

The light of the shop-yard fire, and that of the burning box-car nearer at hand, shone redly through the upper corridor windows, enabling her to go directly to the open door of the superintendent's office. But when she reached the door and looked within, the trembling terror returned and held her spell-bound, speechless, unable to move or even to cry out.

What she saw fitted itself to nothing real; it was more like a scene clipped from a play. Two masked men were covering with revolvers a third, who was tied helpless in a chair. The captive's face was ghastly and blood-stained, and at first she thought he was dead. Then she saw his lips move in curious twitchings that showed his teeth. He seemed to be trying to speak, but the ruffian at his right would not give him leave.

"This is where you pass out, Mr. Lidgerwood," the man was saying threateningly. "You give us your word that you will resign and leave the Red Butte Western for keeps, or you'll sit in that chair till somebody comes to take you out and bury you."

The twitching lips were controlled with what appeared to be an almost superhuman effort, but the words came jerkily.

"What would my word, extorted—under such conditions—be worth to you?"

Eleanor could hear, in spite of the terror that would not let her cry out or run for help. He was yielding to them, bargaining for his life!

"We'll take it," said the spokesman coolly. "If you break faith with us there are more than two of us who will see to it that you don't live long enough to brag about it. You've had your day, and you've got to go."

"And if I refuse?" Eleanor made sure that the voice was steadier now.

"It's this, here and now," grated the taller man who had hitherto kept silence, and he cocked his revolver and jammed the muzzle of it against the bleeding temple of the man in the chair.

The captive straightened himself as well as his bonds would let him.

"You—you've let the psychological moment go by, gentlemen: I—I've got my second wind. You may burn and destroy and shoot as you please, but while I'm alive I'll stay with you. Blaze away, if that's what you want to do."

The horror-stricken watcher at the door covered her face with her hands to shut out the sight of the murder. It was not until Lidgerwood's voice, calm and even-toned and taunting, broke the silence that she ventured to look again.

"Well, gentlemen, I'm waiting. Why don't you shoot? You are greater cowards than I have ever been, with all my shiverings and teeth-chatterings. Isn't the stake big enough to warrant your last desperate play? I'll make it bigger. You are the two men who broke the rail-joint at Silver Switch. Ah, that hits you, doesn't it?"

"Shut up!" growled the tall man, with a frightful imprecation. But the smaller of the two was silent.

Lidgerwood's grin was ghastly, but it was nevertheless a teeth-baring of defiance.

"You curs!" he scoffed. "You haven't even the courage of your own necessities! Why don't you pluck up the nerve to shoot, and be done with it? I'll make it still more binding upon you: if you don't kill me now, while you have the chance, as God is my witness I'll hang you both for those murders last night at Silver Switch. I know you, in spite of your flimsy disguise: *I can call you both by name*!"

Out in the yard the yellings and shoutings had taken on a new note, and the windows of the upper room were jarring with the thunder of incoming trains. Eleanor Brewster heard the new sounds vaguely: the jangle and clank of the trains, the quick, steady tramp of disciplined men, snapped-out words of command, the sudden cessation of the riot clamor, and now a shuffling of feet on the stairway behind her.

Still she could not move; still she was speechless and spell-bound, but no longer from terror. Her cousin—her lover—how she had misjudged him! He a coward? This man who was holding his two executioners at bay, quelling them, cowing them, by the sheer force of the stronger will, and of a courage that was infinitely greater than theirs?

The shuffling footsteps came nearer, and once again Lidgerwood straightened himself in his chair, this time with a mighty struggle that broke the knotted cords and freed him.

"I said I could name you, and I will!" he cried, springing to his feet. "You," pointing to the smaller man, "you are Pennington Flemister; and you," wheeling upon the tall man and lowering his voice, "you are Rankin Hallock!"

The light of the fire in the shop yard had died down until its red glow no longer drove the shadows from the corners of the room. Eleanor shrank aside when a dozen men pushed their way into the private office. Then, suddenly the electric lights went on, and a gruff voice said, "Drop them guns, you two. The show's over."

It was McCloskey who gave the order, and it was obeyed sullenly. With the clatter of the weapons on the floor, the door of the outer office opened with a jerk, and Judson thrust a hand-cuffed prisoner of his own capturing into the lighted room.

"There he is, Mr. Lidgerwood," snarled the engineer-constable. "I nabbed him over yonder at the fire, workin' to put it out, just as if he hadn't told his gang to go and set it!"

"Hallock!" exclaimed the superintendent, starting as if he had seen a ghost. "How is this? Are there two of you?"

Hallock looked down moodily. "There were two of us who wanted your job, and the other one needed it badly enough to wreck trains and to kill people, and to lead a lot of pig-headed trainmen and mechanics into a riot to cover his tracks."

Lidgerwood turned quickly. "Unmask those men, McCloskey."

It was the signal for a tumult. The tall man fought desperately to preserve his disguise, but Flemister's mask was torn off in the first rush. Then came a diversion, sudden and fiercely tragic. With a cry of rage that was like the yell of a madman, Hallock flung himself upon the mine-owner, beating him down with his manacled hands, choking him, grinding him into the dust of the floor. And when the avenger of wrongs was pulled off and dragged to his feet, Lidgerwood, looking past the death grapple, saw the figure of a woman swaying at the corridor door; saw the awful horror in her eyes. In the turning of a leaf he had fought his way to her.

"Good heavens, Eleanor!" he gasped. "What are you doing here?" and he faced her about quickly and led her into the corridor lest she should see the distorted features of the victim of Hallock's vengeance.

"I came—they took the car away, and I—I was left behind," she faltered. And then: "Oh, Howard! take me away; hide me somewhere! It's too horrible!"

There was a bull-bellow of rage from the room they had just left, and Lidgerwood hurried his companion into the first refuge that offered, which chanced to be the trainmaster's room. Out of the private office and into the corridor came the taller of the two garroters, holding his mask in place as he ran, with McCloskey, Judson, and all but one or two of the others in hot pursuit.

Notwithstanding, the fugitive gained the stair and fell, rather than ran, to the bottom. There was the crash of a bursting door, a soldierly command of "Halt!" the crack of a cavalry rifle, and McCloskey came back, wiping his homely face with a bandanna.

"They got him," he said; and then, seeing Eleanor for the first time, his jaw dropped and he tried to apologize. "Excuse me, Miss Brewster; I didn't have the least idea you were up here."

"Nothing matters now," said Eleanor, pale to the lips. "Come in here and tell us about it. And—and—is mamma safe?"

"She's down-stairs in the *Nadia*, with the others—where I supposed you were," McCloskey began; but Lidgerwood heard the feet of those who were carrying Flemister's body from the chamber of horrors, and quickly shutting the door on sight and sounds, started the trainmaster on the story which must be made to last until the way was clear of things a woman should not see.

"Who was the tall man?" he asked. "I thought he was Hallock—I called him Hallock."

The trainmaster shook his head. "They're about the same build; but we were all off wrong, Mr. Lidgerwood—'way off. It's been Gridley: Gridley and his side-partner, Flemister, all along. Gridley was the man who jumped the passenger at Crosswater Hills, and took up the rail to ditch Clay's freight—with Hallock chasing him and trying to prevent it. Gridley was the man who helped Flemister last night at Silver Switch—with Hallock trying again to stop him, and Judson trying to keep tab on Hallock, and getting him mixed up with Gridley at every turn, even to mistaking Gridley's voice and his shadow on the window-curtain for Hallock's. Gridley was the man who stole the switch-engine and ran it over the old Wire-Silver spur to the mine to sell it to Flemister for his mine power-plant—they've got it boxed up and running there, right now. Gridley is the man who has made all this strike trouble, bossing the job to get you out and to get himself in, so he could cover up his thieveries. Gridley was the man who put up the job with Bart Rufford to kill you, and Judson mistook his voice for Hallock's that time, too. Gridley was——"

"Hold on, Mac," interrupted the superintendent; "how did you learn all this?"

"Part of it through some of his men, who have been coming over to us in the last half-hour and giving him away; part of it through Dick Rufford, who was keeping tab on him for the money he could squeeze out of him afterward."

"How did Rufford come to tell you?"

"Why, Bradford—that is—er—the two Ruffords started a little shooting match with Andy, and—m-m—well, Bart passed out for keeps, this time, but Dick lived long enough to tell Bradford a few things—for old cow-boy times' sake, I suppose. I'll never put it all over any man, again, as long as I live, Mr. Lidgerwood, after rubbing it into Hallock the way I did, when he was doing his level best to help us out. But it's partly his own fault. He wanted to play a lone hand, and he was scheming to get them both into the same frying-pan—Gridley and Flemister."

Lidgerwood nodded. "He had a pretty bitter grudge against Flemister."

"The worst a man could have," said McCloskey soberly. Then he added: "I've got a few thousand dollars saved up that says that Rankin Hallock isn't going to hang for what he did in the other room a few minutes ago. I knew it would come to that if the time ever ripened right suddenly, and I tried to find Judson to choke him off. But John got in ahead of me."

Lidgerwood switched the subject abruptly in deference to Eleanor's deep breathing.

"I must take Miss Brewster to her friends. You say the *Nadia* is back? Who moved it without orders?"

"Yes, she's back, all right, and Dawson is the man who comes in for the blessing. He wanted an engine—needed one right bad—and he couldn't wait to uncouple the car. It was Hallock who sent that message to Mr. Leckhard that we've been hearing so much about, and it was a beg for the loan of a few of Uncle Sam's boys from Fort McCook. Gridley got on to it through Dix, and he also cut us out of Mr. Leckhard's answer telling us that the cavalry boys were on 73. By Gridley's orders, the two Ruffords and some others turned an engine loose to run down the road for a head-ender with the freight that was bringing the soldiers. Dawson chased the runaway engine with the coupled-up *Nadia* outfit, caught it just in the nick of time to prevent a collision with 73, and brought it back. He's down in the car now, with one of the young women crying on his neck, and——"

Miss Brewster got up out of her chair, found she could stand without tottering, and said: "Howard, I *must* go back to mamma. She will be perfectly frantic if some one hasn't told her that I am safe. We can go now, can't we, Mr. McCloskey? The trouble is all over, isn't it?"

The trainmaster nodded gravely.

"It's over, all but the paying of the bills. That rifle-shot we heard a little spell ago settled it. No, he isn't dead"—this in answer to Lidgerwood's unspoken question—"but it will be a heap better for all concerned if he don't get over it. You can go down. Lieutenant Baldwin has posted his men around the shops and the Crow's Nest."

Together they left the shelter of the trainmaster's room, and passed down the dark stair and out upon the platform, where the cavalrymen were mounting guard. There was no word spoken by either until they reached the *Nadia's* forward vestibule, and then it was Lidgerwood who broke the silence to say: "I have discovered something to-night, Eleanor: I'm not quite all the different kinds of a coward I thought I was."

"Don't tell me!" she said, in keen self-reproach, and her voice thrilled him like the subtle melody of a passion song. "Howard, dear, I—I'm sitting in sackcloth and ashes. I saw it all—with my own eyes, and I could neither run nor scream. Oh, it was splendid! I never dreamed that any man could rise by the sheer power of his will to such a pinnacle of courage. Does that make amends—just a little? And won't you come to breakfast with us in the morning, and let me tell you afterward how miserable I've been—how I fairly *nagged* father into bringing this party out here so that I might have an excuse to—to——"

He forgot the fierce strife so lately ended; forgot the double victory he had won.

"But—but Van Lew," he stammered—"he told me that you—that he—" and then he took her in his arms and kissed her, while a young man with a bandaged head—a man who answered to the name of Jack Benson, and who was hastening up to get permission to go home to Faith Dawson—turned his back considerately and walked away.

"What were you going to say about Herbert?" she murmured, when he let her have breath enough to speak with.

"I was merely going to remark that he can't have you now, not if he were ten thousand times your accepted lover."

She escaped from his arms and ran lightly up the steps of the private car. And from the safe vantage-ground of the half-opened door she turned and mocked him.

"Silly boy," she said softly. "Can't you read print when it's large enough to shout at all the world? Herbert and Carolyn have been 'announced' for more than three months, and they are to be married when we get back to New York. That's all; good-night, and don't you dare to forget your breakfast engagement!"

Made in the USA
San Bernardino, CA
01 February 2013